The OBSESSION

FILTHY RICH AMERICANS | BOOK TWO

NIKKI SLOANE

For Nick

ONE

Macalister Hale's eyes were liquid nitrogen.

They were so cold, they threatened to burn me in an instant, a flash freeze that would turn my skin white and cause blisters to lift on the surface.

I stared up at the powerful man looming over me, who had one hand on each of the armrests of my chair, and I held in a painful breath. There wasn't any air left in the library or the space between us. He'd used it all when he'd trapped me beneath his inescapable gaze.

Macalister's lips were only a few inches from mine, and for one terrifying moment it seemed like he was considering kissing me. He'd do it abruptly and without permission, claiming my mouth like it belonged to him.

Like I was his prize.

Was I?

He'd just bought me from his son for the bargain-basement price of one hundred thousand shares. At least ten million dollars, and likely more. A roiling sea swelled and churned in the pit of my stomach. Royce had sealed the deal with a gentlemanly handshake. A business transaction agreed upon and completed. And then he'd fled the library without even a glance in my direction.

I don't owe you anything, he'd said.

Maybe it was true.

All I could feel was the cut of his betrayal, sharp and excruciating and deep to the bone. A nasty voice inside my head hissed I should have seen it coming. Betrayal was a staple in the myths I adored, and the mortals always suffered at the hands of the gods. A heavy, expensive ring gleamed on my finger, but my engagement to Royce meant nothing. Marrying him would make me a Hale in name—not an immortal like everyone else in his family.

It just made me a target. A pawn in the game between father and son.

Rather than lower his mouth to mine, Macalister peeled his lips back into a joyless smile. "Marist, you shouldn't find this so upsetting. As I've come to understand, you're a practical girl, and I warned you Royce would sell you out the first chance he got."

I repeated his understated word like it had been punched from my center. "Upsetting?" I wanted to sound strong, but my voice went hollow. "That's . . . not the word I'd use for what just happened."

He reminded me vaguely of Dylan McDermott. He was dark and intense, and looked much younger than fifty-two. His gaze scraped over my face until it settled on my lips. Only this time, it was clear he wasn't thinking about kissing me.

Now he was simply curious about the words I'd produced. He lifted an eyebrow as he evaluated me. "Oh? How would you describe it?"

Unbearable.

I was Ariande, the maiden who'd saved the hero Theseus from the Minotaur's labyrinth, only to be dumped on an island and left to die when I wasn't of any further use.

I swallowed the lump that clogged my throat, blocking the word from escaping. When I didn't say anything, victory flashed through his expression.

"We need to discuss what happens now." He said it in the same dry way he dictated commands to his employees. "While you're living in my house, there are expectations, and you will meet them." He drew in a breath, preparing. "You'll be respectful and courteous, and you will take any directions I give you without hesitation."

My heart, which was already racing painfully in my chest, chugged at a faster tempo. I'd told him he'd never own me, but it didn't make a difference to him. He expected me to bow down to him like everyone else.

"No," I said.

He was ready for that. He charged forward, driving me backward until I leaned over the back of the chair and it dug uncomfortably into my shoulder blades.

"Do I need to remind you we have an agreement? If you're not going to follow through on your end, then you cannot expect me to. My money may have cleared into your family's account, but I didn't get to where I am today by being a fool." His expression was stone, his high cheekbones carved, and his lips chiseled into a tight line. "I haven't removed the lien on your parents' house."

The home I'd grown up in had been in my family for four generations. It was *everything* to my mother, and although it would be a terrible sacrifice to make, was it worth walking away now to get out from under the Hales? What if this was our only chance at escape? In the time of a single breath, I considered cutting my losses.

But my hesitation, or my expression, must have given too much away because a sneer curled on Macalister's lips.

"Your parents signed over authority to their financial manager. He can divert money without their consent, including the five million you just deposited. In fact, he could move every dollar under the Northcott name. He has total control . . . and he's *my* employee."

A strangled sob bubbled in my chest. Macalister could take everything away. I'd fought so hard to save my family from financial ruin, and yet all I'd done was trap them further. I'd given Macalister an opening, and he'd used it to take over.

Oh, my God. I broke inside. He *did* own me.

A single tear wouldn't be contained, and it slid hotly down my cheek. He tracked the path of it with his gaze, and something suspiciously like discomfort flitted through his expression. He was ruthless, but was it possible he had a heart?

No. Unlikely.

It was more probable emotion made him uneasy.

His expression shifted, and he straightened swiftly to his full height. It gave me a reprieve and just enough room to swallow a breath. I swiped the tear away.

"You understand." He nodded. "Good. There are other things to discuss, and I'm glad you're not going to waste our time on a pointless power struggle. While I'm sure this is difficult for you," he said, "I want you to know I'm doing this for your own good. Royce's too."

I gawked up at him. "How is this supposed to be good for—"

"I meant what I said." The ice was back in his eyes. "Your infatuation with each other is dangerous to your partnership."

A sick, bizarre laugh threatened. I no longer knew what—or who—was the bigger danger to my relationship with Royce. It could be the Hale who currently towered over me, or the one who'd sold me out and fled the room like a coward.

"I had to put a stop to it," Macalister's tone was plain, "before things went too far and you both got hurt."

Too late.

But also—*please.*

Like he gave a damn about our feelings. He could hide behind the excuse of wanting to protect his family's name, but I saw this for what it really was. Macalister had been born into tremendous wealth, and it had only grown under his reign as the CEO of the Hale Banking and Holding Company.

He had so much money, he could buy anything he wanted, and a lifetime with hardly any limits made him crave the things no dollar amount could acquire.

Power.

Influence.

Status.

And of course, *control.* He desired dominion over

everything and everyone.

Air stuck painfully in my lungs, making my voice tight. "Is that what this was? The stuff you said"—I could barely force the words out—"about wanting to pursue a relationship with me. It wasn't real. You were only trying to make a point."

I held out hope even when I should have known better. When we'd danced together the night of the initiation, he'd told me he was going to *have* me. Like then, something dark flickered in his eyes, and it was the same as staring at Medusa's head mounted to Athena's shield. It turned me to stone.

"Royce did exactly as I expected he would." His tone was devoid of emotion as he delivered his non-answer. "Now it's your turn. You'll surrender your car keys to me, and I'll have someone on my staff park your Porsche at the stables."

"What?"

He folded his arms across his chest, visibly irritated I'd had the nerve to question him. "Driving is a privilege, and it's one you haven't earned."

Acid invaded my mouth, filling it with the taste of panic. If I couldn't drive . . . "I'm not allowed to leave?"

He scoffed. "Don't be dramatic. You're not a prisoner. If you need to go somewhere, I'll approve it, and one of our drivers will take you."

I repeated his statement in my head and got hung up on the same spot. *I'll approve it.* He was demanding control over every move I made. The strings he'd attached to his five million dollars cinched so tightly around me I couldn't breathe.

His focus drilled into my eyes as he waited to see how I'd react, and it took every ounce of strength I possessed not to fight or flee. I swallowed thickly. "Now?"

He looked pleased at my reaction, or lack thereof. "Yes, Marist. Now."

I rose slowly from the chair to stand on my unsteady legs. The silver lining was at least I had an excuse to get the hell out of this room and away from my new owner.

I found my backstabbing fiancé sitting on the loveseat in the bedroom Macalister had announced was mine. Royce's hands were laced through his thick, dark hair. His eyes were hazy when his gaze snapped to me but, as he shot to his feet, urgency tightened them into focus.

"Marist."

My name in his concerned voice was nearly too much.

I did my best to ignore him and strode to my purse on the dresser. My hands shook as I dug out my keys and, even as I pretended he didn't exist, I felt his stare on my back. It was a hot, unavoidable spotlight.

"Are you all right?" he asked.

The sharp edge of a key bit into my fingers as I clenched them in my fist, but the discomfort held me together. I put my purse down with too much force, and it thudded to the dresser with a loud, angry bang. That was the only response I was willing to give him. Like he'd done to me so many times, I walked out of the room without looking back.

"Just wait a minute. Where are you going?" His swift footsteps announced he had chased me out into the hallway.

I sidestepped the black cat who strolled across the corridor, but Royce must have been so focused on me, he didn't notice until it was too late. A sound of stumbling rang out, followed by an irritated *meow*.

"Goddammit, Lucifer," he muttered. "Always in the way."

The devil cat slowed Royce down enough it prevented him from catching me before I ducked through the doorway.

Macalister and the tension in the cold library were right as I'd left them. He lifted his gaze from the smartphone resting on the desktop and surveyed me clinically. He noted the keys in my hand, then his son at my side who lingered in the doorway like a bad shadow.

"Leave them on the desk," Macalister said, nodding toward the keys in my grip. "Something's come up, and we'll have to continue this tomorrow."

I strode forward and dropped the keys. They clattered onto the polished desktop, and although I was handing over a freedom, I was willing to do it to gain another. Now I would be released for the night, and all I wanted was to be as far away as possible from the entire Hale family.

Since we were still under his father's watchful eye, Royce was indifferent as I brushed past him and made my way back toward my room.

It had a king-sized bed sheeted with a ridiculous thread count, an enormous jetted tub in the bathroom, and a closet so large it had a couch inside. Yet, no matter how fancy it looked, all I saw was my new prison.

Was the boy who followed me a prisoner too? Or was he the warden, making sure I obeyed every rule his father placed on me?

"Get out," I hissed.

Royce shook his head, and determination sprawled on his face. He had no intention of respecting my need for space, and why would he? Everything had been handed to him.

I hated him. I hated even more how, despite everything, he still looked so appealing. And most of all I hated that I'd let this happen. I'd fallen so completely for his manipulation.

His voice was low and urgent. "We need to talk."

"*No.*" It came from me like steel wrapped in barbed wire. "It's too late. I wanted to talk ten minutes ago, Royce, but you shut me out." I narrowed my eyes. "Go use your hundred thousand shares to buy someone to talk to."

He sighed his frustration, pushed back the sides of his suit coat, and rested his hands on his waist. His shoulders were stiff, his jaw set, and tension held his posture as rigid as a statue. He didn't like what I'd said.

Good.

"I'm serious," he said. "I'm not leaving until we have a conversation."

He really was the spoiled rich boy I'd believed he was last year. I stared at him critically, wanting to exaggerate every physical flaw I found and focus in on them. His eyes were too big. His cheekbones too pronounced. He wasn't the most beautiful man I'd ever seen.

I tried to convince myself it was true, but I was helpless.

He was still the boy who'd made love to me in the wine cellar. The only one who I felt had seen the real me. I couldn't reconcile the two parts of him that existed. And if those different sides of him were just a lie, and he really was the hard, indifferent man who didn't owe me anything . . .

God, I didn't want to know. I couldn't stomach it.

He wasn't going to leave this room? Fine. It didn't feel like it was mine, anyway. I'd surrendered my keys to Macalister, but my legs still worked, and I used them to take me away. There came another frustrated sigh from Royce, and he caught my elbow in the hallway, pulling me to a stop, but I shook off his hold while delivering a death glare.

It was so hushed it was nearly a whisper. He didn't want his father to overhear. "Please." His eyes teemed with remorse, but it had to be manufactured. "Talk to me."

"No." Anger made my voice shake. "*I don't owe you anything.*"

TWO

Ominous clouds hovered overhead like dark smoke, but I ignored the approaching storm, barreled out the back door, and marched across the stone patio. My shoes pounded down the outdoor staircase as I hurried toward the lawn and the hedge maze looming beyond.

I was lost. I needed to be lost in every sense of the word.

Harsh wind whipped through the rose garden and splashed my long, dark hair into my face. I'd been forced to color over the green hue I loved, but my snakes were still there, simply concealed under brown hair dye. Medusa simmered in my blood. She'd lain dormant until the initiation, and now she raged in the marrow of my bones.

Quiet relief swept through me once I was nestled in the narrow passage between the manicured walls of evergreen. With the impending storm, it was dark out, and the landscape lighting that dotted the path couldn't seem to penetrate the evening shadows. I stumbled blindly deeper into the maze with no destination, my feet sending pebbles skittering over each other.

I didn't see a flash of lightning. It was only the growling moan of thunder that made me aware of its existence. Maybe Macalister really was Zeus, and this thunderstorm was what had pulled him abruptly away. He was on Mount Olympus, hurling lightning bolts down at the mortals below.

Cold raindrops pricked at my skin, but I pressed on.

I'd never actually solved the maze before, but right now I had no desire to do so. As soon as I'd locked myself in amongst the tall hedges and the marble statues, everything outside of this labyrinth ceased to exist. It kept the fissures in my heart from widening and splitting me in two. The hurt of Royce's betrayal couldn't find me in here.

The clouds darkened. Rain pelted down, stinging and unforgiving. Lightning burst from the sky in a jagged slash, and more thunder followed right on its heels. Only this time it wasn't a low rumble, but a sharp, hateful crack. Like the sound of a slap across a face, magnified a million percent.

I shouldn't be out here, but where the hell was I supposed to go? Back to the house where I couldn't trust anyone? Calling my family wasn't an option. Macalister would take back his deal and his money, and then he'd come after us in retribution. I'd be left with even less than I'd started with.

I'd come much too far to turn back.

The wind swirled around me with unease. It propelled me along the path, ushering me toward the exit. Like it knew I shouldn't stay.

Or . . . perhaps not.

I wiped the rain from my eyes and stared at the decorative

urn before me, surrounded by hedges on three sides. A dead end. There were statues at some of the ends, and urns at the others. This one looked like the rest. Even if I wasn't disoriented, I'd have no idea where I was.

Lightning lit everything in unsettling white light for a sliver of a moment. The booming thunder seemed to anger the wind. It made the hedges come alive and undulate around me. They shook their disapproving branches at me, wagging their fingers at the stupid Northcott girl who'd nearly fallen in love with the prince of lies.

I shuffled along the path as fast as I could. The heavy, frigid rain soaked my clothes and weighed me down. I thought I was headed in the right direction until I turned a corner and lurched into the opening at the center of the maze. It was pouring down so hard now I couldn't tell if the tiered fountain at the center was even running.

I pressed my lips together to stop my bottom lip from quivering. I'd achieved my goal of losing myself, but I hadn't expected to feel so scared and alone. I lifted my gaze to the sky, blinking rapidly against the torrents of rain, and winced as another bolt of lightning ripped from the dark clouds. I pushed back a drenched lock of my hair, slinging away water as I stared at the fountain.

A week ago, Royce had knelt there and asked me to marry him. He'd told me the initiation was just the beginning and hinted things were going to get worse, but I hadn't expected the first hit to come so soon.

Or to come from him.

I turned in place and faced the spot where the hedges

parted, choosing to go back the way I'd come. At least the front section of the maze I was more familiar with.

The storm was like Royce's gaze on me. It didn't let up, no matter how uncomfortable it made me. Perhaps he clouded my thoughts, but when I found myself facing the same damn urn in the dead end, an angry sigh punched from my lungs. I could tell it was the same one from before. Part of a hedge root curled over the edge of the base.

I was smart, and this maze wasn't that challenging. What was wrong with me?

A shiver glanced through my shoulders, but a tingle crept up my spine. I was freezing, but this shiver was something . . . *else*. I turned, and breath caught in my throat.

He had appeared out of nowhere. An oversized black umbrella hovered over Royce's head, shielding him from the worst of the rain. His white dress shirt was untouched. Only the hem of his blue suit pants was wet. He was probably ruining his expensive shoes, but then again, he had more than enough money to buy new ones, didn't he? He'd been filthy rich before he'd struck the deal with his father, and tonight he'd added seven zeroes to his portfolio.

The sight of him made my heart beat faster, and the terrifying thing was I had no idea if it was with anger or relief. Lightning strobed in the sky like giant camera flashes. I gazed at the long, slender metal pole in his hand that lifted the umbrella over his head. Did he want to get struck by lightning? Or did he think he was impervious to his father's wrath?

We stood across from each other, simply staring as the sky was falling around us. God, his eyes. The shadow of the umbrella did nothing to lessen their intensity.

I couldn't take it anymore.

"Are you fucking stupid?" I raised my voice over the unrelenting rain. "What are you doing with that?"

His answer was to pitch the open umbrella to the side. It dropped, bounced to the path at his feet, and I swallowed hard as he let the rain overtake him. It poured over his body, flattening his dark hair and cascading down his shirt. His *white* shirt. It molded to him, showing off every curve and muscle on his powerful frame. He was so fucking perfect. The only reason I knew he was real and not a statue was the way his chest moved with his uneven breath.

All the while he stared at me, his lips were silent. But his eyes? Those were loud and desperate. I couldn't look away or escape, and it broke me. The accusation welled up and burst out, tasting like fire. "How could you?"

His shoulders lifted in a deep breath. "I didn't want to."

I shook my head. It was a lie. I couldn't trust anything he said, no matter how convincing he looked or sounded. The fire flamed out, taking all my strength with it. I repeated my question as a whisper. "How could you?"

"Because no one owns you, Marist. He was stupid enough to buy something from me that's not mine to give." He shifted, uneasy, as if it were hard to admit. "And because I couldn't see another way. I don't think as quickly on my feet as you do." His posture solidified. "You're a hell of a lot smarter than me."

"Don't," I hissed. "We're alone right now. No lies."

His face contorted under the rivulets of water. "I'm not

fucking lying."

"Your father told me," the words were broken and jagged, cutting my tongue, "you'd sell me out the first chance you got, and, fuck, that's *exactly* what you did."

"I know." He took a cautious step toward me. A brilliant line of white light cracked overhead, but he didn't flinch. Royce didn't seem to notice it at all. His focus was only on me. "I'm asking you to trust me. I need a little more time."

With the rain, it was impossible for him to tell if I was crying. I didn't know myself. My tone was patronizing. "That's what you need?" Pain edged into my voice. "I don't think you're in any position to ask me for something. I gave you a seat on the board. My virginity. A whole year of my life." My advance toward him was aggressive and adversarial. "I did what you asked, waited for you. I've given you *everything*."

Maybe even my heart, but I wasn't about to tell him that. I did my best to stand tall under the force of the storm and his devastating gaze.

"I'm done," I said. "You understand me? I'm not waiting anymore, especially for someone who screwed up my entire life." Not just with the initiation either. "Six years ago, you called me a nobody, and nothing's ever been the same."

He took another step, bringing him within striking distance. His face was full of regret, but like everything else, it was a lie. He wasn't capable of remorse—only calculated moves. As the thunder rumbled through the hedges, I swore to myself I wasn't going to fall for his manipulation ever again.

"The plan I had for my life is over, thanks to you," I said. I tugged my shoulders back, lifted my chin, and spoke the threat with the most conviction I'd ever possessed. "Get ready, Royce. Expect me to return the favor."

His lips parted as if he were going to say something but then thought better of it. Had he just choked back an apology? He brushed a hand over his head, slicking back his wet hair, and his gaze drifted down to my left hand. "You're still wearing it."

When he'd proposed, he'd told me that every day I wore the ring, it meant I was still with him. Trusting him no matter what he said or did when other people were around.

"Only because I forgot to take it off," I snapped, although I wondered if it was true.

"You could take it off now." He watched me cautiously. He'd issued the challenge at me, but his uneven voice gave him away. He didn't want me to.

Earlier, the ring had been so heavy when he'd abandoned me in the library, and I had wanted it gone. But he was right, I hadn't taken it off. The weakest part of myself had talked me out of it, but now I was glad. I could use this to my advantage. I'd lie to him and tell him whatever he wanted to hear, just like he did to me. I'd keep my new enemy close.

I toyed with the ring, threatening to remove it. "What if I didn't?"

His chest expanded. "Then I'd tell you those hundred thousand shares are worth a hell of a lot more than buying them on the open market."

I paused. "How so?"

He was a spectacular actor because his pained look was very convincing. "I can't tell you that."

"Why not?" My frustration with him reached a new height. He'd never been forthcoming and hadn't told me his master plan, but obviously it involved some kind of power struggle between him and his father. Royce wanted control of HBHC—he'd said that much.

Was he planning a boardroom coup? No, surely he was too smart to attempt it. Macalister would never allow himself to become vulnerable, and even in the unlikely event that happened, he wouldn't go down without a nasty fight. Plus, board members never voted against their chairman—it was unheard of. They'd always be loyal to the person who'd given them their seat.

So, trying to go against him would be career suicide.

"You can't tell him," Royce said, "what you don't know." Water dripped from his long lashes. It sluiced down over the curves of his cheekbones. "It's better this way."

"Oh, I see." My tone was pure bitterness. "You don't trust me, but I'm supposed to trust you."

"It's not that, Marist. I don't trust *him*." His merciless gaze made the rain and the cold fade until it wasn't noticeable. "If he thinks you know something, he won't stop until he finds out what it is. The only thing he does better than negotiating is extracting secrets."

When I flinched at the bright flash of lightning, he used the distraction to make his move. Royce set one hand on my shoulder, gently pulled me into his arms, and pressed me to his chest. The wet collar of his shirt stuck to my cheek while he smoothed a hand over the back of my head. It may have seemed like a sweet gesture, but it had a purpose. He dipped his lips down to my ear so he could be heard over the thunder surrounding us.

"I'm sorry. I had to." His words soaked in faster than the rain and were just as unexpected. "But I swear I won't let anything happen to you."

My voice was as cruel as I wanted to sound. "Like you did with the initiation?"

He stiffened, and the arms around me turned to marble. There was nothing he could say, no way to defend what he'd allowed. I didn't blame him for that night. I'd gone into the dining room knowing what was going to happen. I hadn't just agreed to it—I'd put my consenting signature down in ink.

But he hadn't protected me. I'd been the one to save us from the worst of it.

If I hadn't, would he still have gone through with it? Would he have stood by and endured two minutes with me on the table, under his father's control?

I'd never ask Royce because I already knew the terrible answer.

He'd sold me to his father, after all, and it was win at all costs.

Layer by layer, Royce softened. His arms were heavy cables around me, not letting go but giving me enough space to draw back and stare up at him. Guilt and shame clouded his eyes. "I promise," he whispered, "I'll do everything I can, so nothing *else* happens to you."

It was like he believed the words he was saying.

I'd strive to be just as good of a liar as he was now, maybe even better.

He searched my face, scrutinizing my dubious expression. It was a statement from him, not a question. "You don't believe me."

"What reason have you given me to?"

He frowned. "When it's just us, I've never lied to you."

Was he kidding? "Oh, really? Tell my why those one hundred thousand shares are more important than me."

Irritation flashed through his eyes. "I can't right now, and they're not more important than—"

"Were you lying when you told your father it was just sex between us?"

The irritation was replaced with relief. "Yes."

I went in for the kill. "Then what is it?"

His eyes heated, cutting through the cold rain. "More."

"More, what?" I demanded.

He didn't falter or hesitate. His hands slid up my back, preventing me from running as he leaned down. He brought his lips right to mine, and they brushed over my mouth as he spoke. "*More. A lot more.*"

"Don't," I warned, although my traitorous insides wanted to melt at his featherlight kisses. He didn't have any right to kiss me, and I tried to pull away. "You traded me away. I'm not yours anymore."

His jaw set, and his expression hardened. "You belong with me. I knew it from the moment I saw you laughing at that bar all those years ago. You're always going to be mine, Marist." He jammed a hand into my sopping hair and yanked me to his lips. "Whether you want to believe it or not."

And then he slammed his mouth over mine, sealing up

my ability to make any kind of protest.

His kiss scalded. When his tongue slipped into my mouth, it singed my bones, and I turned pliant beneath him. The best lies he told with his lips were the ones where he didn't use words. I was thankful for the noisy raindrops pelting the trees and pebbled path because it drowned out the sound of the sob welling in my throat.

This was too hard, too much.

I broke off the kiss, lifted my hand, and struck him across the cheek with a crack loud enough to be heard over the rain. The force of my slap turned his head away from me, and for a long moment he stared off, considering what had just happened.

Or maybe the full force of what he'd done was finally sinking in. How he'd changed things between us forever. He turned slowly back to me with embarrassment lurking in his eyes.

"I'm sorry," he said quietly. He nodded toward the house. "Let's get out of the rain."

The fastest way out of this maze was with someone who knew all its secrets.

I crossed my arms over my chest to hold in my heat as he bent down and retrieved the umbrella. He swung it over our heads as I wiped the rain from my face, and my gaze traced the framework beneath the black fabric.

"You're holding a metal pole in a lightning storm," I said.

The corner of his mouth twitched, but it was gone a moment later. We were already alone in the maze, but being tucked together under the safety of the umbrella felt . . .

intimate. Like we were hidden from the entire world.

"Assuming we survive the walk back," he said, "the first thing we need to do is put a lock on your door."

I kept my tone dry. "Afraid you won't be able to stay away?"

Royce's expression was haunting and deadly serious. "It's not me I'm worried about keeping out."

Oh, my God.

THREE

I BARELY SLEPT MY FIRST NIGHT IN THE HALE HOUSE. IT DIDN'T matter that the king-sized bed was comfortable or that the sheets were soft. The detergent on the linens was pleasant but unfamiliar. Even with the curtains drawn, shadows seemed to move in unexpected ways in the cavernous room. Every foreign sound echoed and jolted me awake, and my gaze shot to the doorknob.

Thankfully, it never turned. Maybe Royce had exaggerated and there wasn't any danger of Macalister coming into my room. Perhaps he'd put the fear in my head as a power move.

When sleep finally came, it wasn't restful. The new room didn't smell like my home, and it certainly didn't feel like it either. Would it ever?

I stayed hidden in bed until the Hales left for work and the house went quiet. With them gone, I could finally think. The most effective way to derail Royce's life was to figure out exactly what he was planning. I thought I'd have the day to explore the house on my own, but my phone buzzed with a text message. Alice, Royce's stepmother, would be sending a car this morning, and she had several appointments set up for me.

Once I'd been whisked to Boston, I met her and a potential wedding planner for lunch. And when that was done, I was delivered to Alice's personal shopper with a long list of occasions I needed to be styled for.

There were fundraisers and charity galas. Golf outings, and regattas, and a whole slew of events I would be expected to attend with Royce. His schedule had been synced with my calendar, and I'd been warned this was only the beginning. More parties and events were coming.

The first one on Alice's list was dinner tonight, because once a week the Hales shared a meal together. So, this evening I'd sit beside my fiancé and be officially welcomed into the family.

In the dining room.

"Are you feeling all right?" the saleswoman asked, worried. She'd noticed my pale face, and perhaps the cold sweat dotting my brow.

"I'm fine," I said as my stomach twisted into knots.

She put me in a short, rose gold dress that had an open back and a beautiful drape. It was business formal—not dressy enough for a wedding, but much fancier than anything I'd wear to dinner with my own family. It looked nice and sophisticated, though, and hopefully it would give me the confidence I'd need to get through this evening.

Royce made good on his promise. When I returned from my afternoon meetings, there was a deadbolt installed just above the knob on my bedroom door. It was brass and matched the décor perfectly, barely looking out of place. Only its shine gave away its newness.

I wondered if the same could be said of me in this house.

At six-thirty, there was a short knock. "Marist," came Royce's voice from behind the door. "It's time for dinner."

I balled my hands into fists, shook out the tension through my fingers, and strode to the door.

He was wearing a stone-gray suit with a charcoal colored tie. Like yesterday, he'd come straight from the office and hadn't changed, but this time he hadn't relaxed his look. The knot in his tie was sharp and perfect. Everything was buttoned down and polished.

Except for the way his hungry gaze roamed over me. It started at my nude heels and worked its way up, flowing over the pink hued fabric until finally finding my face. His blue eyes hinted at his indecent thoughts, and I did my best to pretend I didn't care, nor was I having similar thoughts about the way he looked.

My exaggerated tone was sugary sweet. "How was your day, darling?"

He didn't rise to take the bait. Instead, his appreciative gaze swiped over me once more, before landing on the engagement ring I wore. "Better now."

Damn him. Unwanted warmth bloomed in the center of my chest. I went to push past him, but he put his arm on the doorframe and blocked my exit.

"Grab your phone," he said. "You're going to need it."

That was strange, but I didn't question it. I just did as

I was told.

We walked together in silence through the hall, down the grand staircase, and as we approached the ornate wooden door to the dining room, trepidation turned my legs into unmovable cement. Panic bubbled in my stomach like over-carbonated cheap wine.

"Wait," I whispered.

Royce's warm palm pressed against the bare skin on my back. Not to push me forward, but to connect and calm. "Hey." He matched my quiet voice. "It's okay."

Nothing was okay, though. Behind that door was the long dining table and flickering candelabras and nine men in tuxedos waiting for me—

I'd gone rigid, and Royce's expression hung. "I, uh, can tell him you're not feeling well." He'd done his best to sound convincing, but it was pointless.

"Right. Because that worked out so well for Emily."

Six weeks ago, my sister had tried to get out of lunch with the Hales, but Macalister hadn't allowed it. He'd pushed until she'd made an appearance—one that ended with her throwing up all over his hand during their handshake.

Even if Royce told his father I was sick and that worked, it was only putting off the inevitable. I'd be right back in this situation again next week. Better to face it now and get it over with than live with another week of dread.

I swallowed a deep breath, forcing confidence into my body. "I'm fine. I can do this."

I said it more for me than for him, but Royce nodded. "Yes. If anyone can, it's you."

He pushed the door open, and my lungs squeezed painfully tight.

The room looked so different than it had during the initiation. The curtains were open, and bright sunlight poured in from the oversized windows, chasing away shadows. The candelabras had been shelved on a side table. Even the impressive crystal chandelier overhead seemed transformed. It was elegant and regal, sparkling proudly rather than glinting sinisterly in the darkness.

The table had been set at the end closest to the door, opposite the side where I'd lain naked a little over a week ago and lost my virginity. I tried not to stare at the spot or think about that night. I needed to focus, anyway. The rest of the Hales were already seated, and, judging by Macalister's irritated expression, they'd been waiting for us.

He sat at the head of the table, Alice to his right and his younger son Vance beside her. I worried for a moment the empty seat next to Macalister was for me, but Royce pulled out the farther chair and gestured to it.

"Thank you," I uttered automatically, dropping down into the seat.

Royce said nothing. He sat and plunked his phone face-up on the table beside the silver charging plate. I braced for Macalister to say something about how disrespectful that was. Phones weren't allowed at the dinner table in my house . . . but here everyone had theirs out, resting beside their silverware like it was a required utensil in their place setting.

A woman I hadn't met before, but who was clearly part of the Hale household staff, entered from the kitchen and served us salads. Alice first, then me, and then the Hale men in order of seniority. It was stilted and formal, and so uncomfortable it stretched my skin tightly. No one else seemed to feel it, though. In the silence, they readied their forks and began eating, oblivious to my discomfort.

"Marist. How did you find your first night here?" Macalister's icy gaze locked onto me and refused to let go.

"It was fine, thank you." I despised how weak my voice sounded. Silence followed, dragging painfully, and I felt compelled to fill it. I forced a bright tone. "How was your day?"

It was like I'd just asked him what color money was. He simply stared, making me wince and my skin stretch tighter still.

"It was fine," he said finally. His attention left me so he could stab his fork into his salad, and then he focused on his youngest son. "I volunteered you to Lambert's team for the Marblehead race at the end of the summer. One of their crew members broke a hand, and I told him you would help out."

Vance blinked. He struggled to process the information but failed to conceal the dislike from his boyishly good-looking face. It wasn't the sailing that bothered him. The Hales were the founding members of the Cape Hill Yacht Club, and Vance was an experienced helmsman. He had plenty of racing trophies to prove it.

No, I suspected it was Wayne Lambert who was giving him pause.

Mr. Lambert was the CEO of a giant pharmaceutical company. He had a very large and *very* New York personality, only moving here in the last decade so his daughters could attend Cape Hill Prep. Foul-mouthed and hot-tempered, he had one of those booming laughs that made a room go awkwardly quiet. He was loud in everything he did. And he was new money.

Which meant he was the polar opposite of Macalister Hale.

The two CEOs of Cape Hill seemed unlikely to be friends, so I had to wonder what was going on. Macalister wouldn't put up with Mr. Lambert without a good reason.

"His daughter is also on the crew," Macalister added. "Alice and I discussed it and feel she would be a good companion for the anniversary celebration."

Vance's pointed gaze swung toward Alice, and I couldn't help but think about the last time I'd seen them together. She'd been on her knees, her hands fisted in the undone sides of his tuxedo pants and his dick buried in her mouth.

Her expression toward her stepson now was tepid. "Royce's party was one thing, but this is huge. HBHC is turning one hundred and fifty years old, and you're a Hale. You have to bring a date."

Royce interrupted the wordless conversation going on between his brother and his stepmother. "Which daughter? Lambert has two."

"The older one," Macalister said.

"Jillian," Alice said at the same time.

Royce turned his attention to his brother. "Be careful. She's a stage-five clinger."

Vance arched one eyebrow. "You dated her?"

"Yeah, I think 'date' would be too strong a word." The

amused look on Royce's face froze, as if he just realized his fiancée was sitting right beside him while he was talking about
fucking someone else.

Was I supposed to care about this? Because . . . I didn't.
It certainly wasn't news to me that he'd been a player, and besides—he'd betrayed me. I wasn't supposed to care about him.

He stared at me anxiously, not sure how I'd react.

I shrugged a shoulder. "Good luck, Vance. Last I heard,
she has a boyfriend."

A scoff came from the end of the table.

Macalister's gaze was an avalanche. Cold, terrifying,
and beautiful. "That doesn't matter. When he asks her," he
turned his head so he could decree it directly to Vance, "and
he *will* ask her—she'll be pleased to trade up to a Hale." His
eyes turned smug. "They always are."

If I'd been standing, the arrogance in his tone would
have knocked me over, but he was wrong. My sister Emily
had no desire to trade up to a Hale. She'd been promised to
Royce for years and did everything she could to get out of it,
including getting pregnant.

Alice set her fork down and picked up her phone. "Since
we're discussing the anniversary, I have a mockup of the invi-
tation to show you." She tapped the screen a few times before
presenting it to her husband.

Disdain flooded his face. "This isn't serious. A masquerade party?"

Her lips pressed into a thin line. "This is what you
asked for."

"I believe I asked for something memorable and

sophisticated." He set her phone down and pointed at the screen. "This isn't elegant, it's a junior prom."

Alice tossed a lock of her blonde hair over her shoulder, crossed her arms, and rested them on the table, leaning forward. "This will be elegant, I promise you. It will still be black-tie." Her posture was confident, announcing she wasn't going to be deterred. "You can't be memorable unless you go over the top. Otherwise, it'll just be another bland corporate party, indistinguishable from all the others. You want this to be an *experience*, one people will be talking about for the next one hundred and fifty years."

Macalister wasn't sold, but as he leaned back in his chair, it was clear he was considering what she'd said.

"When people think their identity is obscured, even somewhat," a sly smile graced her lips, "they let go of their inhibitions. Think about the guest list. Wouldn't you love to have an evening where everyone has their guard down?"

My mouth dropped open. She'd just offered Macalister one of the things he valued most. The highest commodity in our elite New England town.

Information.

It'd be his best opportunity to learn all the secrets Cape Hill was desperate to conceal.

His gaze sharpened on his clever wife, and genuine delight flashed through him. He wasn't on the fence about her theme anymore—he was in absolute support of it.

"I trust your judgement," he said. "You understand how important this event is to me and my company." He paused as the temperature of his voice plummeted. "I'm sure it won't just meet my expectations—but exceed them."

It was like he'd just barely left of the "*or else*" threat at the end of his statement, and I swallowed hard on Alice's behalf. She didn't seem affected, though. Either she felt confident in her abilities or she'd been married to him long enough she was used to it.

"Speaking of expectations," his attention returned to me, and I struggled not to squirm in my seat, "after dinner is over, I have some items to go over with you. We can discuss them in the library."

Royce asked it before I could. "What items?"

His father's cool gaze turned to his oldest son. "Things that are none of your business."

My heart launched into my throat, clogging my airway until it was nearly impossible to breathe. The mood in the room sank faster than a company's stock after reporting a huge loss. Alice and Vance tensed.

But Royce's chest puffed up, and he took on a dark cast. "Anything that has to do with Marist *is* my business."

Macalister gave his son a look that screamed, *is that so?* In his mind, Royce had sold those rights away. The oldest Hale laced his fingers together on the tabletop, and as he sat in the ornate chair at the head of the table, he resembled a king on a throne. One who looked very much like he wanted to put the prince back in his place.

"We have an agreement," Macalister said. "I promised to keep her updated on her family's financial situation." His piercing eyes curved back to me. "I don't see a need for Royce to be included on that. Do you?"

Beneath the table, Royce's hand latched onto my thigh, just above my knee. His warm palm tingled against the bare skin of my leg, but I tried not to notice. The action might have seemed affection to anyone else, but this was a warning. He was saying it was dangerous, telling me to be careful.

I understood what was happening and how I was playing directly into Macalister's hand. And while I didn't want to be alone with him, his offer was too good to pass up. Royce withheld information from me, and tonight I would do the same.

I pushed his hand off my knee as I looked at his father. "No," I said firmly. "I don't see a reason either."

The pleased smile on Macalister's face twisted my insides.

Tension rolled off Royce throughout dinner and permeated the room. Not that it would have been an enjoyable meal otherwise. Once the main course had been served, I realized these weekly dinners were merely business meetings for Macalister to preside over and ensure all his family members were carrying out the directions he gave.

As soon as we were dismissed, my fiancé turned in his seat and put a hand on the back of my chair. His voice was low and urgent. "Don't be alone with him."

I sucked in a breath. "Why? What are you worried is going to happen?"

Royce's eyes darted away. "He's manipulative."

I did my best to hold in an incredulous laugh. "Oh, I see. Your worry isn't about me . . . it's what he might say about you."

His gaze snapped back to me. "Let me come with you."

He didn't bother to deny my accusation. My spine hardened, either with pride or vindictiveness or both, and I pushed back from the table. "No."

He followed me up, and his voice edged toward frustration. "Marist, please—"

"This is your own doing. You keep me out of your business, so I'm allowed to do the same."

He frowned and desperation ringed his eyes, but I refused to waver. I couldn't rely on Royce to save me. I'd have to do it myself.

As I marched out of the dining room, he fell into step at my side, not arguing or attempting to slow me down. We both knew his father was waiting for me.

It was fitting the library was on the second floor. We climbed the stairs and ascended toward Mount Olympus while I, the mortal, mentally prepared as best I could for my audience with the god Zeus.

FOUR

Macalister wasn't seated behind the desk like I'd expected. He stood with his broad back to me and appeared to be cataloguing the books on the shelf. While he was already a tall man, the walls lined with bookcases somehow exaggerated his height.

As if he needed any help looking imposing.

The library was warm colors. It had an old-world feel and a relaxed ease, but in his perfect black suit and tie, he looked out of place. At my entrance, he turned just enough to glance at me over his shoulder. "Shut the door." I did as asked, my breath tight in my lungs. He gestured to a chair. "Have a seat."

I lowered into one cautiously, my gaze never straying from him. I had the irrational fear that if I took my eyes off him for a single second, he'd use that moment to strike. It was a ridiculous thought. Macalister wouldn't come at me physically. His attack would be subtle. He'd use precise, surgical words rather than his hands to undo me.

He didn't sit behind the desk. Instead, he took the seat beside me, causing more alert to spike through my body. Perhaps he'd done it to dispel the power dynamic and try to treat me as an equal, but I highly doubted it. More likely, his goal had been to remove the barrier that stood between us yesterday.

He lifted a sheet of paper off the desk and passed it to me. "The situation with your family is more dire than we anticipated. This is a summary of their debt."

I stared at the figures.

Disbelief slapped me across the face. My heart quickened until it beat so fast, blood roared in my ears. This couldn't be right. I tried to read the page through the tears blurring my vision, but then it abruptly became easier. Anger flared and burned the tears up before they could fall.

Five million dollars had been deposited into their account, and it had only made a dent. I'd whored myself out for that money, and it wasn't even enough.

My teeth ground together so hard, my jaw threatened to crack. I tossed the summary report bitterly onto the desk, not wanting to look at the figures another second, wishing I could make them go away just as easily for my parents.

Macalister noted my reaction before speaking. "You're understandably upset. I was too when this was brought to my attention. They've been treading water, hoping for a lifeline to come save them. There was no other plan." His tone was as dark as the black ink he used in his signature. "And that *infuriates* me."

I'd always thought of anger as a blazing emotion, full of

fire and urgency. But in Macalister Hale, anger was cloaked in ice. It was an arctic slide into freezing water, where relentless pins-and-needles slowly trapped and consumed everything.

"I had no idea," I said quietly. "If I had—"

His eyes widened with surprise. "You misunderstand. I'm not accusing you. They shamefully kept this from you and your sister." He set an elbow on the armrest closest to me, and his silver cufflink glinted. "It doesn't change the situation, however. If something were to happen to your parents, their estate would be insolvent. You and Emily would have to liquidate the house, which wouldn't be enough. You'd be left with nothing except the considerable credit card debt you co-signed with your parents."

An invisible hand reached inside my body, and its furious fingers curled around my heart, squeezing to the point of pain. I set my palm flat against my chest. "I should have asked questions."

"Yes, you should have." His expression was plain, but not cruel. "A painful lesson learned."

His gaze wandered over my face, not so much studying it, but tracing each line and curve. He examined me like a financial report he couldn't get to balance. Frustrated and curious, and also intrigued. I dropped my gaze to my knees peeking out below my dress.

"I've set up an account in your name," he said, "with enough money to cover your tuition for your final year at Etonsons, along with general expenses. Any single purchase above five thousand will require my approval, but you will have anything you need."

Surprise drew my gaze back to him, but skepticism took over. I was terrified of what he'd want in return. "In exchange for?"

Macalister's blue eyes blinked. "In exchange for you receiving a first-rate education. I've seen your transcripts and know you're an exceptional student. I only want to see you achieve your full potential."

I stumbled over his words before they truly hit me. "I didn't give Etonsons permission to release my transcripts."

It was the first time I'd ever seen amusement play out on Macalister's face. His full lips lifted just enough to be classified as a smile. "Do you think that was difficult for me?"

"No," I said dimly. I echoed what he'd told me at my interview in his boardroom. "There's no problem big enough money can't solve."

"Yes." He was pleased I remembered. "Your coursework has been excellent so far, but I have some thoughts about your options for next semester."

Of course he did.

"I am curious, though." He leaned closer, like he was capable of holding a friendly conversation with me. "What is it about economics that appeals to you?"

I floundered. How was I supposed to put it into words? I had to give him an answer. "I . . . like variables."

He paused. "Excuse me?"

"Math is precise." I tucked a lock of hair behind my ear as I assembled my thoughts. "You always know the answer, where one plus one equals two. But in economics, everything can be equal and still not give you the answer you expect. The exact same product sold in a perfectly competitive market can be a boon for one company and a bust for another."

I was aware I was speaking in simplistic terms to a man who was likely more intelligent than I was, but he made me nervous. At least I sounded coherent.

"Maybe their manufacturing costs are too high," I continued, "or their marketing was off, or they've priced themselves too competitively. I want to know what's causing it. I like finding the variable."

Macalister made a noise of satisfaction, even as he shook his head. "You like puzzles," he corrected.

"Yes," I said. He wasn't wrong. "I like a very specific type of puzzle."

When a genuine smile expanded on his lips, he didn't look quite so terrifying. He simply looked mortal. "I also like puzzles." He tilted his head an evaluating degree. "How did you find your game theory class?"

The question was innocent, but a sixth sense of awareness tingled down my back. Like I saw the edges of a trap peeking out from beneath its camouflage but disregarded it. "It's been my favorite one so far."

Heat warmed his eyes. "It was my favorite as well. You're so much like me, Marist."

The shudder that clattered through my body was unavoidable. My name on his lips, coupled with the idea I was remotely like him, was too much not to react to. He watched my shoulders quiver, and his expression shifted like he was pleased. He enjoyed having such an effect on me.

My voice was timid when I wanted it to be strong. "We're

not alike."

"You grew into a levelheaded young woman," he said, "despite your financially inept parents, even as they spoiled you and your sister shamelessly. Like you, I grew up with enormous wealth and stayed sensible throughout it." He listed them like bullet points he'd prepared ahead of time. "You speak directly. You do what needs to be done, even when it's difficult. And most importantly, you understand when people need to be saved from themselves."

I launched up out of the chair, literally running from what he'd said. I needed to put distance between us as quickly as possible. But I'd only made it a few steps toward the window when I heard his chair creak, announcing he'd stood as well.

Macalister's voice was surprisingly hesitant. "I don't say this to upset you."

There was a table beside the window, and I set a hand on it for support while I tried to slow my ragged breathing. The glossy black and white pieces of the chessboard nearby were carved figures of art. I wanted things to be like that. Structured rules, clearly defined lines, and to know which team everyone was playing for.

I had to change the topic. "May I ask you a question?"

"Yes."

The word came from just over my shoulder, and I closed my eyes. His proximity constricted every muscle in my body, turning me into one of the chess pieces at my fingertips.

"You don't seem like the type of man to be friends with Mr. Lambert."

His laugh was empty. "That's a statement, not a

THE OBSESSION | 41

question . . . but a correct one. I'm not, nor will I ever be, *friends* with Wayne Lambert." He emphasized the word like it was revolting. "He's just a means to an end."

"You want to see Vance with his daughter."

"Yes. Among other things."

I swallowed a breath and opened my eyes, staring out the window at the manicured lawn that seemed to endlessly stretch for miles around the Hale house. "Such as?"

In the taut silence suspended between us, I felt his gaze fixated on my bare back, drinking in all my vulnerable, exposed skin. The library was cold, and Macalister was colder still, yet when he moved in, there was the dark heat of his breath. It washed down my back and drew a violent shiver from me.

His lips were right beside my ear. "Wayne Lambert is going to get me a presidential nomination to the Federal Reserve."

Oh, my God, of course.

Lambert had been a megadonor to the president's election campaign, was a staunch supporter, and a close friend. It'd be easy for him to whisper a favorable word in the president's ear. And Macalister had plenty of experience. He ran the second largest bank in the country and was scandal-free. He would likely sail through the confirmation hearing.

It shouldn't have been a surprise that this was what he desired. Being the head of HBHC was great, but there was far more prestige and control at the helm of the Federal Reserve. Overseeing the entire U.S. banking system and maintaining interest rates was ultimate power. It was the pinnacle of his career; he couldn't ascend any higher.

"Oh," I breathed.

"I think it's only fitting," his tone was distant thunder, quiet but full of power, "since my family helped build the Fed, that I should sit on its board."

Yet another thing he felt entitled to, simply for being born.

And Macalister would mine Mr. Lambert's connections in multiple ways. They could be equally useful to Vance, who was eyeing a career in politics.

"I'd wish you luck," I said, "but I doubt you'll need it."

I could hear the smile in his voice. "No, I won't."

I didn't get a moment to catch my breath before the mood in the room changed. It shifted and turned darker, as if the air knew his motives.

"This dress you have on," Macalister's tone dipped and veered toward seduction, "I like it very much."

Before I could react, a single cold fingertip kissed my skin and skated like a whisper down my spine. It was barely a touch, but I jolted away from it, sending my hip crashing into the side of the table.

The chess set rattled and teetered, and the tallest black piece with a cross at the top of its crown toppled over onto its side, rolling toward the edge of the table. I grabbed it instinctively to stop it from falling and unleashed my tongue. "I didn't give you permission to touch me."

"You're right, you didn't."

Was that supposed to be an apology? I was trapped between him and the table, and genuine fear snaked through my body. Royce had installed a lock on my door. Emily had said Macalister believed he was entitled to everything, including people. And he'd purchased me like property. He probably believed he had every right to my body, and I'd been so fucking foolish—

"I shouldn't have done that." He abruptly stepped back. "Forgive me. It won't happen again."

I clutched the game piece so hard, the sharp edges were uncomfortable in my grip. A little over a year ago, I'd stood in nearly this spot while Royce touched me the same way, yet the difference was staggering.

"You're . . . shaking." Macalister sounded surprised. "Are you afraid?"

There was no hesitation. "Yes."

He asked it when he already knew the answer. "Of what?"

"Of you." I risked a glance over my shoulder and found him looking, of all things, perplexed.

"There's no need to be scared," he said. "I'm not going to hurt you."

But couldn't he see he already had? He'd driven a wedge between Royce and me, and for what reason?

It was like he could read my mind, and his expression went hard. "I only want what's best for everyone involved. You were too attached."

I said nothing, because there was nothing to say. I couldn't argue. He'd seen me nearly break down last night as Royce had walked out on me.

His command was delivered in a firm tone. "Turn around and look at me."

I filled my lungs with air, turned, and forced my gaze

up over his suit and serious face until I met his icy eyes. In a different setting and with another personality installed in his body, Macalister Hale could be irresistible. He had nearly everything already. Looks, smarts, money, and power. And he was young too. He didn't look fifty, even though he was, and he seemed decades younger than the other CEOs topping the *Fortune* 500 list.

His calculating gaze scrutinized, searching for my flaws and weaknesses and probably finding them in spades, but I didn't dare look away. I gripped the chess piece tightly in my fist and stared back. Was this who Royce would become in twenty-five years?

What if it took him less time to harden into cold, unmovable stone?

What if he's become his father already?

Macalister was dark everywhere except for his pale eyes. "Someday, you'll see how I saved you. You may even thank me for what I did."

Fucking doubtful.

Yet the scariest thing of all was it looked like he truly believed what he'd said. He imagined himself my savior.

I couldn't stand still under his inspection another second. I opened my hand and looked down at the figure in my palm. The carved black piece was intricate and beautiful.

"Would you like to play?" he asked.

"No, thank you." I didn't want to spend any more time in this library than was necessary. "I don't know how."

This idea offended him more than anything else I'd ever done, and he scowled. "Don't lie to me."

"I'm not," I said quickly. Was this really that impossible to believe? My sister hated games. My father didn't have time for them, and my mother only played cards. "No one ever taught me."

His focus fell to the piece in my hand before returning skeptically to me. Behind his eyes, he seemed to be considering something, and a feeling of unease grew in my chest.

"Then I'll teach you."

My pulse sped tumbling along. "No, that's all right. I don't—"

The words died as he held up a hand to silence me. "The piece you're holding is the king." He spoke it heavy with meaning. "When he cannot escape the threat of capture, the game is over."

My mouth went dry. Was he implying he was the evil king and I'd captured him? I hurried to set the piece down on the board. "I'm sure there are things you'd rather be doing than teaching me a board game."

His eyebrow arched so high it was a miracle it didn't knock down the chandelier. "Chess is a sophisticated game of strategy and tactics. You will enjoy it very much."

If he was going to be my partner? Again, fucking doubtful.

He wouldn't be dissuaded, even when I'd made it clear I didn't want to play. He didn't care, knowing he'd get his way. As he picked up the board and carried it to the desk, I stood rooted to my spot and looked longingly at the door. As long as I was here, I had to follow his orders. There wasn't a way out, but perhaps I could get something for my misery.

He wanted something, but I did too.

"I want a job at HBHC," I said.

He was arranging the board and paused, his fingertips still on a figure of a horse's head. "Excuse me?"

"Royce doesn't have an assistant. I was thinking I could be his until my semester starts."

"No." He didn't bother to consider it. He just resumed his task, as if it were that easy to shut me down.

"I need something to do, rather than sit around the house all day, waiting for Alice to summon me." Like I'd done today.

This time when he paused, he wore his irritation like his expensive suit. "It wouldn't look good to have you working for him. If you need help occupying your time," his tone threatened, "I'll find something for you."

I kept my voice soft and pleading, not wanting to challenge him. "You could call it an unpaid internship."

His irritation climbed to the top of the bookshelves. "Why would you want that?"

"Experience," I choked out.

Oh, I was going to have to get much better at lying if I was going to survive the Hale family.

Macalister's jaw set. "That's an acceptable answer, but it's not your reason. Tell me now before I lose my patience with you."

I went with a vague version of the truth. "Royce shuts me out to the point I don't know who he is. You had me move in so we could get to know each other better, but he's at the office so much . . . I thought this could help."

What it would really do was help me figure out what Royce was planning. I'd have total access to his schedule, see who he was meeting with and talking to. I had no qualms about spying on my fiancé to discover all the secrets he wouldn't tell me.

Macalister ran a hand over his jawline. "You understand you'll be around him the majority of your day, and at the house in the evenings, in addition to all the events and obligations he has."

"Yes."

He didn't smile with his lips, but it lurked in his eyes. "Royce won't like that."

"No," I said, "I don't suppose he will."

He straightened abruptly as if it had been settled. "I will allow this on two conditions."

My hands hung at my sides, hidden in the folds of my skirt, and I bunched my fingers into fists, bracing for impact.

"First, because you two will be working so closely and living together, I think a little distance is needed. You'll refrain from physical contact except when it's necessary. For instance, if you're in public and some display of affection is required, that's acceptable. But there's no need for it in my house."

I knew it was coming, that Macalister would forbid Royce and me from any kind of physical relationship. It was the next logical step in splitting us apart, and a small part of me was relieved by this constraint. Royce was masterful at seduction, and now his best tool of manipulation had been shelved.

But a much larger part of me mourned the loss of it. The only time Royce and I truly seemed to connect was when I acted on my feelings. I'd waited so long, just barely gotten him, and already he was being taken away. It was unfair, but so much of my life was right now I was growing used to it.

My voice was hushed and uneven. "All right."

Macalister nodded, pleased. "My second condition is we play a game of chess together here every night."

My heart ground to a halt. "For how long?"

"Until you beat me." His grin was downright evil. "Do we have a deal?"

FIVE

ROYCE WORE A NAVY THREE-PIECE SUIT, A WHITE DRESS SHIRT, and a pale silver tie with matching pocket square. He had his laptop bag hung on one shoulder and a cup of Starbucks in hand, and he strode down the hall toward his office looking both at ease and in command. He was so perfectly Wall Street it was like he'd just come from a stock photo shoot.

When his eyes locked onto me seated behind his assistant's desk, he pulled to a stop. He stared, unable to believe what he was seeing, two separate universes colliding.

This morning, he'd gotten up earlier than anyone else to hit the gym and hadn't returned by the time I'd left. Thankfully, the ride into Boston hadn't been as awkward as I'd feared. Alice and I sat in the back of a Mercedes and Macalister up front with the driver, and neither of the Hales glanced up from their phones the entire drive.

"Marist?" Royce asked. His unsure gaze floated around the HBHC executive hallway like he needed to confirm where he was. "Do we have an appointment today?"

"No. Your father wants to see you when you get in, though."

He was bewildered. "Okay, but what are you doing here?"

"Me?" I feigned my own confusion. "Oh, I work here now."

"I'm sorry, you what?"

I gave him a Cheshire Cat grin. "I'm your new assistant."

His eyes clouded. "Right."

"Go see your dad. Someone from IT is supposed to be here soon to set up my email."

He flopped his laptop bag on my desk with a thud, but set his coffee down with more care, as if the contents of the cardboard cup had greater value than the MacBook in his briefcase.

"I'll be right back," he said, "and then we'll see about that."

He did an about-face and returned to the elevator at the end of the hall. Even though he was on the board of directors now, he wasn't on the top floor yet with all the other chief-level executives.

How long would it be before he was named chief operating officer? He wouldn't be thirty for another four years, and that still seemed awfully young. He was hungry, though. Maybe his ambition made up for some of his lack of experience, and his last name did the rest of the work.

The doors peeled back, he stepped into the empty car, and I leaned over the desk to watch him as he turned to face the doors. The smirk on his face was so large, it read all the way down the hall to me. He was such an arrogant prick.

I hated how much it turned me on.

The doors sealed closed and carried him up to his father's office, where he'd do his best to undo the move I'd made last night.

While I waited, I returned my attention to my phone and the article I was reading about chess theory. I'd lost my first game last night so quickly, it had been embarrassing. I had to get much, much better if I didn't want to spend the rest of my life closed in the library losing to Macalister.

I was still installing a chess app on my phone when Royce's shadow fell across me. I glanced up, and his furious expression made my heart stop.

"My office," he growled. "*Now.*"

Holy shit. The dark timbre of his voice was scary and . . . a little exciting too.

He didn't wait for me. He was a blur of navy wool and silver silk as he snatched up his coffee cup and laptop bag and pounded through the doorway into his office.

Royce didn't have to issue the order for me to shut the door—his attitude made it perfectly clear the conversation we were about to have was serious. Beyond the glass wall at the back of his office, the city was different hues of gray. The concrete, the steel, and even the overcast sky were all cold and unemotional. Was it because the storm was brewing here in my fiancé's eyes?

"He said you *asked* for this job." He jammed a hand in his hair, visibly unsettled. "What did you give him?"

I put my hands on my hips. "It's none of your business."

My answer angered him further, and I enjoyed the unease that simmered in his expression. He stared at me, silently demanding I explain.

I sighed. "I gave him nothing."

His gaze narrowed. "He doesn't give people what they want, ever, and definitely not out of the goodness of his heart." Royce clenched a hand into a fist and pressed his knuckles against his desktop. "He doesn't even have a heart. So, I'm asking again. What did you give him?"

"It's nothing," I repeated, my voice giving away nothing about how unsure I felt on the inside. "I have to play him in chess every night."

There was no reaction. He was a statue. "For how long?"

"Until I win."

It sounded ridiculous when I said it out loud, but tension corded his muscles, making his shoulders stiff.

"Great," Royce snapped. "Did he mention he played competitively when he was at Harvard?"

I deflated a little. "No."

He let out a tight breath and straightened, setting the full power of his intense stare on me. "So, now you'll have to go to him every night. He'll wear you down, Marist. He'll get inside your head and turn you against me."

"He won't." A part of me wanted to laugh. Right now, Royce didn't need his father's help turning me against him. He was doing just fine all by himself.

"Something you need to understand about my father is he doesn't play a game unless he's sure he's going to win."

I swung my gaze away. Royce's office was so professional and impersonal, decorated for the persona he projected. Did he think other people would see it as a sign of weakness if he acted like a human? Was that how his father had taught him?

For being a family company, it was like he hid that part

of himself.

"I wish you'd let me go with you last night," he said.

"Yeah? Well, I wish you hadn't sold me for one hundred thousand shares, Royce. You don't always get what you want."

"But I do." His tone softened. "I wanted you, and now here we are."

His statement rankled. "You *don't* have me. You gave me away."

He was abruptly right in front of me, wearing a determined look while heat warmed his eyes. It distracted me long enough for him to get his hands around my waist.

I squirmed in his hold. "No. We're not allowed to—"

Everything from his expression to his voice was dark and aggressive. "Yeah, he told me all about how you agreed to his stupid 'no contact' deal. But *I didn't.*"

It stole my breath the way he kissed me. He was a roller-coaster. Thrillingly dangerous even when there was no threat to my safety. I wasn't going to die. All the danger was manufactured, but it didn't feel any less real.

It was just a kiss, anyway. Breaking Macalister's rule wasn't going to cause the end of the world.

Was it?

Royce's hands slid around my back as his tongue slipped into my mouth, and before he'd made the deal, I would have enjoyed this, but now all I could taste was his manipulation. I couldn't trust him when his mouth was pressed to mine. And I couldn't trust myself not to cave.

"No," I said, stepping back.

My retreat left him adrift, but he recovered with lightning

fast reflexes. His eyebrow arrowed up. "No?"

"You just take whatever you want and demand I trust you, but trust doesn't work as a one-way street. Until you get that, I'm not sharing any part of me with you."

Oh, he didn't like that. His jaw set, and I was struck by how much he could look like his father when he was challenged. But he relented, one layer at a time, either returning to the man he was when we were alone . . . or shifting tactics.

He grabbed my hand and squeezed the engagement ring he'd given me. "I know it doesn't seem like it, but we're in this together. I can't protect you if you shut me out."

Fire ignited inside my belly. "Except you never let me in." I pulled away. "And I don't *need* your help, Royce."

By the end of the week, I was second-guessing every choice I'd made.

Working as Royce's assistant was a joke. He spent his days in meetings and conference calls and long lunches, all of which I wasn't allowed to sit in on. There were no paper trails or clues in his immaculate office. No hushed conversations for me to overhear. His email wasn't run by me, and I didn't screen his calls.

I'd also been distracted with wedding planning. Alice was focused on the anniversary party and demanded I step in and oversee the coordinator she'd hired. My future step-mother-in-law was the CEO of my wedding. I was just middle management, executing her vision.

Every night, I lost the game of chess.

Last night, Macalister accused me of trying to lose too quickly. Subconsciously, perhaps I had. While I spent every free minute practicing on my phone, anxiety crept in as soon as I walked into the library and found his icy stare waiting for me.

I wanted it over as soon as possible.

On Friday, the stock market dipped and put Royce in a foul mood. After our silent car ride together this morning, he'd skulked into his office and shut the door without a word. He didn't come out for lunch. At three o'clock, he emerged, and the somber expression he wore made suspicion coil in my belly.

"I'm heading out early." His eyes met mine briefly then shifted away. "I'm not feeling well."

HBHC stock was still falling since this morning, and it seemed like a really bad idea for anyone named Hale to leave early, but I didn't say that to him. Instead, I stood and gathered my things. "I'll go with you."

I'd hoped for pushback. If he were up to something, he wouldn't want me tagging along. But he gave a slight nod and waited dutifully for me to finish. He wasn't sneaking off to some clandestine meeting.

Maybe it wasn't a lie that he was unwell.

As we sat on the leather seats and the town car whisked us away from Boston, Royce ignored the phone he had clasped in a hand and resting on his knee. He chose to stare blankly out the window.

Gone was the confident, cocky man I'd worked with

all week. He didn't act or even look like himself. A troubled Royce made me worried, and even though I didn't want to care about him, it was impossible not to. Concern stole into my voice. "Are you okay?"

"Today was a bad day."

That was all he said the entire fifty-three-minute ride back to the house.

He vanished into his room, and as I did the same, unease grew ten-fold inside me.

Royce owned a massive amount of stock in his family's company. The drop today had likely cost him a million or more, so it was understandable to be upset, but . . . it was temporary. I'd bet my great-grandmother's necklace that one of Macalister's first lessons to his sons had been that the markets fluctuate. You couldn't be reactive. It might take a few weeks for HBHC's price to bounce back, but it would.

The stock market was a marathon, not a sprint.

My fingers paused on the book I'd pulled from my nightstand.

Perhaps that was causing Royce's dramatic mood shift—not the loss in money, but the loss of time. Maybe the drop in the market had thrown a wrench into his plans.

If that was true and his master plan was disrupted, why didn't I feel better? I clenched my teeth and simmered with self-irritation.

I snatched up my latest book on Greek mythology—this one a collection of essays—made my way to the back of the house, and down the stone steps toward the hedge maze. I'd always been drawn to it, and I'd found reading to be much easier when I put distance between me and Royce.

He was a distracting puzzle of a man I couldn't figure out.

The puzzle of evergreen trees was easier. It hadn't rained since the night I'd gotten lost, and, refusing to be conquered, I'd used the last three days to learn every passage in the maze. I could quickly find my way to the center now and on to the exit on the other side. I'd learned all its secrets, but not its magic. It still lingered amongst the leaves and statues.

As I'd done yesterday, I sat beneath the tiered fountain, moving over on the circular bench every ten minutes or so to stay in the shadow its cascading tower cast on me. The afternoon sun was as merciless as the July humidity.

The final essay in the book was about Hera. She'd been beautiful, and Zeus wanted her, and when she wouldn't submit to his advances, he tricked her. Knowing she loved all creatures, he changed into a cuckoo bird stranded out in the cold. Once she rescued him and took him inside her warm room, he changed back into his true form and raped her.

The shame of it would have been too much, and she was forced to marry Zeus to keep it a secret.

Queen of the gods, she was also the goddess of birth and marriage, which was ironic. Zeus was the *worst* husband. Every time she had her back turned, he'd run off to take another mortal lover, even though she stayed constant and faithful.

But her jealousy grew until she was only beautiful on the outside. Her wrath twisted her into an ugly goddess, full of vengeance and fire.

She'd never been my favorite in mythology, but I felt for her.

When I closed the book, my stomach growled, and reluctantly I wound my way back through the walls of evergreen, seeking the kitchen. There was a full-time chef on staff at the Hale house, but I didn't bother her for dinner. I pulled together some leftovers from earlier in the week and ate alone at the large table, my gaze out on the side garden.

Alice was there, pruning the white roses that bloomed along a trellis. She could have had one of the landscapers do it, but she enjoyed gardening. Her blonde hair gleamed in the golden sunlight, and as she paused to wipe sweat from her forehead, her eyes locked onto me. She waved, but didn't smile, and went back to work.

Did she know about the deal her husband had made with Royce? How Macalister had bought me for one hundred thousand shares? Macalister was Zeus, but she wasn't Hera. At least, not in jealousy or fidelity—I'd seen her and Vance together, after all.

I stared down at the wood grain running through the table and tried not to think about it.

At seven-thirty sharp, I peered up at the closed library door, and trepidation twisted in my core. The sensation was becoming familiar. Macalister was already in there because I could hear his heavy footsteps moving around. I filled my lungs with a deep breath, grasped the knob, and pushed the door open.

Awareness ghosted across my skin like a whisper. Something was . . . different. The room looked the same with its bookshelves full of colorful spines, and the smell of leather and oak was as I was accustomed to. The man who stood by the window wore one of his many impeccable suits, not a cuf-flink or a hair out of place.

But he didn't have to say a word for me to know some-thing was wrong. The nearly empty tumbler of amber liquid in his hand did.

I'd never seen Macalister Hale drink.

The night of the initiation, he'd toasted with a glass of champagne, but he'd only taken a single sip before handing it off to his wife. In fact, I wouldn't have been surprised to learn he'd merely pressed the glass to his mouth and faked the action of letting the alcohol past his lips.

He demanded precision in all aspects of his life. I as-sumed he didn't drink because he wouldn't want anything to impair his judgement or make him vulnerable. But there was a bottle of Macallan 1926 on the table that was half empty, and an unused glass rested beside it.

Macalister's shoulders rolled back, and he straightened to his full, daunting height. His gaze pierced into me while accusation swamped his eyes. "What are you doing here?"

Was I early? I wanted to shrink back into the shadows, but there was nowhere to hide. I bit down on the inside of my cheek to muster the words. "It's seven-thirty."

His arm extended out before bending at ninety-degrees, pulling back his sleeve and making the Cartier watch on his wrist visible to him. He checked the time and frowned. "So it is."

Rather than take a seat at the desk where the chessboard waited for us, he stayed at the window and finished his scotch. Not in savoring sips as it was supposed to be done, but in one huge swallow.

The whole day had been weird, but nothing set me more on edge than the way Macalister looked now. The only emotions I'd seen from him were the hard, shallow ones. Anger. Disappointment. Envy.

This man now was barely recognizable. He looked exhausted.

And utterly human.

I hadn't taken my hand off the doorknob yet. Like a chess piece, I'd moved but was still considering before committing to it. "Do you want to postpone?"

"No." He strode to the desk, put down his empty glass and refilled it, then poured a few sips-worth into the other glass. "You'll join me in a drink while we play."

It wasn't a request, and his order made me squirm inside my skin. Sharing a drink with my future father-in-law should have been a nice gesture, and the scotch he'd poured wasn't an 'average day' kind of whiskey—not even for one of the richest men in America. It was far too fine, too expensive.

I didn't like how it made the evening seem like we were friends. We'd never be *friends*. He was more than twice my age, and the power dynamic between us was wider than the Atlantic.

"I'm, uh, not a scotch drinker," I said.

He wasn't fazed and held the glass out to me. "I don't remember asking."

My heart sank. I closed the door and went to him, mumbling a *thank you* as I took the scotch. At least he hadn't poured heavy and was only wasting a few thousand dollars on me. Like a gentleman, he waited until I sat before he did. Two months ago, I wouldn't have warranted this sign of respect from him. For years, he hadn't noticed my existence.

Not until his son showed an interest.

Macalister's steely eyes weren't as focused as they normally were. While we played, his moves were still deliberate and cunning, but they were slower. Last night, he'd gone on the attack, and even the way he'd set his pieces down was sharp and aggressive. It had been a quick death.

Now, it was slow and agonizing. He slid the marble pieces across the black and white checkerboard like soap slicking across skin.

"You haven't touched your scotch," he said as his queen glided to a new spot close to my king. "Check."

I'd learned that the game of chess was played in three phases. The opening, the middlegame, and the one we'd just entered—

The endgame.

I picked up the tumbler and sipped the scotch while pretending to consider my options. There weren't any, really. I knew how it was going to end no matter what I did. Royce's words echoed in my mind. *He doesn't play a game unless he's sure he's going to win.*

Macalister's heavy gaze drank me in as the flavor of burnt rubber rolled across the tip of my tongue. I guarded my reaction carefully. He didn't need to know I hated his expensive scotch or the way he looked at me. Chess wasn't the only game we played every night. The stakes on the unspoken game were much higher.

I moved my bishop to block in a futile attempt, sacrificing it and only prolonging the inevitable.

His voice was unsteady, rather than gloating like he usually did. It was as if he were sad the game was over. "Checkmate."

It was the longest game we'd played yet, but he wasn't satisfied. As I rearranged the pieces into their starting positions, I tried to ignore the man who'd won and his strange behavior.

He said it quietly. "You're improving."

"Still a long way from beating you," I grumbled, then sucked in a sharp breath. I hadn't meant to say that out loud. I finished arranging the pieces into their starting positions and stood from my chair, relieved to escape—

Only to be frozen in place by his command.

"Stay."

There was a hint of desperation in the word, so faint I wasn't sure if I'd imagined it. I didn't want to stay. This mortal version of Macalister was the scariest of all.

My voice went soft, not wanting to disturb the shadows in the room. "Is everything all right?"

His expression shuttered, like I'd uncovered a dark secret. "Why do you ask?"

"I've never seen you drink before."

His gaze fell to his hand wrapped around the glass. "I do, once a year."

He lifted the drink to his lips and fixed his stare on me while he drank. His Adam's apple bobbed with each slow, deliberate swallow. It made me uncomfortable. He looked at me like he'd rather be savoring me than the liquor. When he finished, he set the glass down and ran his finger along the rim. It was an absentminded gesture, but it rang false. Everything he did was calculated and measured.

"Once a year?" I asked.

"Yes." The pad of his finger curved another loop around the edge of the glass. "The day my wife died."

SIX

My heart slowed to a stop. "That's today?"

Macalister's expression was vacant stone, matching the marble chess pieces. "Losing Julia was the second most difficult day of my life, so you'll have to forgive the scotch. I've done it for the last fifteen years, and it has become a tradition of sorts."

I sank back into my chair with breath clutched tightly in my chest, hoping that if I didn't breathe, I couldn't hurt for him.

Fifteen years ago today, the Hales had gathered in a hospital room for the last time as a full family. I'd only been six years old when she'd had the equestrian accident, but I'd heard the Hale men had been there when she'd passed. Royce had been ten.

Oh, God. Royce.

This was why he'd been so withdrawn today. It had nothing to do with the stock prices or money. The ache in my heart tore in two. One side hurt for the man who'd lost his mother, and the selfish other side was wounded he hadn't shared the meaning of this day with me.

I snatched up my neglected glass of scotch and took another sip. Maybe Macalister would think my bleary eyes were caused by the whisky, rather than the bomb he'd dropped.

"I didn't know," I said, stumbling over my words. "I always liked her. She was so pretty and nice."

I cringed, bracing for how he'd respond to my ridiculously childlike statement. He didn't look irritated, though. Sadness swept into his stormy eyes and was quickly blinked away. He shifted in his chair, visibly uncomfortable with showing emotion.

"Yes," he said finally. "She was quite beautiful."

In my awkwardness, I couldn't keep myself from babbling. "I thought Royce was upset about the hit to the stock market."

Macalister's eyebrow lifted with interest. "Royce was upset?"

"I . . . maybe upset isn't the right word. He was quiet today, and it was obvious something was bothering him."

"But he didn't mention what it was?"

"No," I said softly.

He poured himself another drink, then rolled the liquor around in the bottom of the glass as he considered my statement. "Hale men typically aren't forthcoming, especially when it comes to emotion."

"I'm learning that," I said dryly. The glass was cold in my fingers, even as the burn from the whisky lingered in the back of my throat. "You should be sharing this drink with him."

A sound erupted from his chest, too cruel and bleak to be considered a laugh. "No, I don't think so."

I must have had a confused look on my face because he set his elbows on the desk and leaned forward, seriousness wiping his expression clean.

"The most difficult day of my life was the one where I buried her . . . by *myself*. Vance was too distraught, and Royce refused to go."

I inhaled so sharply, it hurt.

I hadn't thought about that day since, but at the time, I'd wondered why neither of the Hale boys had been at Macalister's side during the burial. The only reason I'd been there was for moral support. My parents had thought Emily and I could somehow help, even though we weren't close friends with the boys.

"He refused?" I asked. I pictured Royce as I remembered him back then, a wild, stubborn brat who always got what he wanted.

The muscle along Macalister's jaw hardened. "He blamed me for her death, because Julia and I had argued that morning, and he believed she wouldn't have taken her horse out if we hadn't. He said a number of awful things that day."

Sadness cloaked me like a heavy, stifling blanket. "I'm sure he didn't mean it. He was only a boy who'd just lost his mom."

"The staff was able to get him into the limo, but when we arrived at the cemetery, he wouldn't come out. I am not a man who begs, Marist, but I did that day. I wanted closure for my son. I needed him beside me during the most difficult task of my life, and instead I felt tremendous shame and disappointment at the boy who could only think about himself."

Oh, Jesus. I wasn't sure which Hale my heart broke for in that moment. Was it the stoic man who had stood beside the mound of dirt and the newly carved stone bearing his wife's name? Or the boy wearing a formal black suit no little boy should own, crying his eyes out alone in the back of the stretch limo?

"Macalister." My voice broke on his name, teeming with emotion. "He was ten."

It was the wrong thing to say because a dark pall spread through his expression. "I was younger than him when my parents died, and I did what was required of me."

How was I supposed to respond to that? The only stuff I knew about the Hale family was the history lesson he'd given me during the initiation. I'd never met any of Macalister's family, but I assumed it was his terrible personality that had pushed them away, not that he had some tragic backstory.

"People grieve in different ways," I choked out.

He gave me a pointed look. "Yes, and Royce made it abundantly clear he would prefer to do it by himself."

I couldn't argue. He hadn't told me what today's date meant to him. My fiancé was an island, unconnected to anything or anyone.

"Well," I said, searching for an out, "Vance, then. You shouldn't drink alone."

"I'm not alone." His eyes were like an exposed live wire. Electric and beautiful and extremely dangerous. "You're here."

"I don't count. I'm not a Hale."

"No, not legally, of course, but that's a formality. You live in my house, you work at my company, and you've sworn yourself to this family. You're a Hale, Marist." His tone was absolute. "One who I've made a considerable investment in."

I could read it all in his confident body language and heated eyes. He expected me to pay dividends. Not to his son, but to him personally. The thought made my throat swell closed and my mouth dry up.

"I would like to know," he continued, "whose idea was the lock on your bedroom door? His?"

I bit my lip, unable to answer, but it was all the confirmation he needed.

"You're a smart girl, so I assume you've asked yourself why." Macalister recapped the bottle, his fingers turning methodically, and I couldn't help but think of a torturer turning a screw. "I own this house and everything in it, including access to any space whenever I desire. The lock is unnecessary, as you are perfectly safe while you're here. Royce knows this."

My heart clanged in my chest louder than the bell on Wall Street that opened the markets.

"The lock's protection is an illusion." The deep, stern timbre of his voice made him impossible to ignore. "It's not to keep things out, but hold them in."

I strove for confidence when I felt absolutely none. "Such as?"

"Before he suggested it, were you concerned about not having one?"

I frowned. "No, but—"

"And now I suspect you lock it every night and worry

what would happen if you don't."

I glanced away, unable to look at him as he proved his point. Was it true? Had Royce's demand for the lock on my bedroom really been manipulation? A way to ensure my distrust of his father?

"A cage may open from the inside," Macalister said, "but it's still a cage."

My eyelids were heavy from the false eyelashes the makeup artist had applied, and as I stood in the shade of one of the trees on the Hale grounds, I stared at the branches above and silently prayed for one of them to break off and crush me to death.

"Marist," the photographer said, "let's have you put your back against the tree. Royce, lean into her. Hand on her waist and the other on the tree by her head."

I took her directions and leaned against the tree trunk, its rough bark against my back, and steeled myself as Royce stepped into my space. He clasped my waist with a confident hand, and the heat of his palm seared through the thin silk of the dress I wore. But it didn't compare to the fire in his crystal blue eyes.

He was so fucking good at pretending. Was this just a production for our engagement photos? Or was any of it real?

The crew buzzed about us. Two men held white screens to bounce the light, and whenever the photographer was busy adjusting settings on her camera, the makeup artist dabbed at me with powder. It was a thousand degrees outside, but I was sure there wouldn't be a speck of shine or bead of sweat on my body. The pictures would be flawless.

They had to be. Alice said several high-end magazines had requested engagement photos of the happy couple. *Brides* had offered to do a full spread.

They wanted pretty pictures to go with the pretty lie.

The photographer adjusted her stance and angled her camera at us. "Kiss her."

A smug smile curled on Royce's lips the moment before he leaned down and pressed them to mine. In his office, I told him this wasn't allowed, but now that he'd been given free rein, he was happy to take advantage.

It was impossible not to fall into his kiss, not with the way he moved against me. It was a seductive dance. His tongue delicately slipped into my mouth and stroked so softly, I felt it deep between my legs. He made me melt so badly, there was no way the makeup artist had enough powder to cover it all.

"Very nice," the photographer said, subtly nudging Royce that she'd gotten the shot she wanted, and it was time to move on. But Royce didn't take orders from the servants. The prince of Cape Hill got whatever he wanted, and right now, he wanted this kiss to continue.

His hand curved around my waist until it was wedged between my back and the tree, and he used it to urge me deeper into his demanding kiss. He drew the fingertips of his other hand along my jaw so he could cup my face and prevent me from ending it.

Wars raged—one in my head, and one between our mouths. What was happening was a cruel tease. I couldn't lie like he did, so when I kissed him back, the meaning was real. As hurtful as his kiss was, it didn't mean I wanted him to stop. Oh, God, how I wanted him to keep going. I wanted the entourage of people to fade into the trees and disappear so this moment wouldn't end.

Royce adjusted the angle so our mouths could better meet, and when he pressed the rest of our bodies together, I felt fully possessed by him. The connection was so powerful, it was nearly as intimate as sex.

Someone let out a nervous, uncomfortable laugh, breaking the spell between us. As Royce lifted his head, malice flashed through his eyes. He didn't like being interrupted.

The photographer had a wide smile and gave us a wink. "Save some of that for the next setup."

My face burned hot, and it had nothing to do with the heat outside. It was caused by the man who twined his fingers with mine and pulled me away from the tree, out into the harsh sunlight. And once we were linked, he refused to let me go.

We were posed in a half-dozen different locations on the Hale grounds, but my heart climbed into my throat when Royce suggested the site where he'd asked me to marry him. The photographer looked delighted and had him lead the way. We were a parade, marching through the maze until the bubbling fountain came into view.

"Oh, how romantic," she gasped. "This setting is fabulous."

I stood motionless as the makeup artist slicked gloss over

my lips, but like a thirsty gazelle sharing a watering hole with a lion, I watched Royce with wary eyes. He looked effortless in his tan suit without a tie, full of carefree confidence. The enormous privilege he carried weighed nothing.

The photographer tossed a finger at the stone bench. "Royce, why don't you sit beneath the fountain?" When he did, she added, "Great. Marist, we'll have you sit sideways in his lap."

To the rest of the people, my fiancé just looked thrilled with this idea, but all I saw was his devious smirk. I begrudgingly marched toward him and refused to let the excitement deep inside me make an appearance. He held his arms out, welcoming me into his lap, and the masculine scent of his cologne invaded my senses. It was bad enough he looked good. He didn't have to smell amazing too.

I forced on a smile, matching his dazzling one while the camera's loud shutter clicked away.

"Good, good," the woman said. "Can you put your arm around his shoulders? Tilt your head down and look at him."

It was uncomfortable sitting on him, and the dress rode up high across my bare legs, but I did as I was directed. When I shifted, trying to find a better position, it worked a grunt from him that was probably too quiet for anyone but me to hear. It was loaded with pleasure.

His hand gripped my knee for a moment before it slid a few inches up my leg, and my breath caught. His fingertips were hidden beneath my skirt. It lingered right at the edge of being inappropriate, and the way my body responded to it was *completely inappropriate*. Despite the summer heat, goosebumps pebbled across my skin.

His touch gave me tunnel-vision. The photographer said something to Royce, perhaps telling him to straighten his back, but everything outside of him went fuzzy. It barely registered when the woman commanded me to kiss him. My body was already clamoring for it, so it wasn't hard to give in.

"Control yourself this time," I said. Hopefully my scolding tone masked the very real plea beneath it.

"Not a chance."

Today, he wasn't Hades, the king of the underworld—he was Ares.

God of war.

I wasn't going to win against him right now, not under his brutal kiss, but at least the surrender was sweet. Like when he'd proposed, time slowed. He stripped away the armor I'd put up to protect myself, one seductive kiss at a time, until I was laid bare. Then he delivered the final blow with a sweep of his tongue and left me trembling.

His mouth carved a path down my neck.

"What I'm doing right now? This is nothing." His voice was whisper soft but still packed its defiant punch. "Every party we go to, every time we're out together, I'm going to have my mouth on you. My hands all over you." As he spoke, his lips brushed over my sensitized skin. "I don't give a fuck who's watching or if we make a scene. I want you, Marist. I want you so badly it scares me."

Desire snaked through my veins like a drug he'd administered.

My resistance to him might have cracked, just a little,

which was incredibly dangerous. He'd slip inside the fractures, fill them up, and split me open. I'd become the foolish mortal worshiping at the temple of a god who didn't care. He wasn't capable.

Was he?

"Your phone is ringing," the makeup artist said abruptly, jarring me from my thoughts. Since my dress didn't have pockets, she'd offered to hold on to it for me, and now she thrust the phone my direction.

I scrambled up off Royce's lap and took the phone. One look at the screen and worry sliced through me. My mother never called, not unless something was wrong. I tapped the screen, and before I'd brought the phone to my ear, she started speaking.

"Marist," she said in a panicked rush. "We're taking Emily to the emergency room. I found her—"

"What? What's wrong?"

"—and there was so much blood. It's just awful. Will you meet us there?"

Cold dread froze my limbs in place. "Mom, slow down. What happened?"

Hearing the fear in my voice had Royce on his feet. I turned away from him, not wanting the concerned look streaked on his face to distract me as I tried to focus on what she was saying.

"She'd been cramping all morning, but I thought it was normal. I had some spotting with both you girls." Her tone was crushed with guilt. "I told her not to worry, Marist. I thought if she took a nap, she'd feel better."

I couldn't catch my breath, and without thought, my legs started churning, carrying me through the maze toward the house. I needed my car keys. "Which hospital? Port Cove?"

Cape Hill was too small to support a full hospital, but the next town over had one. Surely it wouldn't be Mass General. That was at least forty minutes away.

"Yes. We're in the car now."

"I'm on my way." I hung up as I scrambled up the stone steps, only to jerk to a stop at the top—

A warm body slammed into me and nearly knocked me over, but then Royce's hands were on me. "Whoa."

I hadn't realized he'd been right on my heels and didn't take the time to think about why that was. All that mattered was getting to my sister. "I need my car keys." I glared at him like it was somehow his fault I didn't have them. "Your father took them."

"I'll have a driver out front in ninety seconds." He took one hand off me to pull out his phone, and I watched his thumb slide across the screen with surgical precision, texting his order. "What's going on?"

My pulse was a chaotic, fluttering mess. "I don't know. I think Emily's having a miscarriage." Everything felt out of control, and the sensation was horribly disorienting. "I don't want a driver, Royce. *I want my keys.*"

Strangely, he didn't rise to match my intensity. He was a ship in a storm, even-keeled and staying the course. "I know you do, but my way is faster." He gripped my hand and pulled me toward the house. "Let's go."

It wasn't until we were seated in the back of the town car

and Royce was buckling my seatbelt that I realized what we'd done. "The photoshoot . . . We just left everyone back there."

The sedan jerked to a start and barreled down the tree-shaded drive toward the main road before he'd finished buckling his own seatbelt. "Are you kidding? Don't worry about them."

"Right," I lashed out. "How stupid of me to think about anyone other than myself. Sorry, I'm not a Hale, so I'm not used to doing that."

I'd expected my dig to earn me a scornful look or a sharp comeback. He was supposed to get angry. Instead, he said nothing. He laced his fingers with mine, and his tone was soothing. "It's going to be okay."

The pain in my chest was acute. Emily's pregnancy wasn't *exactly* planned, but she had made it clear she wanted her baby with all her heart, even when the father didn't. I clutched Royce's hand so hard, my knuckles turned white. She wasn't just my sister . . .

"She's my best friend," I whispered.

He leaned across the seat and pressed his lips to my forehead. "I know. I promise you it's going to be all right."

"How can you promise that?" I cried.

His eyes were as pure and unforgiving as the diamond on my finger. "Because I have more money than God, which means I can make it so."

SEVEN

My mother was a mess. Not physically, of course. Her tailored white blouse was impeccable, and her black slacks were wrinkle-free. Her statement necklace was a vivid red, giving her a punch of color, which she needed right now. Her face was pale, and likely in her worry she'd rubbed off most of her makeup. My father sat beside her, his arms crossed and his vacant stare boring a hole into the tile floor of the emergency waiting room.

"Mom," I said.

Relief at my voice brought her to her feet, but when her gaze wheeled around to find me, she did a double take. She blinked her stunned eyes, taking in my silk Dior dress and perfectly executed hair and makeup.

And then she spied Royce beside me and stiffened.

He wasn't his father, but he was still a Hale, and that made her nervous. Her focus darted from me to him and back again.

"They took her back for an ultrasound," she said.

"Is she okay?" It was a stupid question to ask while standing in a hospital, but I needed the answer to be yes.

My mother frowned and nodded slowly as she twisted the tissue in her hand tighter. "Emily's doing all right now, and the baby still has a heartbeat, but that's all we know at this point."

"Oh." An ounce of relief loosened my chest so I could breathe. "Well, that's good, right?"

Her gaze drifted slowly downward until it landed on my hand, and she flattened her lips together with displeasure. I didn't understand until I tracked her eyeline and discovered my hand curled around Royce's.

When the hell had that happened?

When I shook free of his hold, something that looked strangely like disappointment blinked through Royce's expression, but it was gone so fast it couldn't have been real.

I sat in the empty set of chairs across from my parents, and my surprise continued when he sat beside me. I was grateful for his help getting to the hospital, but what was he doing?

My mother's tone was full of judgement. "You two look nice."

"We were shooting our engagement photos when you called," Royce said.

"Oh." She lifted her chin. "I see. And how are the wedding plans going?" Her posture was stiff and awkward, and she forced pleasantness into her voice. "I haven't been told much. Being the mother of the bride, I thought I'd be more involved."

A thousand thoughts raced through my head. I had barely been involved, and I was the bride. I hadn't even picked out what I was wearing right now. Everything was selected by Alice and approved by Macalister, and I was sure when the time came, it would be the same of my wedding dress. I wanted to remind my mother again that our family wasn't paying a cent toward the wedding, and that meant we'd relinquished the right toward any decision.

The two Hales at the top had made it known that Northcott input would not be needed. My wedding had nothing to do with me. It was a merger, and the reception afterward was a promotional opportunity.

My loudest thought was the one that spilled out of my mouth. "Really? You want to whine about this now?"

She took in a marked breath, like a bee she hadn't bothered unexpectedly stung her anyway. "I'm not whining, but I think it's ridiculous I haven't been asked to be a part of the most important day of my daughter's life."

Frustration balled my hands into fists, but before I could snap back at her—

"I agree," Royce said. "I'll speak to Alice about it." An easy, disarming smile breezed across his lips. "She doesn't mean to do it, but she has a habit of taking over."

My mother's demeanor changed faster than the direction of the wind. Her eyes brightened. "Thank you, Royce. I'd appreciate it."

And just like that, he'd won over his future mother-in-law.

"Northcott?" a voice called from down the hall.

We were ushered into Emily's room, where my sister

looked tired and small, but other than the IV hooked into her arm, she appeared fine. I hurried to her bedside and crushed her in my arms.

"I'm okay," she said. "Everything's all right." She released me and gave me a once-over, then shifted her gaze to take in the rest of the room. "They said everything looked okay on the ultrasound, but the doctor hasn't come by yet." She turned her weary focus toward the man at my side, and the warmth faded from her. "Hello, Royce."

"Hey," he said. "Glad to hear you're okay. Your sister was worried."

"Enough to drag you here, I guess."

"Oh, no," I tried to explain. "We were—"

He waved a hand, cutting me off. "I decided to tag along."

A fast set of knocks rang out on the door behind the curtain before it slid open and a woman in blue scrubs and a white doctor's coat strolled in. She ignored everyone else in the room and focused only on Emily.

"I'm Doctor Spenser, head of obstetrics. I've looked over your tests, and I can say things look good with the baby. He or she appears to be doing just fine. Now, the placenta is lower in your uterus than typical. It's a condition called placenta previa, and it's the most likely cause of your bleeding." She softened her voice. "Unfortunately, you're probably going to have more during the pregnancy. As long as it doesn't get too heavy or painful, it's nothing to worry about. It does mean you're looking at a C-section when we get to the finish line."

She slipped her hand in her pocket, pulled out a small tablet and stylus, and continued talking as she wrote orders on the screen.

"Your iron is low, and you're dehydrated, plus your blood pressure is high, so I want to get you in a room upstairs and keep an eye on you. Let's see if we can get your numbers looking better tomorrow."

In my peripheral vision, I saw Royce pull out his phone, and his thumbs fluttered over the screen. Was he already texting for the driver to come fetch us? Because he could go without me. I wasn't going to leave while my sister was being admitted to the hospital.

Once again, I was irritated that my car, the one I was completely capable of driving, was off-limits. Next time I was at the Hale house, the first thing I'd ask Macalister about was getting my keys back. I'd done everything he asked all summer. Now it was winding down, and soon school would start, and I was desperate to regain any independence I could.

After the doctor finished answering Emily's questions and left, Royce's phone rang. He glanced at the screen and looked pleased. "Excuse me for a minute." He swiped to answer the call and strode toward the door. "Hey, Nigel, thanks for calling. You got something for me?"

The rest of his one-sided conversation was drowned out by the sliding door and then muffled beyond the glass, but suspicion brewed inside me. Macalister's personal assistant's name was Nigel. Why would Royce be talking to him?

I needed to find out, and standing around wasn't going to make that happen.

"I'll be right back," I said to my family.

Royce had his back turned as he faced the empty hallway,

his phone pressed to an ear and his other hand on his hip. I cracked the sliding door as quietly as possible so I could make out what he was saying.

"Good. How soon can we get him on a helicopter?" Royce paused, listening to the other side. "Great. Call me back if there're any problems." Like he was abruptly aware, he turned and looked directly at me. A slow smile spread on his face. "Oh, and Nigel? Thanks. We appreciate your help."

He tapped the screen and slipped his phone in the interior pocket of his suit coat. His eyes were playful.

"Were you spying on me?" he teased. He gestured across the way to the unused room, and our faint reflection in the dark glass.

Oh, my God, I was an idiot. I stepped out of the room and closed the door behind me. "Who are you putting on a helicopter?"

"Dr. Zetsche from Johns Hopkins." He said it like that would clear everything up. When it didn't, he added, "I asked Nigel to get me five names of the best obstetrics doctors in America, and Zetsche happened to be the closest. We'll meet him when he lands at Mass General."

My brain couldn't keep up. "What?"

"We'll have Emily transferred to the Phillips House. It's the top floor of Mass General, and it's, uh . . ."—his expression faltered as he searched for the right phrase—"been a while since I've been there, but it has some of the nicest suites in the country."

I grasped my elbow with my other hand, using the awkward posture as a defense mechanism, like it could shield against the pang of hurt I felt for him. He had to be talking about his mother, and the last time he'd been there was when she'd passed away. Like the anniversary of her death, he didn't elaborate or share his feelings with me.

"I don't understand," I whispered.

His expression was a mixture of sadness and determination. "Your sister deserves better care than Port Cove, don't you think?"

I didn't flinch or shrug him off as he cautiously set a hand on my hip. I liked the connection.

The corner of his mouth quirked up into a half smile. "Think of it this way. One of the perks of marrying me is you get the best of everything."

"No," I said. "What I don't understand is why you're doing this. Why you came with me, why you stayed." I gestured to the empty hallway. "There's no one here, no cameras to document this. You won't get credit for caring about my family."

He solidified, hardening into stone. "You're right. Honestly, I don't care about your family." His hold on me was firm, locking me into place. "But, as much as I've tried not to, I *care* about you. I know you don't believe me, and I haven't given you a reason to, but you're mine, Marist. My fiancée, and my partner, and . . ." He turned his head to the side, staring down the long hallway as he assembled the words in his mind. When he had them, his focus snapped back to me. "Where you go, I go. Whatever you want, I'll give it to you."

The distant sounds of the emergency room faded to nothing, so all I could hear was the furious beating of my heart. Royce's expression was pure conviction. Maybe it was a lie, but I chose to believe what he'd just said was the truth.

"Then tell me what you're planning," I whispered.

His lips parted.

But nothing came out, like he was hanging on the cusp of revealing his master plan. Confliction ran visibly through him, and he retreated at the last second. "I can't, not yet. But I promise you, when it's in motion? I will." His advance had been so subtle, I hadn't realized I was completely in his arms. He tipped his head, so his lips brushed against my hairline, and his voice matched my whisper. "I'll tell you fucking everything."

I sighed, closed my eyes, and didn't fight him as his arms squeezed me into his embrace. Right now, I didn't care about Macalister's stupid rule that I'd agreed to. I greedily accepted Royce's affection, whether it was real or manipulation.

For a long moment we stood in silence, hugging in the quiet hospital corridor. I didn't want to admit to myself how good it felt to lean on him, both physically and emotionally, and it was hard to say because the words had a bitter taste. "We're beyond broke, Royce. I don't know how my family can afford—"

"Shh." He lowered his mouth to mine. "We're in this to-gether, remember?"

It was after midnight when the town car brought Royce and me home from Boston. My sister had been transferred to the top floor of Massachusetts General Hospital, into a spacious suite with a full sitting area, 1200-thread count sheets, and beautiful bay views.

The car pulled to a stop in the circle drive, and we sat motionless as the driver shut off the engine, climbed out of his seat, and rounded the back of the car to open my door. The silence between us wasn't uncomfortable, but it was heavy.

Filled with all I wanted to say but couldn't seem to get out.

There'd been a party at the marina tonight, and we were supposed to have made an appearance. Instead, Royce had spent it with my family. He was understandably uncomfortable with his memories of the hospital, but he hid it well. During the walk to the elevator this afternoon, we'd passed the Julia Hale Memorial fountain, and he'd turned his head the opposite direction.

When the driver opened my car door, I stayed put. I *had* to say something. Royce had done so much today.

"Hey. Thank you," was all I got out.

It was woefully inadequate, but his smile was bright, shining better than the overhead light in the back seat. "I'm glad I could help."

We climbed the steps to the front door, and as we went inside, I was struck with the realization that I'd referred to the Hale house as 'home' when talking to my family this evening. It didn't feel like home, but then again . . . after the years of lies my parents had told me, the house I'd grown up in felt less like home every day.

If home wasn't a place, but the people you surrounded yourself with, I was losing where I belonged.

"Good night," Royce said when we'd both reached the

doors to our bedrooms.

I gave him my first genuine smile in weeks. "Good night."

He disappeared through his doorway, and a second later Lucifer's lecturing meows rang out. The cat seemed to run on a schedule and grew irritated whenever Royce deviated from it.

There was a lamp shining in the sitting area of my room, which I assumed someone from the staff had put on when Royce had told them we wouldn't be back until late in the evening. I set my purse down on the dresser and kicked off my shoes, so tired I considered climbing under the covers with the Dior dress still on, but then thought better of it.

Movement off to the side caught my attention, and by the time I turned to look at him, the man was already on his feet.

"Fuck," I gasped. My face flushed hot, and I instantly hung my shoulders in embarrassment. "Macalister. You scared me."

His expression was cold and indifferent, but icy fire burned in his eyes, threatening to incinerate me. "You're late."

Late? Was he serious? I gave a skeptical look. "For our game of chess?"

Most nights when we played, he'd come from the office and was still wearing his standard two-piece suit, but when Royce and I had backed out of the marina event, he must have gone in our place. He'd worn a three-piece but shed the jacket at some point before entering my room, leaving him in a smoke gray pinstripe vest and matching pants. The silver bar on his black tie glinted as he took a step in my direction.

The air dropped ten degrees with that action.

He stood and stared at me in such a demanding way that my pulse raced. It felt like I'd done something horribly wrong and he expected me to apologize.

"My sister's in the hospital."

Irritation simmered in him. "I am aware of that. It was my helicopter that brought in her doctor."

He didn't charge at me. He put one steady foot in front of the other in a slow march, an enemy advancing to invade.

"Oh. Thank you." I couldn't stop myself from backpedaling; it was the dresser that handled that. The drawers rattled as I bumped into it, and the sound stole his focus. Macalister was curious, like he didn't understand why I was backing away from him.

We'd spent the last few weeks building a rapport, but it didn't exist here in my room. This was supposed to be the safe space where I retreated after losing to him each night. But even this was an illusion. This room wasn't mine—everything was his. Including me, he'd argue.

His presence was unrelenting.

"It's late," he said. "And you've kept me waiting."

Was there extra meaning buried in his statement? I didn't want to find out. I ripped my gaze away and padded on bare feet to the door. "Okay, I'm ready. Thank you for waiting."

He followed me out of the room, and by the time he'd entered the library, I was already in my seat, my legs tucked up under the skirt of my dress and my white pawn positioned in my opening move.

Every other time we'd played, it'd still been light outside

and it streamed in through the large arched window. It was a moonless sky tonight, making the library dark and intimate. The light from the single desk lamp wasn't powerful enough to reach the edges of the room, and the sharp edges of Macalister's cheekbones were carved with extra shadows.

He sat opposite me and considered his opening.

I didn't let out the tight breath I was holding as he placed his pawn exactly where I'd hoped he would. I leaned forward eagerly on my knees and slid another pawn forward two places.

When he was caught off-balance and his guard was down, he was a beautiful man. He looked wise and distinguished, practiced and skilled with age. But his eyes were deceptively young and treacherous.

They widened as he stared at the board, then narrowed to slits when he realized what I'd done.

He picked up his queen, set her beside my pawn, and the air whooshed from my lungs like a hole burst in a balloon.

Checkmate.

I'd lost in two moves.

Anger ringed his eyes. "We'll play again."

I was so drained it was a struggle to push myself out of my chair. "It's been a long day."

"No." His tone was pure authority as he reset the board. "Fool's Mate is not acceptable."

"I held up my end of the—"

His fist banged on the desktop, rattling the chess pieces. *"Sit. Down."*

My stomach turned over as I dropped back into my

chair. I blindly snatched up a pawn and moved it forward, desperate to appease him. I understood what this really was. He craved control in everything, but he couldn't control me from losing.

Right now, he couldn't even control his own emotions.

Macalister closed his eyes, pinched the bridge of his nose, and let out a calming sigh. "Forgive my tone. As you said, it's been a long day, and I've been looking forward to our game all evening."

My breath caught with his admission.

His eyes opened and captured me. "I enjoy the time we spend together." He picked up a pawn and moved it, and I felt his fingers wrapped around me, squeezing tight. "I hope it's the same for you."

What the fuck was I supposed to say to that?

"Mm-hmm." I peered at the board, acting like I was too deep in thought to really process what he'd said. I took my turn and sat back in my seat, tucking a lock of hair behind my ear.

His tone was casual and conversational. "How is Emily? And the baby?"

"They're okay, but the doctor wants to keep her a few days."

We moved our pieces in turn as he volleyed more questions at me. "What about the father? Is he in the picture?"

I grimaced. The asshole hadn't spoken to Emily since she'd told him she was pregnant with his child. "No."

"And who is he?" Macalister captured my rook and deposited it off the board.

I swallowed thickly. "I think she'd prefer I didn't say."

Was that a smile hidden in his eyes? "No, that's probably wise. It's a bit of a scandal, after all. I'm told her professor's married."

My mouth fell open, but I promptly shut it. "Of course,
you already knew."

It *was* a smile. He looked so fucking pleased with himself. "Yes. Royce was supposed to marry your sister. I had to
know who was responsible for disrupting those plans." He
relaxed in his seat, watching me as I positioned myself to defend my queen. "He's a terrible man."

I paused. "Because he cheated on his wife?"

"Because he made the wrong decision at every turn. He
chose to sleep with a student, to get her pregnant, and to
abandon her and their child."

"You're right." It was strange to agree with Macalister on
anything. "He is a terrible man. I wish I could say it's surprising, but Emily's always had terrible taste in men."

The second it was out, I wanted to take it back. I hadn't
meant to be mean or talk behind my sister's back, but the day
was bleeding into the next, and I was stretched thin. I went
to move my knight—

"No, that piece is pinned."

Meaning I couldn't move it because it'd expose my king
to check. "What? Where?" I scoured the board and found his
bishop in position. "Shit."

Macalister's eyebrow arched. "You should find better
language to express yourself."

My brain was no longer functioning at full capacity. It

had to be the reason I was dumb enough to challenge him right now. "Well, I read that cursing is actually a sign of intelligence."

"Yes," he said. "Fluency in swearing can demonstrate a mastery of the English language, but just because you have a skill, doesn't mean you always have to *fucking* use it."

Stunned wasn't a strong enough word. I was glued to my chair. "I've never heard you swear before." My voice fell to a hush. "I . . . didn't think you knew how."

He looked dubious, and then something even more shocking happened.

Macalister *laughed*.

"I'm no saint, Marist. I was just like you when I was your age." He sobered. "But since then, I've become much more selective with the words I use. Language is a tool, and I prefer a scalpel to a hammer."

This side of him was disorienting. I'd been flipped upside-down, and he shook the idiotic thought from my head. "But I like using the hammer."

He gave an amused smile. "Sometimes it's the right tool." His focus shifted back to the game between us. "Check."

With two more moves, the game ended and he won again, but this time he seemed satisfied with his victory. Now was as good a time as any.

I went with the sincerest tone I possessed. "I was hoping you'd consider giving me back my Porsche."

His movements didn't slow or miss a beat. "No."

Frustration forced a sigh from my lips. I'd been perfect since I moved into the house, following every command like a trained pet. "I've done everything you asked."

He stopped, and his icy gaze zeroed in on me, like he was evaluating me from top to bottom. "You haven't earned it yet."

Royce's warning drifted through my mind. *He doesn't ever give people what they want.* I straightened my posture, trying to exude confidence. We were about to negotiate. "What do I have to do to earn it?"

He leaned on the armrest of the chair, looking regal and powerful and very much in control. "You're not ready."

I shook my head. "Try me. Royce had to call for the car today, and it made me feel powerless."

If ever there was something Macalister could respect, it was that. He tilted his head, made his final decision, and rose from the desk. I watched with cautious eyes as he shifted a stack of books to the side on the top shelf of the bookcase and retrieved a black box from behind them. Eagerness fluttered in my stomach. He'd kept my car keys in here this whole time?

He turned, set the box down beside the chess set, and my excitement crashed, plummeting into apprehension.

The box was laced shut with a black satin bow.

Like a gift.

A cold draft rolled down my back, causing the hairs on my arms to stand on edge. One thing was certain; fear was inside the box. He had no reason to give me a gift. If it was, it'd come with ulterior motives. Was his goal to tangle me in all his strings, like a spider's web?

I hesitantly reached for the box, but Macalister put his spread fingertips on the lid, stopping me. "Not yet." He lowered deliberately into his chair, pulled the box back toward him, and steepled his fingers together. "Do you like chess?"

I took a breath and considered my answer. The game we'd played with the marble pieces was over, but now a different, more strategic and dangerous one had begun, and I needed to make my moves carefully.

At least it wasn't a lie. "Yes."

His blue eyes warmed a single degree. "Good. I thought so. I've enjoyed teaching it to you immensely. So much so, I'd like to play a new game."

My pulse kicked as a warning. "What kind of game?"

He paused to either drag it out or let the silence build my anticipation. "I want to teach you about pleasure."

EIGHT

EVERYTHING IN ME WENT WHITE AND STILL. "I'M SORRY, WHAT?" When Macalister leaned over the desk, I could practically taste his excitement. It was dark and wicked.

"We're not supposed to speak about the initiation, and we won't, other than to say it was clear that night my son had done you a . . . disservice."

His eyes were electric. I couldn't look away, like a person who'd touched a power line and the current kept them holding on, no matter how badly they wanted to let go.

"You're young. There's so much more to pleasure than you've been shown," he said. "Young men are fools. They believe the point of intimacy is to rush to an orgasm—*their* orgasm. Older men have patience, both in and out of the bedroom. I've learned how to wait, how to control my body. I know how to take my time and appreciate every moment."

"Uh—" Every muscle in me clenched, and I went rigid, but Macalister didn't care how uncomfortable I'd become. He just pressed on.

"Foreplay doesn't start when I have a woman beneath me. It begins hours before, or days." His voice dripped with seduction. "Weeks, even."

My chest heaved as I couldn't catch my breath. Everything was spinning out of control. I wanted him to stop talking, but a sick part of me didn't mind it so much.

"So, I'll make my desires perfectly clear," he said. "I'll teach you, Marist. I have enjoyed being your instructor these past few weeks, and this would be satisfying for both of us. I have far more skill and experience than a man half my age. I'll work to master your orgasms."

"Oh, my God," I breathed.

"I'll enjoy watching what each one does to you, the way I make your body flinch, how I'll leave you breathless and trembling. I'll give you so many, I'll savor it when you can't keep count." His smile was loaded with sin. "Yes. I will require that you count them."

"*Oh, my God,*" I repeated in a rush. My mind was blank with shock, and I gripped the armrests of my chair, desperate to flee. But his voice was so powerful, it chained me to my seat. There was no other noise, not even the beating of my own heart. Macalister's words were the only sound left on earth.

"Older men understand the way the world works. We know how to dress. What to eat." His expression was beautifully perverse. "How to *fuck.*"

It was scary, what he'd said, but far more terrifying was the way my traitorous body responded to it. Heat pooled in unwanted places.

He put his fingers on the top of the box and inched it

forward. "Open it."

I used the last scrap of power left in me to speak, and it came out as a plea. "I don't want to."

One of the most famous Greek myths was Pandora's Box. Pandora had been a mortal given a gift from the gods but told not to open it. Unable to keep her curiosity in check, she disobeyed them, and from the box sprang all the evils of the world, like death and sickness.

Whatever was inside the box before me, I was sure as soon as I opened it, I'd wished I hadn't.

His look said I'd just turned down a once-in-a-lifetime offer, and I had better reconsider. "I'm giving you a gift."

My hand trembled as I reached forward and tugged at the satin ribbon. The knot slipped free, and the ribbon un-threaded as I lifted the lid. The interior was black velvet with a gold fabric insert, and in the center was a black, U-shaped object accented in shining gold. The packaging was sexy and luxurious, filling me with heat and leaving me cold in the same instant.

"What is it?" I whispered.

His eyes were liquid. "Pick it up."

I unseated the thing, which was smooth, flexible, and covered in slippery soft silicone. One side of the U was longer and much wider than the other end. I turned it over in my hands like examining it would help. Was the band actual gold?

When the thing hummed to life, the powerful vibrations nearly made me drop it, and once I realized what it was, I did. It stopped buzzing immediately after, and as I lifted my accusing gaze to Macalister, he set his phone down on the desktop.

He'd given me a vibrator.

And he had control of it.

"This is . . ." I started, not able to find a word that could encompass the way I felt. In the end, I went with one that worked, but was much too simple. "Inappropriate."

He had the audacity to look confused. "Why?"

Had he lost his mind? "Because you're married. Because I'm engaged to your son."

"As I'm the one who orchestrated all of that, do you think I'm unaware?" He gave me a direct look, pinning me further to my seat. "What I'm offering tonight isn't physical. There are different kinds of pleasure, just as there are different forms of sex. Some don't require contact, or even a partner. Before you came here, you said you masturbate nearly every day, so am I safe to assume you have done so while in my home?"

Oh, my fucking God.

My mouth dropped open all the way to my toes.

The answer was yes, of course. I'd told Royce he wasn't allowed to touch me, but the weeks had worn on me. Night after night I'd squirmed and writhed under my own hands as I thought about the man in the next room over. I'd had to keep my moans quiet so he wouldn't hear what he was doing to me.

These days, the lock on my door wasn't keeping him out. It was holding me back from caving and going to him.

I treated Macalister's question like it had been rhetorical. If I said yes, it gave him even more power, and if I said no, he'd know I was lying. The guilty expression on my face gave it all away.

His knowing smile was sinister.

"The game is simple," he said. "Every night at ten-thirty, wherever you are, you'll turn the device on and use it. There are instructions in the box. I control the speed and tempo, and the session will last as long as I think it needs to. When it's over, you'll text me the number of orgasms you received."

My eyes were so wide they had to be as big as dinner plates. "No."

He ignored me. "These are the only orgasms you're allowed. If you need an additional session outside of our regular time, I will do my best to accommodate that. But from now on, it will be my responsibility to provide you with pleasure, and you will give me absolute command over your experience."

This time it was harsh and firm from me. *"No."*

Displeasure flared in his eyes. "I own you, Marist. You want your independence with your car, then you will surrender a freedom to me in exchange. What I'm asking for is not challenging, and we both know how far you're willing to go to get what you want."

It was like he'd slapped me. His cruel, true words forced tears into my eyes, but I blinked them away.

His tone softened. "It's just like we've done with chess. Play the game every night and earn what you want. I wouldn't even be in the room."

"That isn't a game," I spat out, "it's extortion—not to mention—super fucked up."

He crossed his arms over his chest. "That is my offer."

I finally found freedom from the chair and stood so fast the legs scraped loudly across the hardwood. "My answer is no."

"I told you that you weren't ready." He reached across the desk to collect the vibrator and put it back in the box. "Let me know when you are."

The restaurant at the country club had ocean views and a great seafood menu, and they embraced the aquatic theme. It was maritime chic. The modern pendant lights over every table were designed to look like schools of white fish swimming with the current.

Sophia Alby was already seated when I arrived, and she brightened as soon as she spotted me.

Nerves rattled in my stomach as I made my approach. One off-handed comment from Royce to Sophia about how I was a nobody, and the next five years of my life had been irrevocably altered. Her whispered rumors were all-powerful and far-reaching.

But high school was over. Did she still have that kind of pull in her social circles?

I was banking on it.

"I was excited when you messaged," she said, flipping her phone over so it was face down on the tabletop beside her menu.

I squeezed out a smile and tried to be the manufactured,

Instagram version of myself as I sat across from her in the booth. "I'm glad this worked out. Thanks for meeting me."

"Of course." She leaned over the table that was uneven planks fashioned to look like a deck. "How's your sister? I heard she's in the hospital."

Cape Hill was small, but it still amazed me how fast news could travel. It seemed like all roads of information flowed toward Sophia, though.

"She's doing better," I said. "They sent her home this morning."

"Oh, good." She took a sip of her water. "Nothing serious, then?"

At least she didn't know why Emily had gone to the hospital. My sister had just started her second trimester, wasn't showing yet, and wasn't ready to announce her pregnancy. "No, nothing serious."

The waiter came by, took our lunch orders, and once he was gone, Sophia couldn't contain her curiosity another second. "What did you want to ask me?"

As she stared at me with her big doe eyes, perfectly sculpted nose, and gorgeous blonde hair, I couldn't help but flash back to high school. She'd been Aphrodite. The most beautiful girl at Cape Hill Prep, queen of society and decider of who was popular and cool.

The girl I'd been five years ago was now pissed at what I was about to do, but it was necessary. *Win at all costs.*

"So," I started, "this is kind of embarrassing. You might not remember much about me in high school." It was likely the only thing she remembered was not to bother remembering a *nobody* like me. "But I wasn't close with a lot of people. I've been so busy, I didn't make many new friends at Etonsons either." I paused, playing up my nerves, which wasn't a stretch by any means. "At Royce's party, you asked to take a picture and said . . . we were friends."

Her smile froze and unease clouded her eyes. Did she think awkward Marist Northcott was going to ask to be her new best friend? I wanted to laugh when her gaze instinctively flicked toward the exit. She was thinking about running before I got clingy.

"Royce has a ton of friends," I continued, "which means he'll want a big bridal party."

When it clicked, her gaze snapped back to me, and suddenly she very much wanted to be Marist Northcott's new best friend. "Yeah," she said enthusiastically, "he's a great guy."

I tried to keep my eye from twitching. "Right. So, I know it's a lot to ask, but I'm hoping I can talk you into being one of my bridesmaids."

Her eyes widened. "Oh, my God, yes! Of course, yes." She pressed her palm flat to her chest like she'd just accepted an Academy Award. "I'm so honored, Marist."

"Awesome." It came out overly bright, not that she noticed.

Her excitement was so big, she nearly vibrated out of the booth. "I mean, it's going to be the wedding of the century. The Northcotts and the Hales. Who do you think I'd be partnered with?" She gave me a hopeful look. "Tate?"

"Tate . . . Isaacs?" I hadn't thought about him in forever. He'd gone to Cape Hill Prep and, like Sophia, was two years older than I was. If she'd been the queen, he'd been the king, once the mantle had been passed down from Royce. My eyebrows pulled together. "I didn't know Royce was even friends with Tate."

Sophia peered dubiously at me. "Seriously? Did they have a falling out? I thought they were best friends."

"Oh." I bit my bottom lip. "No, I'm sure everything's fine." There was still so much about Royce I didn't know.

"You should have seen him at the fundraiser thing the other night." She pretended to fan herself. "Sweet baby Jesus, I swear Tate is Cape Hill's very own Michael B. Jordan." Realizing she'd gotten sidetracked, she refocused. "I assume Vance is the best man?"

"Yeah," I said with faked confidence. I assumed as well, not knowing if it was true.

"And Emily will be your maid of honor, so they'll be partnered together. Not that I'd complain about being paired with Vance. He's so cute, but he makes me feel like a dirty old woman."

I blinked. "You're a year older than him."

"Exactly. Women are at least five years ahead of men in maturity, so it's like he's not even legal yet. And I've always been into older men, anyway."

Macalister's words from last night echoed in my mind, and I shifted uncomfortably in my seat.

"Okay, so I've got to ask." Sophia's voice dropped low and she turned serious. "What's it like living there?"

"With the Hales?"

"I'd die. I wouldn't be able to function around all those hot men."

I gave a strained smile. "I survive. I've gotten used to Royce," I lied, "and Vance is hardly ever there."

She seemed to be waiting for more, and when it didn't come, "And Macalister?"

"What about him?" My mouth went dry as I understood what she was asking. She thought Macalister was hot. "Really?"

"Are you kidding?" She stared at me like I was crazy. "He's the best one out of the bunch. I mean, you *have* seen him, right? Or how when he walks into a room, everyone just . . . stops."

They did that out of fear, not his looks. "Because he owns Cape Hill."

My statement was ignored. "And those blue eyes he has." She closed hers, and a dramatic shiver shook her shoulders. "They're gorgeous. Plus, he's so powerful and, like, bossy. I know it's wrong and he's the same age as our dads, but fuck. Macalister can *get* it."

It was perfect role reversal how I now eyed the exit, wondering if I could extract myself from the situation. But I'd come with a mission, and I wasn't leaving until it was accomplished.

"He's good looking," I agreed. "But I can't think about him like that. He's going to be my father-in-law." I swallowed a breath. "You remember he's married, right?"

She snorted. "Like that matters here." The smile froze on her face. She'd realized she might blow the opportunity I'd given her and needed to correct course. "At least you know Royce is only going to get hotter as he gets older."

She had a point. "True."

"So, when did you guys really start dating? I usually hear things, but you two weren't on my radar until recently. Someone said you hooked up with him at his graduation party last year, but then I also heard he went on a date with Emily, so I thought maybe they got you and your sister mixed up."

Surprise jolted through me. "Who said I hooked up with him? Because we just fooled around a little, we didn't—" *Stop talking, Marist.* I slammed my mouth shut.

She laughed lightly. "Oh, my God, you're embarrassed. That's so cute. I think it was Ally who told me. She saw Royce come out of some room and then you were right behind him. She said you both looked like something had gone down in there."

My cheeks warmed at the memory of Royce's fingers between my legs, my hands gripping the bookshelf.

Wait for me, he'd ordered.

The server appeared, set our lunches down in front of us, and flitted away. Sophia readied her fork but paused before digging into her salad.

"Good for you," she said. "After Emily, I knew he wasn't dating, but I didn't have a clue why. I should have, though. A guy like Royce doesn't just give up women for a year. You guys hid your relationship so well." She grinned widely. "You had all of us fooled."

My insides solidified. What had she just said? My brain wouldn't accept it.

No, she had to be mistaken. Royce had ordered me to wait, but I refused to believe he'd done the same.

She took a bite of her food, but her chewing slowed when she noticed I wasn't eating. I hadn't even moved.

"You okay? Is your order wrong?"

I forced myself to act natural, jamming my fork into a pile of linguine. "No, it's fine." I pulled my lips back into what I hoped looked like a bliss-soaked smile. I wanted her to take my comment at face value and not hear the subtext hidden beneath. "Sometimes it's still hard to believe I'm going to marry him."

"Yeah, I'm sure. You're both young, but at the same time, it's kinda undeniable you're in love. It's a fairytale the way you look at each other—it made everyone jealous at Royce's promotion thing, you know. We all want what you have."

I shoved a forkful of pasta into my mouth so she wouldn't hear the huge gulp of air I'd just swallowed. What she thought was a fairytale romance was only a carefully crafted lie.

For the next twenty minutes, I ate silently while Sophia prattled on about work and her parents' remodel of their second home in Barcelona. I waited until she'd spent enough time talking about herself that she was relaxed and comfortable before I made my first move.

I crossed my arms and leaned my elbows on the table, tilting my chin down to my chest. My voice was quiet and secretive. "Can I tell you something?" Then I uttered the phrase she wouldn't be able to resist. "And it needs to stay just between us."

There was a spark in her eyes. "Of course. What is it?"

I hesitated for effect. "I don't know if Royce is going to take over for Macalister when he retires."

It was as if I'd just said her credit card was declined. "What?"

I pushed my hair back behind my ear and leaned even closer, like I was worried someone might overhear. "I've been working as Royce's assistant, just until school starts back, and I'm beginning to see how he is at the company. I thought Macalister was grooming him to step up as CEO one day, but instead of giving him more responsibilities—Macalister seems to be taking them away."

Confusion continued across her face. "Why?"

I lifted my shoulders. "I don't know. Maybe he can't cut it? Maybe Macalister thinks he won't be any good as CEO. That's kind of the feeling I get from the executive suite. No one's comfortable with Royce being anything more than a figurehead."

It was a total and complete lie.

My time at HBHC had been brief, but so far, Royce had seemed dedicated, competent, and valuable. And everyone, except for his father, loved him. There'd been meetings that ran long where I'd had to fake fires for Royce to put out, only so he could use it as an excuse to get on to the next meeting.

Perhaps I should have felt bad, but I didn't.

This was only fair.

Five years ago, Royce had told a simple lie, and the effect had been catastrophic. It was poetic I was doing the same, right down to using Sophia Alby to do it. At least, if my plan worked.

"But," she asked, "if Royce doesn't succeed Macalister, then who? Vance?"

I shook my head. "He doesn't want it. I don't know what Macalister, or the board, is planning to do."

"Wow." She collapsed back in the booth, the information overpowering her. "That's crazy."

"I know, right? But promise me you won't repeat it."

I hoped what I was asking was impossible for her. She'd always been such a gossip. With any luck, she'd go home and tell her father, who'd spread the rumors of instability at HBHC far and wide.

Sophia had been Aphrodite, but today I needed her to be my Hermes—messenger to the gods.

"I promise," she said. The corner of her mouth lifted into a sardonic smile. "Who would I tell?"

Everyone.

She'd tell *everyone*.

While I waited for the black Mercedes to pull up, Sophia and I Instagrammed our lunch date. We projected the image of two new best friends, pressed tight together with huge smiles, but it was fake and hollow. She had to feel that way too, at least a little. We were just using each other to get what we wanted.

Business contacts in a shared space.

It was irritating to sit in the back seat of the car as the driver took me back to Boston, when all I wanted to do was drive and think about what Sophia had revealed. She had to be wrong. She wasn't the all-seeing Oracle, and just because

Royce hadn't dated anyone last year didn't mean he'd stayed celibate like me.

When I got back to HBHC headquarters, he'd just finished up his lunch meeting, and I followed him into his office, shutting the door behind me.

"What's up?" he asked as he thumbed through emails on his phone. "I've got to leave for another meeting in ten minutes."

What was he talking about? His schedule on Tuesdays after lunch was one of the only times he actually got to spend more than twenty minutes at his desk. "With who?" I asked lightly. "I don't have it on the calendar."

"Don't worry, I've got it. I'll be back before the budget meeting at three."

He didn't look at me when he spoke, and I couldn't help but think he was pretending to act distracted and purposefully being vague.

"You're going out for it?"

"It's coffee with a friend."

I narrowed my eyes as he rounded his desk and sat down behind the computer. "I thought you said it was a meeting."

He finally set his gaze on me with a hard, direct look. He wanted me to drop it. "It's both."

My suspicion increased ten-fold, but I did my best to hide the excitement from my voice. "Which friend? Tate Isaacs?"

Royce's blue eyes widened with surprise and then emptied completely, like he'd forced any emotion out from them. He asked it like he didn't really care, although I was sure he did. "Where'd that name come from?"

I strolled to his desk, and the air in his office thickened. He watched me cautiously, the same way I usually watched him. He was smart enough to know to be wary of my intentions right now.

"I had lunch with Sophia Alby today."

He settled back in his chair, and even though I was standing, he still thought he was the one in control. "I didn't know you two were friends."

"We're not."

I sat on the side of his desk, crossed my legs, and didn't miss how it caught his attention. *Good.* His gaze skated across my bare legs and disappeared up my skirt, and desire cracked into his expression. Warmth spread through my body, but I had to push it aside.

"I asked her to be a bridesmaid."

He considered this information for a long moment, and then his tone was guarded and cool. "That was dangerous."

Royce understood how Sophia worked. Macalister Hale was the wealthiest person in Cape Hill, but secrets and gossip were their own form of currency, and that made her the second richest person in town. She wielded a kind of power that was harder for the Hales to buy and control.

"She told me something interesting," I said. "About you."

Tension flooded through his chest and shoulders. He was trying very hard to look indifferent. "Yeah? What?"

"She said you weren't with anyone at all last year. She thinks it's because we were dating in secret."

He made a show out of checking his watch. "I don't really have time for this. Can we talk about it later?"

"Why? Is your coffee meeting important?" I batted my lashes at him, pretending to be hurt. "More important than your fiancée?"

He didn't match my playful attitude. Instead, he was deadly serious. "I don't lie when we're alone, so no, it's not more important than you. But, Marist? It's a close second."

It was so convincing that for a half-second I believed him, but then I wised up. He was avoiding confirming or denying what Sophia had told me, and instead he was trying to distract.

Two could play that game. I was eager to see how much he liked being manipulated.

I stood, leaned over him, and put my hands on the armrests of his chair, bringing our faces level with each other.

His mouth curled into a sexy smile, and his voice was sexier still. "What are you doing?"

I walked his chair back, rolling it away from the desk to make room. Since I was leaning over him, his focus zeroed in on my bra and cleavage that was exposed by the hanging neckline of my top. It kept him hypnotized enough, he didn't say anything when I folded my legs under me and knelt in front of him.

A smile seared across my lips.

He'd probably think me on my knees meant I was submitting to him, but he was about to learn who was in control.

NINE

THIS TIME WHEN ROYCE ASKED IT, HE WASN'T AMUSED—HE was angry. "What are you doing?"

I'd run my palms up his spread thighs until I found what I wanted. He made a half-hearted attempt to push my hands away, but I was persistent, and he began to grow hard under my touch.

He both did and didn't want me to keep going. "I thought that wasn't allowed."

I stroked the bulge thickening down one leg of his suit pants. "Technically, I only agreed not to while we're at the house."

When I reached for his belt, his grip on my wrist was more serious. "My door's not locked."

"But it's closed." There was office etiquette—a closed door was treated as a locked one. Plus, Royce was a Hale and sat on the board of directors. "Only someone with career suicide would walk in here."

I undid his belt buckle with one hand while cupping him

with the other, and a nearly inaudible groan came from him. God, it was hot. He stared at me with his beautifully conflicted eyes, silently pleading for me to stop but also to hurry up already and get his zipper down. My unpracticed hands shook, but it was mostly with excitement.

Outside the office window, sunlight bounced off the brownish-blue bay far below. He had Boston and his fiancée at his feet, and his fingers curled tight around his throne as I pulled him free from his pants.

A big part of me was thrilled with this plan, no matter how risky it was. Macalister's constant supervision and inappropriate offer had left me feeling weak and powerless. I needed to take some control back. I'd push the rules just as I pushed Royce now.

"There you go, Medusa," he muttered. He tipped his head toward his lap and his rock-hard erection. "Turning me into stone again."

A half-laugh bubbled from my chest, but then I closed my hands around him and stroked downward. Last time I'd done this, he'd told me to do it like I meant it, and so I did now. I slid my firm grip up and down, wringing another moan from him.

This was his purest self. The only time I knew beyond a shadow of a doubt he was being true. His body wouldn't let him lie.

He was breathing hard, and his maroon tie rode his heaving chest like it weighed fifty pounds. It was undeniable how we looked. The prince being serviced by one of his subjects. His heavy cock throbbed in my hands, and I relished the way it felt. So soft and yet hard.

"Oh, *fuck*," he said appreciatively, but then he glanced at his watch and torment twisted his face. "Fuck."

Rather than pick up the pace, I slowed my tempo.

"You're making me late."

An evil smile bloomed on my face. "Then go. I'm not making you stay."

"Oh, you aren't, huh?" He gripped my hands and urged me to pump on him faster, both with his action and his furious eyes. "Harder," he barked, "and faster. Finish what you started."

"I'll do it how I want, *thank you very much*."

Between his spread legs, I shifted on my knees so I had better leverage. The carpet was stubby against my skin and probably going to give me rugburn, but it was a small price to pay to watch the pleasure work its way through him. He slumped, banging his head back against the chair while the muscles along his jaw flexed, and he let out a deep sigh. It was the perfect mixture of satisfaction and misery.

"Jesus, you gotta . . ." he choked out. "I need . . ."

My voice was dark and patronizing. "To come? Or to not be late for your very important meeting?"

He said it through clenched teeth. "Yes."

My hands ground to a halt, leaving him pulsing in my tight fists. "You poor thing. It's so hard when you can't have every little thing you want."

I thought I was in charge, but no.

He launched forward in the chair and latched a hand around my throat. Not to strangle or hurt me, just to seize my undivided attention. Even after all he'd done, didn't he know he always had it? His eyes were only an inch from mine, but I could see everything in them. How badly he wanted me. How frustrated he was.

And how desperate he was to hide it.

"I might not have everything I want right now," his expression roared with absolute power, "but you better fucking *believe* I'm going to get it."

When I let go of him, he didn't release me. His free hand went to his cock and began to pump. I stared down at it with fascination.

"Are you going to help?" he asked. "Or was your plan to leave me like this?"

"You love to walk away from me." I wanted to sound strong, but every glide of his fist over himself was undoing me, stroke by sexy stroke. "I'm just following your signature move."

Except I couldn't walk away. His hand on my throat and his other hand twisting and sliding on his cock had me locked in place. I didn't want to go, anyway. There was nowhere else the lustful part of me wanted to be. It demanded I enjoy the show.

"All right," he said. Desire drenched his expression. "I'll just do it like I do every night, when I lie in my bed and wonder what the hell you're doing in the next room, and why you're not naked in my bed right that fucking second."

My heart skipped and tumbled. How many times had I had the same thought?

Just every night.

"I'm thinking about," he said, "the sound you make when I slide my fingers inside you." The tendons in his hand strained from how hard he clenched his fist. "The way you taste." He jacked himself faster, pushing skin through rough skin. "I'm thinking about how hot and wet you were when you rode my dick in the wine cellar."

My chest tightened as his words wrapped me in an immobilizing vise.

As he continued to stroke, we studied each other's reaction with intensity. His pupils were dilated. His pulse throbbed in his neck. He began to violently jerk his hand along his length, and the force shook the chair.

He wasn't touching me to give me enjoyment, but it didn't matter. I felt the same physical pleasure he was experiencing just from his words and the memories he gave me.

"You want to know what always sends me over the edge?" His hand on my throat tightened, although he probably didn't realize he'd done it. He was right on the cusp of losing control. "I think about how it'd look if you went down on me. I'd wrap your green hair around my fist and fuck your pretty red mouth. My dick going in so deep . . . your eyes water . . . and then you make me . . ."

We shuddered together as he clamped his fist over his tip and came with a heavy groan. He kept his gaze locked on me the whole time, delivering his patented stare while satisfaction crawled along his expression.

And then it slowly drained away.

All his dirty talk had heated me to the core, but it was the tiny detail that had made me threaten to combust. He fantasized about me with green hair, not the way I was now. He pictured the color I would have chosen if I had any say. If I were allowed to express myself, rather than be the brand-approved Stepford wife his family demanded.

Royce crushed his lips to mine, but the kiss was over almost as soon as it had begun, and the ache for more lingered in my mouth. He finally released me and yanked a tissue from the box on his desk, hurrying to clean up the mess in his hands.

I sat back on my heels, surveying him as he shoved himself back in his pants and zipped up.

"I'm going to have to run," he grumbled.

"You mentioned that."

"No, I mean literally. I should have left five minutes ago."

He shot to his feet, largely ignoring the evil look on my face, but he wouldn't miss my patronizing tone. "Oh, did I fuck up something you had planned? Because if so . . . I'm not sorry. I warned you."

He finished buckling his belt and straightened his suit jacket. "Am I looking forward to showing up sweaty and late to a meeting and then ask for an obscene amount of money? No, not really." His expression hardened. "But it's not going to change anything. I'm still going to get what I want."

I went still as a statue. "What?"

He gave me a final glance before heading for the door and lobbed the comment over his shoulder. "Feel free to try that again anytime, though."

It barely registered because the confusion was still too loud in my brain. What the hell did he mean, he was about to ask for an obscene amount of money? He'd just gotten one hundred thousand shares from his father, and the promotion to the board came with its own salary and bonus.

I have more money than God, he'd said.

So why the hell would he ask for more?

The door to his office swung shut with a thud, leaving me alone with more questions and desire than I knew what to do with.

My goal to derail him had failed miserably, and the unsatisfied thirst snaking through my body was the only thing in control right now. I stared out the window at the landscape while I tried to flush away the heat. The vision he'd painted in my mind of his fist tangled in my seaweed colored hair made me long for it to be real. Not just the hair color, but the physical connection.

But it couldn't be.

Besides the deal I'd made, everything was approved by Macalister, even the outfit I wore today. I'd been instructed to dress feminine—he preferred women in skirts rather than pants whenever they were in the office. It was some sexist bullshit, but I couldn't complain about it.

I wasn't allowed to do anything or be who I was. How long could I live like this before I lost myself? Even if I wanted to rebel, any change I effected would be temporary and corrected. Hair would be recolored, wardrobe revised, behavior modified, and then it would be like it never happened.

Like I never existed.

I needed something permanent. Something that couldn't be undone. Something only for me.

Like a symbol I could look at and remind myself who I was, no matter how much the Hales tried to change me.

Oh, God. I swallowed dryly as the idea formed.

I could do it. But to carry it out, I'd have to make a deal with the devil.

As Macalister and I played our nightly chess match, I was a towering stack of blocks, and every move he made was another brick being pulled from the base of my foundation. The mood in the library was always tense, but this was a new level. Our conversations had lessened and become stilted since he'd unveiled the black box, and tonight I swayed and teetered in the silence.

"Checkmate." It simmered with irritation from him because he found the victory hollow. "You were distracted tonight."

My pulse mirrored a frantic trader on the floor during a massive selloff. "Yeah, I . . ."

Was I really going to do this? There'd be no turning back.

I said it quickly before I lost my nerve. "I'm ready to play the other game."

There was no reaction from him, other than his calculating eyes assessing me for the truth. Whatever visual test he'd given me, I must have passed, because he rose from his chair and went to the spot where he'd tucked the dreaded box away.

But once he had it, he didn't give it to me. He stood with the black box in his hands, the black bow at its front taunting me. "What makes you think you're ready now?"

"I'm motivated," I said.

He lifted a curious eyebrow. "Why?"

The question had an agenda. He wanted to know not only what had happened, but how badly I was motivated to see if he could squeeze even more out of me.

I crossed my arms over my chest. "I need a space that's my own."

He scowled. "You have a room here. If Royce is not respecting that, tell me, and I will take care of it."

Of course he'd think Royce was the problem and not himself, even though he'd been the one waiting for me in my room the night Emily had gone into the hospital.

"I'm not really talking about a physical space," I said. "I need a place free from rules and obligations, where I'm the one in control and making the decisions."

He appeared to find the answer satisfying. He set the box on the desk but left his hand on it, his turn not yet complete. "Explain to me the rules, so I know you remember how we're going to play."

Oh, Jesus. I swallowed hard. "At ten-thirty I use what's inside the box. When it's over, I text you the number."

His face took on a wicked cast. "The number of what?"

My heart was in my mouth and got in the way of my tongue. "Orgasms."

If I wasn't so anxious, I might have appreciated the way he looked when he was satisfied. It was such a rare event.

"Are you allowed orgasms outside of our arrangement?"

"No," I said.

"And so we're clear," he pushed the box to me, "by accepting this, you are entrusting your experience to me and surrendering control."

It was impossible to catch my breath, but I got the word out. "Yes."

The box was heavy, weighed down with a million reasons why I shouldn't have agreed to his deal.

"Excellent." His low, seductive voice was a fog that enveloped the room. "I look forward to receiving your text this evening."

I said nothing as I wrapped the box in my arms and fled from his lust-filled blue eyes.

TEN

Ten-thirty came much too fast. Time seemed to go impossibly slow whenever I was with Macalister, but now I was locked alone in my own room, and the minutes raced by.

As soon as I'd left the library, I'd hurried down the hall and was thankful I didn't run into anyone else. It felt like I was carrying a bomb and it'd explode if Royce saw me with it. So, I stumbled into my room, shoved the box under my bed, and pretended if it was out of sight it ceased to exist.

But the goddamn clock kept ticking, and soon I'd have to unleash all the evils inside Pandora's Box.

At ten, I changed into a pair of sleep shorts and a tank top, curled up on the couch, and tried to read, but every few sentences my gaze would drift over to the bed. Where would I do it? There? And how exactly did the strange vibrator work?

I only made it ten minutes before I sat on the floor, my back against the side of the bed and the box on my lap, the ribbon undone. My mouth went dry as I read the instructions. Half of the thing—the smaller end—went *inside* me.

The wider, fat end would press against my clit.

Of course, I considered not using it and faking the ordeal, but I was sure he'd know somehow. And it was wrong, but I couldn't help but be a little curious.

I'd never admit it to Macalister, but I'd never used a vibrator before. Like a fool, I'd thought my parents watched the credit card statements, and I would have been too embarrassed to be caught buying a sex toy with their money. Plus, I'd been a virgin and able to get myself off just fine with my own hand, so I never had much drive to seek out additional help.

When the time drew near, I was strangely numb to all emotion—other than anxiety—like I'd been with the initiation. It seemed weird to have the lights on, so I turned them off, and only moonlight lit my room as I climbed onto my king-sized bed. I pulled off my clothes, wiggled under the covers, and sucked in a deep breath.

At the other end of the hall, Macalister was likely in his room, thinking about me. Would he touch himself as we did this? Or would he be completely focused on me? Maybe he'd multitask during the session and check how his personal stocks were performing.

Alice wouldn't be around because they didn't share a bedroom. It wasn't their loveless marriage that kept them apart. Their sleeping patterns were total opposites, as Macalister was an insomniac and Alice needed a minimum of eight hours of rest to function.

My fingers crept down across my stomach, inching lower. I closed my eyes and pictured Royce today, wearing that stunning black suit and maroon tie, his pants undone and his hard cock clenched in his hand.

As he stroked in my mind, my fingers rubbed over my swollen clit. I didn't want to think about why I was already wet or what had turned me on before I'd even started the fantasy. All that was important was that I be ready before the clock hit ten-thirty.

Breath escaped my lungs as I pushed the black vibrator inside me. It was cold and smooth, and the other end fit tight against my slit. It wasn't . . . uncomfortable. If anything, it felt good.

But the waiting? That was agony. I lay in my bed, my hands balled into fists at my sides, so tense I was ready to explode. Was this part of the session? To build anticipation until I was—

"Oh!" I gasped.

Vibrations buzzed against my center. The sensation wasn't like anything I'd experienced. Instant, acute pleasure burst between my legs, so great it made me flinch. I gripped handfuls of the sheet beneath me, needing to hold on as warmth spread along the length of my body.

It stole my breath and my thoughts.

All I could focus on was the pulse, both inside and out, which made me want to twist and writhe. I turned my head and groaned into the side of my pillow. Holy fuck, it felt good. I just had to lie there and take it, surrendering control.

By the time I got a handle on the sensations, the pattern changed from a steady vibration to a slow building one. It would crest and ebb, and with each cycle I clawed my way reluctantly closer to an orgasm.

I was alone in the room. If I were controlling the vibrator on my own, this would mean nothing. Royce's only issue with me using a toy would likely be that he didn't get to participate.

But I wasn't in control.

And that made all the difference. The walls between Macalister and me were only an illusion of propriety. What I was doing was *wrong*. Worse was the sick appeal of it. Royce had denied me for a year, gotten what he wanted, then traded me away. I could argue it served him right that he'd allowed this to happen.

I crossed a line, and now it felt too good to stop.

My breath came and went so quickly it left me lightheaded. Sweat beaded at my temples as my orgasm approached. It was useless to resist, and I gave up holding back. The only worry now wasn't if I would come, but if I could stay relatively quiet as I did it.

A tremble worked its way up my legs, my eyes slammed shut, and I jammed my hands into my hair. I wasn't going to come—I was going to break apart. Even if I was able to piece myself together afterward, I wouldn't be the same. There'd always be this stain on my insides from where I'd let Macalister in.

Win at all costs.

That was what I had to do. Losing the battle was all right as long as I won the war.

I rolled onto my stomach and released a pleasure-soaked moan into my pillow as I came. The orgasm tightened my muscles until I wasn't in control, and they tweaked and contracted like a marionette's strings being pulled. Ecstasy purred and buzzed, sizzling on my nerves until everything was tingling.

It was so, so good until it was too much.

I reached down and yanked the vibrator out, overly sensitive. It continued humming, quiet as a whisper as I blew out a long breath and struggled to slow my heartrate. When I was no longer tingling and the fog had cleared in my brain, I grabbed my phone and thumbed out the message.

Me: One.

Five seconds later the vibrator died, and it was painfully silent in the room.

Macalister: Tomorrow you will have two.

I lobbed my phone onto the other side of the bed, hoping it would take the wicked excitement along with it.

My Porsche was waiting for me in the circle drive the next morning, washed clean and gassed up to go. I climbed into the driver's seat and wrapped my hands around the steering wheel, letting the feeling of being in control calm me. Every mile of road I put between myself and the Hale house lifted more pressure off my shoulders.

I'd told the Hales I was going to visit my sister, but I drove out of the way to Port Cove first. The tattoo shop was nicer than I expected, with upscale furniture and flooring and a sexy vibe. Arturo, the artist, was short with tattoos crawling all over his skin, and he listened thoughtfully as I explained what I wanted.

"I have a picture," I said.

I pulled out my phone, opened Instagram, and searched for it on my profile. As I scrolled, it was sickening how long it took to get through all the fake posts I'd made before finally getting to the real me. I'd buried myself under an avalanche of selfies with my daily outfits, curated office shots, and vapid party pictures. I'd posed with people who didn't care about me, only what I could do for them.

When the consultation was over, I drove to my parents' house.

It was the first time I'd been there since I moved in with the Hales, and it was beyond strange. Everything felt . . . smaller. The lights didn't shine as brightly, and the rooms seemed overwrought with items my parents didn't need. It had a claustrophobic effect I'd never noticed before.

Emily was in her pajamas and in bed when I arrived, her back propped up by pillows. It didn't look like she'd showered today, and there were dark circles under her eyes. Concern made me collapse beside her.

"I'm tired all the time," she said. "This baby is sucking the life out of me."

I didn't miss the way her gaze slid over me, taking in my designer clothes, my rich brown hair, and perfectly manicured nails. Envy wasn't something I'd ever seen in my sister's eyes before. Was she wondering if this was what her life would have been if she hadn't gotten pregnant?

I wanted to tell her it was like my Instagram feed—nothing was as glamorous and perfect as what I projected. She didn't know Royce had sold me out, or who he'd handed me over to. I wanted to confide in my sister and best friend what I'd had to do to earn the right to drive myself here today.

But I couldn't, because that meant I'd have to admit it out loud, and I couldn't stand to see the judgment twist on her face. Not to mention, she was on bed rest, and I shouldn't cause any additional stress.

There was a third, shameful reason I didn't say anything. I still wasn't over what she'd kept from me. Her affair with her professor, her pregnancy, and the rumor she'd heard about the initiation. I wanted to move past it, but I struggled.

No one was who I thought they were, and it felt like my whole family was slipping away.

"It's going to be all right." I tried to make it sound convincing but faltered. So, I curled up in bed beside her and watched Netflix while we talked about things that didn't matter. She probably wanted to escape as much as I did.

"Marist," our mother said when she came in and discovered me in bed beside Emily. "Were you even going to come say hello?"

"Of course," I said. "I thought you were going to join us."

She scowled. "No. I wish I had time to sit around and watch TV, but I'm too busy."

Her passive-aggressive statement sliced through my mood and turned my tone sarcastic. "I'm sure."

She ignored my attitude. "I need to leave soon. I have an appointment at Barney's."

Tension tightened the muscles in my back. "You're going shopping?"

"I need a dress for the anniversary gala." She put her hands on her hips. "Don't worry, I have a budget." An idea must have taken hold in her mind because she abruptly straightened and brightened. "Do you want to come with me?"

A hundred thoughts hit me at once, but the cynical one was the loudest. What was her motive for asking me to join her? Did she genuinely want to spend time with her daughter . . . or was she hoping I would be able to pay for her dress?

I'd go with her, if for no other reason than to make sure she stuck to her budget. I'd have to save her from herself.

It was like I'd just swallowed ice and it sat as a frozen lump in my stomach.

I sounded like Macalister.

At twenty-three, Jillian Lambert was two years older than I was. When her hair was down, it was long and wavy, but tonight her honey brown tresses were pulled back into a high, sleek ponytail. Her black dress had fluttering shoulders, and it walked a perfect line between casual and dressed up.

She'd chosen wisely. I still hadn't figured out exactly how to dress for the Hale family dinners either. I took my seat beside Royce and flashed a sympathetic smile to her across the table. She looked nervous as hell and like she'd rather be anywhere else than seated beside Vance.

Sophia had told me Jillian had a nasty, very public

breakup with her boyfriend at the marina fundraising event Royce and I had missed. I had the sneaking suspicion Vance had played a part in it. His guiding hand had orchestrated the thing somehow to make sure she would be single.

Because his father wanted Jillian with Vance, and the Hales always got what they wanted.

"Thank you for joining us this evening," Macalister said to her.

Her voice quavered. "Thanks for having me."

"How is the training going? Are you prepared for the race?"

She glanced at the man seated next to her like she needed his approval.

"Yeah, we're ready," Vance said.

Macalister was irritated his son had spoken in her place. He refocused on Jillian. "Does your father think you have a good chance at winning?"

She nodded. "We're all hopeful."

Macalister eked out half of a pained smile. Her answer lacked the kind of confidence he demanded from both his family and his employees. He couldn't say anything, though. She was his link to her father, who was Macalister's link to the president, and he wasn't going to risk falling out of Wayne Lambert's good graces.

"Vance has been so helpful," she added. Her amused gaze darted to him. "Always telling us what to do and stuff."

I snorted. "What did you expect? He's a Hale."

Oh, my God. What the fuck did I just say?

Every pair of eyes at the table turned to me, and the room went so quiet no one was breathing. I was Medusa again. Everyone had turned to stone.

"Yeah," Royce said finally. "You'd better watch out or he'll make himself captain." His teasing tone released the tension and let the air back into the room, and I was so grateful. I flashed him an appreciative look.

"Vance doesn't want that," Macalister said. "I'm sure your father is an excellent captain." His voice was cool and pointed. A warning to Vance to stay in line.

A tight smile pressed on Alice's lips. "May I shift topics for a moment?"

Her husband nodded. "Yes."

"The masquerade masks for the gala," she said. "I keep thinking it would be better if we had a consistent look for the family. It's the Hale Banking and Holding Company, and we'll want a picture of all the Hales represented."

Disinterest colored his expression. "What did you have in mind?"

"I was thinking black and white? Or everyone in gold?" She pursed her lips, unhappy with the answers she was giving. "I'm still working up ideas."

"How about the Greek myths?" Royce said.

"What?" Alice and I asked at the same time.

He tossed up a hand like he was literally throwing the idea out onto the table. "Marist has all these books about the myths, and some of them are—"

"We're not Greek," Macalister said.

My fiancé wasn't fazed. "I think it could be something different and unique. That's what Alice said we needed, right?" He shrugged as if he didn't care either way. "I don't know, I kind of like the idea of being a god."

Alice tilted her head as she considered his statement, before her gaze latched onto me. "This was the stuff you used to post on social media."

"Yeah," I said.

Macalister peered at his wife. "I worry the whole evening lacks sophistication, but the masquerade is your concept. I leave the smaller decisions to you."

In Macalister-speak, that meant he was giving up control because he thought it wasn't worth his time. Costumes were beneath him.

Alice wasn't sold, but not ready to dismiss Royce's idea either. "Maybe Marist and I could pull some pictures together."

Outwardly, I nodded and looked enthusiastic to help. On the inside, I wanted to slump my shoulders and scowl. Was this another part of me the Hales would modify and skew to fit their brand?

"You're going to a masquerade party?" Jillian asked. "That sounds fun."

Macalister's glare carried the heat of a thousand suns, and it was shocking that Vance didn't burst into flames. He obviously hadn't asked her to be his date yet, but he rolled right into an easy smile. "It will be fun, and you can come." His eyes sparkled with charm. "I'll even let you be my date."

"Oh." She laughed nervously. "That's okay. We're just friends."

He didn't miss a beat. "Well, *friend*, I need a date."

Jillian's hesitant gaze darted around the table, searching

for help, but she didn't find any. Her shoulders tightened as her chin dropped toward her chest. "I just got out of something serious."

Vance's expression darkened. "Yeah, with a serious douchebag. Screw that guy. Show up on my arm, and he'll see how much you've traded up."

She looked torn. The idea had appeal, but her gaze flicked over to Royce for a second. Was she thinking about how awkward it'd be since she'd slept with Vance's older brother?

I couldn't picture them together. Jillian was pretty, and she'd been popular enough in school, but they had nothing in common. It had probably been a one-night stand, and he'd been his fake persona with her. Playing his role as the cocky bastard who made all the girls swoon. She hadn't seen the other side of himself that he'd shown only to me.

I knew it, because I couldn't stand anything else to be true.

It was clear Vance wasn't going to be able to close the deal, and Macalister wasn't going to let that happen. "I invited your father personally," he said. "Please, I insist."

That settled it. She couldn't refuse the king.

Her voice was timid. "Okay."

"Excellent," Macalister said.

Jillian's gaze fell to her plate, and she looked like a trapped animal, resigned to the cage closed around her. Was that how I'd looked the day I'd made the deal to marry Royce? It felt like a lifetime ago.

I stared at her across the table, feeling nothing but dread. This family was going to eat her alive.

All through dinner, Macalister hadn't so much as glanced my direction. His indifference toward me made me question if what had happened last night had been real. I was terrified to be alone with him and answer the questions I knew he was going to ask.

But a deal was a deal, and I had no choice.

At seven-thirty, the door to the library was open and Macalister was already waiting inside. But unlike the other nights, he wasn't seated behind the desk. He stood beside the leather reading chair, his attention on the black cat knotted in a ball on the top of the high chair back. I expected Macalister to shoo Lucifer away.

He lifted a hand, set it on the cat's head, and stroked all the way down its back.

Lucifer's apple green eyes popped open and peered up at the man petting him and, after a moment's consideration, he decided he would allow it. As Macalister stroked the cat again, Lucifer stretched and gave a rumbling, content purr.

Macalister was in side-profile to me, unaware I was watching him. As his face softened into a smile, I fractured. Maybe all the Hales had two sides, but I didn't want to see this other version of him. I could only deal with him as Zeus—uncaring god of the mortals. He was complex enough like that.

"Royce told me you hated the cat," I said quietly.

Macalister straightened and dropped his hand like Lucifer had burned him. He wasn't pleased I'd caught him being affectionate and tried to hide his embarrassment with a dark glare. "And I told you that you shouldn't trust any-thing he says."

He strode to the chessboard and sat, which meant I had to shut the door and join him.

"What is it about mythology that appeals to you?" he asked as we began playing.

I didn't want to have this discussion. "I'm not sure I can explain it."

He found my lack of answer unacceptable and let me know with his sharp tone. "Try."

I sighed. "So, you have these gods, who have power and immortality and are supposed to be superior . . . and yet, they're so much worse than the mortals. They're spiteful and jealous, full of lust and wrath. They don't care about anyone but themselves." I tried not to get distracted by talking. I had to focus on the board and defend my queen. "They're people's terrible, basic instincts, but amplified."

"You're saying you enjoy reading about horrible things happening to horrible people."

Was he *teasing* me? His sense of humor was so dry, I could rarely tell when he wasn't being serious. He was in such a good mood tonight. Getting Jillian to agree to be Vance's date must have been the reason. All his ducks were lining up for him to get everything he wanted.

"When you're a god," I said, "there are no consequences, so power corrupts absolutely. It makes for some pretty fasci-nating and messed up stories."

There was a long moment of quiet. I couldn't tell if he was thinking about what I'd said, or his next move.

"Then," his gaze lifted from the chessboard to meet mine, "after I've won this game, you'll pick out one of your books for me to read. I'll start with your favorite."

My heart clunked in my chest. Him reading my favorite book was almost as intimate as him giving me a vibrator. I swallowed thickly, searching for a way to distract. "Who says you're going to win?"

He blinked slowly. "My knight, most likely. I'm taking your queen in two moves, and then it will all be over."

Confounded, I stared at the board. How the hell was he going to—

I deflated as I saw what he anticipated.

"You're a clever girl," Macalister said, "but you get lost in the game. You're thinking about each move you make, while I'm at least two moves ahead."

Just as predicted, in two moves he carried out his plan. My queen was captured, and without my most valuable piece, it was only a matter of time before he had me locked in checkmate.

A victorious smile burned across his lips. "I'll wait here for you to bring me my book."

I sighed and climbed out of my chair. I used the short walk to my bedroom to try to figure out which title to give him. Would he want the most literary and sophisticated one from my collection? Or the one I thought he'd tolerate the best?

When I returned and presented the book to him, he examined it with disdain. "This is your favorite?"

"Yes," I lied.

"And, being that it's your favorite, I assume you've read it multiple times." He thumbed through the book, showing off its pristine pages and unmarred spine.

"Uh . . ." I was so busted. I'd only read it once. "I thought this was the one you'd like best."

He shut it with a loud slam and thrust the book toward me. "That's not what I asked for, though, is it?"

"No, I'm sorry." His disappointment was so heavy it was crushing, and I needed relief. "I'll be right back." I grabbed it from him and took off for my bedroom.

When I returned with the black book and its well-worn gold embossed cover, Macalister's displeasure faded. He took the hardcover book from me, his gaze scanning the printing on the front before opening it and reading the inside flap of the dust jacket.

He asked it without looking at me, as if he were only mildly curious. "Are you looking forward to tonight?"

His question opened me up and filled my interior with concrete.

"It's all I could think about today," he added.

It became impossible to breathe. Everything in me was too tight, too strained. "Macalister," I pleaded.

I couldn't have picked a worse thing to say. His eyes lidded with desire, and he licked his full lips, like I looked delicious and was about to be devoured.

"I enjoy the way you say my name." His expression teemed with dangerous lust. "Like it's nearly unspeakable—a word too filthy to say out loud."

I pressed my hand to my chest and took a blind step backward, but he matched it with a step forward of his own, keeping me only an arm's length away.

"You'll say it tonight," he said.

What? I shook my head. "No. I won't."

He hardened at my refusal. "You will. You'll think about me, and when the pleasure is too much, you'll say my name."

"*No.*" I found my footing and my spine. He'd gotten me to do a lot of things, but . . . "You can try to control me all you want, but you can't tell me what to think. You can't *make* me think about you."

Excitement danced in his vibrant eyes. "You gave me complete control over your experience. That was the deal we agreed on. You say I can't make you think about me, but I'm already two moves ahead, Marist." His voice swelled with power. "I can, and I *will.*"

ELEVEN

Royce lurked outside the library, leaning against the wall on the other side of the hallway, his thumbs hooked inside his pants pockets. He took one look at my flushed face, straightened from the wall, and his gaze flew to the library door in accusation.

"What did he do?" he demanded.

Nothing I didn't agree to.

"Nothing," I said quickly. "We were just talking." I was still terrible at lying, but at least this was merely a bend of the truth. Macalister hadn't actually done anything to me.

Not yet. But worry spread through my veins like a virus replicating itself. He was a relentless man who was never satisfied, which meant he wouldn't stop. Not even when he got what he wanted.

"Did you need something?" I asked.

My breath caught as Royce moved in, taking up all the space in the hallway so he was the only thing I could see. He was high cheekbones, dark hair, and gorgeous eyes that penetrated all the way down to my bones.

"Yeah." His voice was low and thick. "Let's go out. I don't care where, just someplace that's not here."

To make sure there was no misinterpretation of his intentions, he put his hand on the wall beside my head and his knee between my legs, leaning in. The contact of his thigh against the cleft of my body looked tame, but I shuddered. He shifted his leg, rubbing against me and creating tension and fire.

It drove me to put my hand on his chest, and I marveled at how steady his heartbeat was. Mine was rapid and uneven.

"Or do you want to stay in and break some rules?" he murmured. His seductive voice wasn't playing fair. I wanted that very much.

"I can't." As I eased him back, my body mourned the loss.

"No?"

"No," I whispered. Because of what I'd done with his father last night, and what I had to do again tonight. My betrayal seemed slightly less awful if I wasn't intimate with Royce at the same time. I just needed one more day with my freedom to get what I needed.

Plus, I couldn't go anywhere with him, anyway. I had less than two hours before I had to play Macalister's fucked up game.

"Is everything okay?" he asked. "What were you talking about in there?"

"Nothing."

He frowned. "Tell me. Maybe I can help you."

Help me? How was I supposed to say what my issue

was? And asking me to tell him was awfully rich. I pushed away from the wall and gave him a hard look. "We all have our secrets, Royce. I'm tired and going to bed. Good night."

My body was taut with anticipation. It gripped me so hard, everything ached from its nervous clench. I actively tried not to think about Macalister as I prepared, but that backfired. Trying not to think about him made it impossible not to. He'd turned my brain against me.

At ten-thirty sharp, the vibrations kicked in, and I welcomed the sensation. My mind emptied of thought, other than how good the toy lodged inside my body felt. And once my mind was cleared, then I imagined it was Royce at the helm, controlling my pleasure.

I pictured him now, wearing one of his best suits, kneeling on the bed between my spread legs. He had his phone in his hand and a dastardly smile on his lips. His gaze would focus on the toy pulsing and watch how my hips moved in little circles, desperate for release.

The vibration pattern changed into a sharp staccato rhythm, and I stifled a moan. Heat blasted down my spine, but goosebumps lifted on my skin. In my head, Royce's expression dripped with desire, and the sight of me writhing under his command was too much. He smoothed a hand down the fly of his pants and gripped the heavy bulge swelling there. I'd never seen the sight in real life, but my imagination was so vivid. The picture I painted was carnal. His expensive watch peeking out from under his shirt sleeve and cuff of his jacket, his sexy hand squeezing back his pleasure.

I wanted him.

I'd had him.

And I wanted him still, worse than I had a year ago.

Grinding against the motorized silicone and empty sheets wasn't enough. At this moment, I didn't care if he'd told me nothing but lies, I would settle for what we had. I'd let him use me, and I'd use him, and after enough time pretending, maybe the feelings would become real between us, matching the way our bodies longed to be together.

"Fuck," I groaned to myself.

In my fantasy, Royce couldn't get his pants undone fast enough. His hands were clumsy with eagerness, ripping down his zipper. He tossed the tail of his tie over his shoulder and out of our way before he lowered down to meet me. I wanted to feel his weight against my body. The pressure of him. I needed to tangle my hands in his thick hair and bite his lip as he tried to kiss me.

I lost control the moment I imagined him shoving himself inside me with one deep, unapologetic thrust.

My orgasm was fire. I cried out as ecstasy swept through me, burning along my nerves in pinpricks of heat and bliss. Instinct took over, and I reached down, turning off the overwhelming vibrator because the pleasure was so acute, it hurt. The buzzing ceased, plunging the darkened room into near silence, punctuated only by my uneven gulps of breath.

The orgasm was so mind-numbingly powerful, I lay on the bed for a long while, unable to move or think, only recover.

Slowly, reality came back to me, and I picked up my phone.

Me: One.

The message delivered, then said it had been read, but no dots appeared to indicate Macalister was typing. Instead, my screen turned to black, his name flashed across it, and my ringtone punched through the quiet.

Holy. Shit.

Panic made my stomach bottom out. What was I going to do? I couldn't *not* answer his call, but how the fuck was I supposed to talk to him now? I closed my eyes and held my breath, praying the phone would miraculously stop ringing. Was there any chance he'd called me by mistake?

Don't be so fucking stupid, Marist.

I tapped the screen, and my voice was a ghost. "Hello?"

There was no greeting, only his angry question. "Why is it off?"

"Because it was too intense," I blurted. "And I already came, so I thought—"

"Turn it back on, now. I'm not finished with you."

My heart halted painfully, but in the aftermath of my orgasm I was weak. I fumbled with the phone as I followed his order. "Okay," I said on a shaky breath. "It's on."

"And it's inside you?"

I bunched a handful of the silky duvet in my fist. It was barely a whisper. "Yes."

"I don't believe you. You'll take a picture and send me the proof."

My brain went black as it short-circuited. He was insane. There was absolutely no way I was going to take a picture of me wearing the vibrator and text it to him. "*No.*"

"No?" I could picture the arrogance on his face on the other side of the conversation.

The vibrator leapt to life, and as I jolted in surprise, a shameful moan burst from my lips. I was still sensitive, but after the first few seconds, it lessened and I could think over it.

"That was rather convincing, Marist." His deep voice was much smoother than the scotch he'd poured for me weeks ago. "How did your orgasm compare to last night's?"

Oh, my God. I couldn't catch my breath. "I can't . . . talk, while you're—"

"If you don't want to talk, then you'll send the picture. Otherwise, I need to listen to ensure you're still following my rules."

The speed revved up, like he'd turned the dial from low to medium, and it forced a whimper from me.

"Good. Was your orgasm tonight better?"

I blinked rapidly, unable to focus on anything around me in the dark bedroom. There was only his inescapable voice. That was the moment it settled on me, what he'd meant about being able to force me to think about him. I couldn't drown him out. Even if I pictured Royce, he'd have Macalister's voice.

"I can't do this."

"Of course you can." Irritation tinted his words. "It's a simple question."

"No, I'm hanging up."

His voice seethed with cold fury. "Then you'll give your keys to Royce, and I will explain to him why you lost your privilege."

I put my hand over my mouth, covering the cry just before it pealed from my lips. I'd walked voluntarily into Macalister's trap. He hadn't even needed to disguise it; I'd been that stupid.

"What will it be?" he demanded.

I couldn't tell Royce what I'd done. Even after he'd hurt me so deeply, I was reluctant to do the same to him. But I'd foolishly thought I could keep this all a secret. I wasn't a god. There were going to be consequences for what I'd done.

The silver lining to the disaster I'd allowed was the freedom in giving up. With no options left, at least that meant there were no more decisions to be made. I had no power left as I spoke. "It was . . . better tonight."

"Why?"

I lashed out, wanting to knock him down a peg. "Because I was thinking," I gulped down air, "about *him*."

He laughed, but it was devoid of warmth. "I still have more work to do, then. I'll break you of this ridiculous infatuation. You deserve a man who knows your value, Marist. Not some boy who threw you away."

It put me in the strange position of wanting to defend Royce to the very man he'd sold me to. But I didn't get a chance. The pattern on the vibrator slowed to a crawl, and the vibrations shifted.

"Oh," I gasped. It was a completely different sensation, and it took a long moment to realize that both sides, inside and out, were now pulsating.

"I'll tell you what I think about." I pictured him sitting

on the leather couch in his bedroom, wearing his suit with his tie still knotted perfectly at his throat because he never relaxed. He didn't do casual. "I think about how you denied me. I am still owed my two minutes."

My pulse roared from the pleasure, but the rest of me was frozen in place.

"And you will give them to me."

The phone was crystal clear, so it sounded like he was right beside me. He wasn't in the room, and yet he filled every inch of it.

"I won't," I whispered.

"I'm going to tell you how I imagine it. You'll allow me to peel you out of your dress and everything else until I can see every beautiful inch of you. This time, no one will be in my way. It'll only be us."

The way he said the word *us* gave me a chill.

"I'll run my hands over your skin. Perhaps you'll shiver, but I'll make sure I'm the cause. There's no place I'll leave untouched because I'm a thorough man. Dedicated and relentless."

I felt his imagined hands on me, sinking me further into the bed.

"Your knees will give out from the way my fingers feel sliding over you, so I'll have to lay you down. Now it will be my mouth's turn. I'll explore and taste, starting with your lips, taking note of every sigh you make and how your body responds as I move lower."

My ragged breathing was so fast my heart couldn't keep up. Blood roared in my ears.

"I'll have to hold your breasts steady in my hands while I give them the attention they deserve. You'll be breathing as hard as you are right now. Once I've had my fill, I'll venture lower. You'll squirm. You tell yourself you don't want it, but— oh, Marist. *You do*."

The vibrations increased, bringing terrible pleasure with them.

"You're desperate by this point. There's a need that I created and only I can satisfy, and I'm going to, because once I start something, I don't give up. I don't walk away."

The unwanted heat building in me was too strong to ignore, too powerful to stop. I grabbed a fistful of the thick duvet and shoved it over my mouth, my teeth clenching down on the fabric.

"I score my fingers down the insides of your spread thighs, hard enough to leave marks. The pain is temporary and necessary. It wakes up your nerve endings and will make your orgasm stronger."

Macalister reigned on Mount Olympus, hurling down his devastating words like lightning bolts, each one making me jolt and flinch.

"If I've done everything right, by this point you're shaking. You want my mouth on you, but you can't bring yourself to ask. You won't need to." His voice was seductive and commanding at the same time. "I understand what you need, and I'm going to give it to you."

Once more, the vibrator picked up speed, and I groaned into the bunched duvet covering my mouth.

He was abruptly angry. "I can't hear you."

Oh, God. I pulled the bedding away just long enough to gasp it. "I'm here."

Just those two words in my tight, breathless voice was enough to give away how much he'd affected me. It was impossible not to visualize what he was describing, no matter how much I didn't want to.

For once, I could relate to all those stupid mortal girls seduced by the gods, but I hated it. I despised how my body was reacting to him. How the fucked up side of myself wanted to hear the rest of Macalister's terrible fantasy.

"Is your cunt wet?" he asked.

I flinched like he'd slapped me. It wasn't just the question that was so shocking, but the language. His carefully selected vulgar word for maximum effect.

"It will be. You'll cry out when I run my tongue through it. If your hips buck, I'll hold you still and keep my mouth exactly where I want it. I'll trace my tongue over every inch because, as I mentioned, I am a thorough man."

I was breaking apart. I needed him to stop . . . I needed release . . . I *needed*—

"I want you to picture what that looks like. My head buried between your legs, my mouth fucking you as I watch."

I saw it. His icy blue eyes evaluating me as his tongue fluttered over my clit. The sensation wasn't that different from the vibrations teasing me now.

"I'll find the place that makes all the words disappear from your mind." His voice picked up in urgency, like he knew I was right on the edge. "Every word except for one, and you know which word that is, don't you?"

I didn't want to say it, but a dam burst and spilled out in a tidal wave of pleasure. *"Macalister."*

As I came, a shuddering moan seeped out like he'd wrestled it from my body. Hot flashes coursed down my limbs, spiraling out from my core.

The buzzing ceased, giving me a reprieve and prolonging the pleasure. There was nothing else to do but enjoy it, and I rode each wave until I felt like I was finally back in my own body again.

Realization as frigid as the polar vortex moved in and took hold.

"I don't know if I've heard anything better than the way you say my name," he said. "Especially when you're coming while you do it." He paused, drawing in an uneven breath. "We'll talk again tomorrow. Good night, Marist."

I was a frozen statue, unable to say anything, even after the line went dead.

The clear bandage pulled at my skin, and my form-fitting dress rubbed on it uncomfortably whenever I moved my arms, but it was worth it. Since I had an unpaid internship, and most days Royce didn't even need me, I'd taken the morning off and driven to the tattoo shop in Port Cove. I'd told everyone I had a dentist appointment, and they seemed to believe me, but I still checked my rearview mirror periodically as I came and went from the shop.

Macalister had security on staff—spies, as Royce liked to

call them. But no one had followed me.

I sat at my desk and stared across the hallway at Royce's closed door. He'd been in a meeting since I'd arrived hours ago, and I was starving. I'd ordered us lunch from the Chinese café that had recently opened one block over and put our food in the kitchen while waiting for him to finish.

There were only three days left of my "job," and it had been a total failure. I wasn't any closer to figuring out his master plan, or if the man he was with me behind closed doors was the real version of himself.

Twenty minutes later, his door swung open and he emerged with the heads from the finance department. The team dispersed with quick goodbyes. The meeting had run long, and everyone was late for their next appointment. Tension was still high at HBHC. The stock prices hadn't bounced back like the rest of the market—it continued to tick downward.

Was it possible this was Sophia Alby's doing?

I hoped so. I was a student of economics, and information was a commodity, so it was fascinating to me the impact a simple rumor could have on this huge, global company.

Royce's gaze landed on me. "Hey."

"Hey," I answered. "Do you mind if we have lunch together?"

He liked the idea until he checked his watch. "I wish I could, but that meeting blew up my schedule, so I don't—"

"I had it delivered and put it in the kitchen. I thought we could eat in your office."

We didn't eat at his desk. Instead, he sat beside me on

the couch in the small sitting area of his office, his open take-out container balanced on his lap. "Did you get that meeting with Frank Davos on my calendar?"

I made a face similar to the one I'd made yesterday when he'd forwarded me the email. He didn't usually ask me to schedule stuff, and it likely took him longer to forward the message than for him to do it himself and enter it on his phone.

"Yeah," I said, trying to keep the irritation from my voice. I could handle a simple task. "It's done."

"Okay." He looked relieved. "It's, uh, important. I wanted a second set of eyes on it."

He considered a meeting with his personal broker, a man who worked *for* Royce, important?

"You don't like your lunch?" he asked, interrupting my thoughts.

I looked down at the hand-pulled noodle dish. "No, it's good. I'm . . . nervous."

His chopsticks paused. "About what?"

I set my container down on the low table in front of us and put my sweaty palms on my knees. "I need to show you something."

His expression clouded, but it dissipated when I stood and turned to face him, my hands moving behind my back. I found the top of the zipper on the back of my dress and pulled it down slowly, going tooth by tooth.

Royce's eyes hooded as I shrugged out of the straps of my top, pulling the dress down and exposing the lacy bra I wore. He abandoned his lunch, tossing it down on the table with a messy thud, and then settled back on the couch, casting one arm along the back of it. His posture was confident and relaxed, and his wide smile was inviting. He thought I was stripping and wanted me to continue the show.

But I grabbed my left bicep with my right hand and pulled it toward my chest, showing off the newly inked skin along my ribcage.

He sat forward to get a better look, then stood and set one hand on my waist, the fingers of his other hand tracing the edge of the bandage. His delicate touch lit up my skin.

"Medusa," he said simply. "It's beautiful."

A sliver of relief worked its way through my system. "You like it?"

"Yeah, I do. When did you get it?"

"This morning."

It hadn't taken long for the artist to do the design. Arturo had sketched it out last night and texted me the sample, and this morning he'd inked Medusa painfully into the skin just below the band of my bra. It was one of the only places on my body that I'd see and likely no one else. Well, except for my future husband.

Who stared at the small, single-colored tattoo like it was a work of art.

And it was. She had a classically beautiful face, surrounded by locks of coiling snakes. He'd captured her as young and confident—more of a sexy temptress than an evil monster.

Royce's fingers continued to outline the edges, carefully avoiding my irritated skin, and his touch sent goosebumps rippling along my arms. "Did it hurt?"

"Yeah," I said. Shame colored my voice. "And I deserved it."

He hesitated, his fingers stopping in their tracks. "What?"

"I did something awful." I stepped away and struggled to push my arms back into the straps of my dress. "Your father controls everything, and I couldn't take it anymore. I don't recognize that girl in the mirror. Not the way I look, or the clothes I wear, or what I post to stupid fucking Instagram. I know this sounds insane, but I feel like I'm . . . disappearing."

My voice broke as the emotions swelled in me, and the worry in his expression skyrocketed, but I had to keep going.

"I needed this tattoo. Something he couldn't take away from me."

Royce's arms circled around me. "Marist, it's okay. Believe me when I say I fucking understand, and—"

But he wouldn't, not when I told him everything. "To get this done without him knowing about it, I needed my car. You remember when you told me he doesn't just give people what they want?"

His arms around me hardened into stone. "What'd you do?"

"He wanted to play another game." My pulse quickened. "It was really fucked up."

"What happened?" When I didn't say anything, his mind must have gone to the worst possible scenario because all the color drained from his face and horror filled his voice. "Did you fuck him?"

"No! God, no." I swallowed a breath. "But . . ."

I couldn't get my words out, and it was clearly killing him. "Jesus, just say it."

"He gave me a vibrator."

Royce's face contorted, not understanding. "Uh, okay."

I could read his thoughts through his expression. He didn't like it, but it also didn't seem that bad. "I don't—"

"He has control over it."

His arms went slack, releasing me, and his demeanor went cold. "I'm not following. You're saying he used it on you?"

"Yes. Wait—no. Not like you're thinking." I pressed my lips into a flat line. "He wasn't in the room. He can control it with his phone."

The distance grew between us, and not just physically, and I didn't like that he was slipping away.

"It was twice," I said, "and that's it. I was stupid, and didn't realize how far he'd push, but I promise you it's over now. I'm not going to play his game again. I'm so sorry I did." I stepped forward, closing the space between us. "I'm sorry I did that to us."

A wide range of emotions played out on his face. Anger. Distrust. Sadness.

And finally, resignation. "Why are you telling me this?"

"He wants to tear us apart." I took a deep breath. "Please don't let him." Maybe if I laid myself bare, he'd open up to me. "I don't want to keep secrets. I screwed up, but I'm still yours, Royce."

I placed my left hand on his jaw, and he covered it with his own, his thumb brushing over the engagement ring sparkling there. The symbol of my commitment to him, even when I had nothing to show for his.

"Are we okay?" I asked hopefully.

He didn't use words to answer me, instead he leaned in. His kiss was restrained, but I accepted it greedily. It was certainly a better reaction than I'd hoped to receive. When the kiss ended, he drew back, and his gaze shifted away from me.

Darkness lurked in his eyes.

It was like I didn't exist. He was too busy contemplating his next move.

My heart sank. He wasn't going to tell me anything. No matter what I did or how honest I was, he still didn't trust me.

Was I foolish to have expected anything else from him?

I picked up my half-eaten lunch and tossed it into his garbage can with a bit too much force. "I'll let you get back to work."

"Marist," he called when I was halfway out the door. His voice was heavy with meaning. "Thank you."

I didn't know if he meant for lunch or for admitting what I'd done. So, I nodded and pushed my way out through his office, my new tattoo throbbing the whole way.

Later that afternoon, Alice forwarded me an email from *Vanity Fair*, announcing they planned to do an article about me, like I was somehow special and interesting now because of the family I was marrying into. They were requesting an interview with Royce as well, and when I pulled up his calendar, the meeting with Frank Davos caught my eye.

Royce had said he wanted a second set of eyes on it, so the least I could do was confirm I'd put the time and date in correctly. I scrolled through my inbox until I found the email and double-checked. Everything was right.

I'd been too focused on the scheduling last time to notice the email was part of a longer conversation. The back and forth replies spanned several weeks. Curious, I scrolled to the beginning and began to read.

The original email had been a check-in on Royce's portfolio, but the conversation meandered through other topics. Frank considering selling his Red Sox season tickets. Royce's frustration with an iOS update that made his devices temporarily stop syncing. It was mostly friendly things with some light business sprinkled in.

But as I read on, excitement ignited in my chest.

Royce had been gobbling up stock in one specific company, and Frank told him they'd reached the threshold. Any more would put him at a five-percent stake in ownership, and he'd be required to declare his intentions to the Securities and Exchange Commission. Meaning he'd have to tell the government whether he intended to buy the company, or simply maintain a controlling interest.

Royce referred to the company in one of the most recent emails as CRNE, but I wasn't familiar with whatever business that was an acronym for. Google wasn't any help either. All the results were either the Canadian nurses' exam or a privately-owned sanitation company in Chicago that didn't trade.

I sat back in my chair and frowned. None of it made sense.

A notification popped up in the corner of my screen telling me that the final bell had rung on the markets, and HALE had closed at the price of $102.82. Down another sixty-two cents from yesterday. My gaze flicked to Royce's office.

The one hundred thousand shares he'd sold me for had lost $62,000 in value since yesterday.

My focus settled back on the computer screen, and I stared at the ticker symbol. Rather than use their acronym, HBHC had chosen the name Hale as their identifier on the New York Stock Exchange. I sat up straight and punched the keys on the keyboard, looking up to see if CRNE was a stock ticker symbol.

It was.

Ascension Bank and Trust wasn't as big as HBHC, but the rival bank wasn't small either. They were still a *Fortune* 100 company, and they'd been around almost as long, although a merger had changed their name a few years ago.

Before then, they'd been Crane Bank Corp and they'd kept the CRNE ticker symbol after the name change.

My mind raced with a new question. Why would Royce invest so much in another company, and a competitor at that, if his life's goal was to run HBHC? I couldn't see any other reason to buy such a large stake in a rival company, except ownership. He was going to buy Ascension—it was what he needed more money for.

With that puzzle piece in place, the others fell in, and I finally saw the whole thing. He couldn't buy his family's company out from under his father, he'd need another company to do it. And Ascension was perfect.

Holy. Shit.

Royce was plotting a hostile takeover of HBHC.

TWELVE

Macalister sat behind the desk in the library, looking like he was a king and ready to hold court. If he expected me to bow and cower, he could think again. The sting of the needle that had buried ink in my skin was still there, and I used the pain as fuel.

He'd crossed a line last night, and I was determined to push him away, back over to the side where he belonged.

"Good evening," he said. There wasn't a smile on his face, but it lurked in his voice.

I locked down my shoulders to prevent the shudder from rippling out and focused on my task. I sat in my seat and moved my pawn, not giving him any of my attention.

Even though my gaze stayed focused on the board, I sensed his hesitation.

"Don't be rude." He said it like a threat.

I lifted my defiant gaze to his and matched his cold tone. "Hello."

He looked dissatisfied with my short response but made

his opening move. "I read your book."

I moved another pawn, using that to make my statement. "Aren't you curious to know what I thought of it?"

"I'm sure you'll tell me, regardless."

Oh, he didn't like that. His eyes went to slits. "I do not appreciate your tone when I'm trying to hold a conversation with you."

"And I didn't appreciate what you did last night, so no more conversations. I'm here to play chess, and that's it."

He didn't take his calculating eyes off me as he moved his knight. "Am I to understand you're upset that I gave you two orgasms?"

I wasn't going to take his bait or blush at what he'd said. I reached into my pocket, pulled out my keys, and surrendered them to the desk. "That was the last time I'll play your game."

"Is that so?" He glared at the keys, offended by them. "I believe I told you to turn those in to Royce. I think he should know why you're giving them up."

"I agree," I said. "That's why I already told him this afternoon."

His reaction was subtle, but I caught the way his shoulders straightened, and his eyes widened. My move had caught him off guard. "I don't believe you."

"Call him in here and ask him." I crossed my arms over my chest, touching the sore spot beneath my arm where Medusa lived. "I'm not a good liar, but I'm not a Hale yet. I'm sure I'll get better."

Macalister's eyebrow spiked up so high it was a perfect upside-down V. "You should think very carefully about the next thing you say to me."

It was silent for a tense moment before I spoke, and I meant it in more than one way. "It's your move."

Anger simmered through his expression, but then it faded as he brought it under control. "I won't allow you to quit when we've barely begun."

I shook my head. "I'm done."

He'd told me to think two moves ahead, and I had. I couldn't win—the only way was to not play at all.

"No," he said. "We had an agreement."

I didn't acknowledge his protest. "When we're done with our chess match, I'll bring the box back to you."

"*No*, Marist." He looked strangely human and desperate. "I'm not ready for this to be over."

His admission seemed shockingly genuine and froze me in place.

After a heavy pause, his shoulders lifted on a deep breath. "I realize now I came on too strong last night. I apologize. Going forward, we can move at whatever speed you feel comfortable with."

He still didn't get it. "Macalister, there is no going forward. I'm never going to feel comfortable with what we did, and we're never doing it again."

His hand was resting on the desktop, and it curled into a fist, his thumb brushing back and forth over his fingers absentmindedly. He was deep in thought, figuring out how to get what he wanted.

"Keep it," he said abruptly. "It was a gift, and you'll change your mind."

My voice was steel. "I won't."

The setting sun outside the window cast a soft glow across his face, but the warmth didn't touch him. His expression was absolute.

"We'll see."

Since I'd confessed my sins to Royce, he'd largely steered clear of me. There were no more offers to leave the grounds and go someplace where his father's rules didn't apply. We continued our charade of being a lovestruck couple when we were in public, but as soon as we were safely out of view, he'd drop my hand and dig out his phone.

To be fair, he did have a lot on his mind.

I hadn't let on that I'd figured out his plan. I wasn't sure what to do with the information, partially because I only knew the broad details. I had no idea when he was going to pull the trigger on it, or if his offer to buy Ascension would be friendly or hostile.

And even if he acquired his target company, what then? He had a lot of HBHC stock personally, but once Macalister got a hint of what his son was planning, he'd employ all the defenses available to keep his company in his hands.

Takeover attempts were expensive for everyone involved, and most of the time they failed.

The odds were so heavily stacked in Macalister's favor, it was shocking to me Royce was even considering it. Yet he'd been planning this thing for a while. It had to have taken him years to accrue that much Ascension stock on the open market.

I could disrupt his life so easily now. One careless mention to Macalister as we played our nightly chess game, and Royce's plan would disintegrate. And it was probably in his best interest if I stopped him now, before he lost everything. Macalister would take away Royce's seat, and what was left of their strained father-son relationship would implode, but at least my future husband wouldn't go broke.

I had good reasons to tell Macalister what I knew, and yet every night I couldn't bring myself to do it. For weeks, we played, he talked, and I lost each night. It was like we were stuck on repeat.

The first week of my final year at Etonsons was surreal. It felt like I was back in my old life. I sat in the lecture hall, disappearing amongst all the other faceless students . . . until I noticed the magazine the girl in the row in front of me was reading before class began.

Our engagement pictures had been released to the media last week. Alice had selected two. One where I was sitting on Royce's lap beneath the fountain, and a closeup where he was kissing my hand, showing off the stunning engagement ring. The first time I'd seen the photos, they'd taken my breath away.

Sophia Alby had said Royce and I were a fairytale, one that everyone wanted to be a part of. But I was convinced no one truly wanted that fairytale story more than I did. The camera made a very convincing liar out of me. It all looked so real.

On a Friday, I met Alice in the lobby of the dress store. Donna Willow, the designer who'd dressed us both for Royce's promotion party, had flown in exclusively to show us her designs for the anniversary gala. It was quite the contrast from the shopping experience last month with my mother who, as I'd feared, had tried to exceed her budget and asked for my help convincing the financial manager to give her more money.

She had caviar tastes and would never get used to having to live on a tuna fish budget.

The designer, wearing all black, stood next to a rack of her dresses and supervised her assistant as the girl steamed wrinkles out of the garments. When she saw us, Donna smiled and gestured for the assistant to stop.

"Alice," Donna said, "I swear you look younger every time I see you. How are you?"

I stood awkwardly by my future step-mother-in-law's side while she chatted with her friend. It was only the first week of classes, and I already had a ton of work to do, so I was hoping this appointment would go quickly.

Donna pulled a peacock blue dress down off the rack, handed it to Alice, and sent her off toward the dressing room. There was no discussion between the women. No comments about color or any other options presented.

"Now," she set her sights on me, "do you trust me?"

Of all the people I'd gotten to know over the last few months, ironically, Donna Willow was the person I trusted most. "I do."

"Good. Don't let Alice tell you it's too costume-y." She

dug through the rack and had to use both of her matchstick thin arms to support the full dress as she pulled it out for me to see.

"It gorgeous," I breathed. And it was beyond perfect.

She beamed at me. "It's also quite heavy, so if you don't mind?"

"Of course." I eagerly took the hanger from her, scooped up the bottom half of the garment in an arm so it wouldn't drag on the floor, and hurried to change into it.

It was strapless like the red dress, but not a corset. The fit and flare style dress hugged my figure all the way to my knees before bursting out into a skirt full of volume and layers. The silhouette was flattering, but that wasn't what made me fall in love. It was the rich green fabric with slightly different tones that gave it a texture quality. Clear beading was carefully placed, flashing a hint of sparkle when I moved, like a scale catching the light. It gave a subtle nod to the interpretation of a snake, including the train trailing behind me like a tail.

I was the modern Medusa, a serpent ready for a black-tie event.

Alice was already on the pedestal out front, scrutinizing herself in the mirrors. The off the shoulder blue dress fit her like a second skin, flaunting her statuesque form. The outer layer of the skirt was tulle and see-through, and it trumpeted outward while the underskirt stayed straight. Like a peacock's fan of feathers against its svelte body.

I was Medusa, but she was the perfect vision of Hera, queen of the gods.

"You look amazing," I said.

"Oh." Alice pressed her fingers to the hollow of her neck as a shy smile teased her lips. "Thank you."

Her gaze met mine through the mirror, and she took in the green dress I wore, and for a moment she looked . . . displeased. But the emotion retreated. She flashed a vacant smile, stepped off the pedestal, and gestured for me to take her place.

I fell even more in love with the green dress when I could see it from all the angles, but Alice gave me a hard look in the mirror. "I'm not sure about this one."

"I am," a male voice said.

I didn't have to see him to know who it was, but my heart fluttered as I turned and gazed at Royce over my shoulder. I'd been so busy with school I'd barely seen him all week, and . . . was it possible he'd gotten hotter? There was a brightness in his eyes that made my knees go soft.

"What are you doing here?" I asked lightly. Could he hear I was happy to see him?

He shrugged. "I had time." His gaze left mine and swept slowly down the lines of the dress. "Green is my favorite color."

A nervous laugh bubbled from me because he'd said it so seriously, and the way he looked at me made my fluttering heart worse. "You only like it because it's the color of money."

"Well, all of my favorite things are green." His expression was cryptic. Unreadable. "Or they were, at some point."

I flashed back to our first night together more than a year ago when he'd cornered me in the library. I'd had green hair and red lips, and he'd told me I was beautiful.

God, if he kept this up, I was going to need to sit down.

"Do you like it?" he asked me.

I nodded, hoping it could shake loose the fog he created in my mind. "It's perfect."

His lips lifted into an effortless smile, and my insides went boneless. Had something good happened? It was like a switch had been flipped in him, and the man he'd been with me before had returned.

Royce's focus shifted to Alice, but he nodded back toward me. "Mind if I steal her for a moment?"

She waved a hand, dismissing us, and went back to admiring herself in the mirror, pulling at the waist of the dress where she wanted a tighter fit.

His hand was warm as he grabbed mine and led me back to my dressing room.

"It's been weird not having you at the office," he said.

"Missing me?" I teased.

His intense eyes drilled into me as he pushed the door closed. "Yes.

And then he launched himself at me like he couldn't hold himself back another second. I was jerked into his kiss, our mouths smashing together and cutting off my sound of surprise.

The way his mouth dominated mine ripped me open and poured fire inside. The desire for him flared white-hot, a fuse being lit on a stick of dynamite, ready to explode. He wasn't soft or gentle. He was firm and rough as he claimed me, like I was his and could never, *ever* belong to anyone else.

A tremble started in my knees and graduated to my

center when his demanding tongue pushed inside my mouth. He didn't ask for permission or give me a chance to stop him. Royce overtook me. His hands slid up my front, and he cupped my breasts, crushing and massaging me through the dress.

He squeezed a throaty moan from me, and the satisfied sound clung in the air of the dressing room.

Where have you been? I wanted to ask but didn't. I should just be happy he was back and that I hadn't lost him.

"I'm sorry," he said, sandwiched between two mind-numbing kisses.

His mouth roamed down the column of my neck, and when he sucked on my pulse-point, it felt like it was directly between my legs. It made it impossible to think about what he could be sorry for. Surely it wasn't for what he was doing this very second, because it was the only thing that felt right.

"Hmm?" That was the best I could manage to ask for clarification. My hands were inside his suit coat, my fingers stroking over his dress shirt and wanting to get at the hardened chest beneath. It was exciting how he seemed to be having as difficult of a time breathing as I was.

"I've been avoiding you." He carved a path with his mouth down my neck, across the center of my throat, and back up the other side. "You told me everything, and I didn't do the same, and it wasn't fair. It didn't feel right."

I pulled back. "And it does now?"

His eyes were lidded, and he looked vulnerable, but I wasn't deceived. He was more dangerous than ever like this. "No, but it will. I'm going to make it right." A smile hinted.

"But also, I'm an impatient motherfucker. I've been waiting for this day for . . . a while."

The way he'd said it, you'd think he'd been waiting years.

Perhaps he had been. Maybe tomorrow I'd read in the finance section of the news that he'd tendered his offer to buy Ascension. The question was on the tip of my tongue, but then he was there, his mouth pressed to mine again, and all the words fell away.

He eased me back against the mirror in the dressing room, and I gasped as my bare skin pressed to the cold glass. It was immediately followed with a heavy moan because the rest of him pushed against me, all hot and urgent.

A female voice carried loudly through the closed door. "You're not damaging all my hard work, are you, Mr. Hale?"

We both froze at Donna's question. A wild, guilty smile splashed on Royce's face, and—*fuck*—it was so sexy, it was indecent.

"No, ma'am." He straightened away, like a kid caught with his hand in the cookie jar. His gaze assessed every inch of me, and I could see him weighing his options. He could have me right here and now, if I was willing. Which—oh, yes—I was.

His money meant he could do whatever he wanted. Pay off the staff in the shop to leave us. Tear this dress off me and hire whoever Donna would need to make a replacement in time. Everyone in Cape Hill, and especially the Hales, viewed wealth as a superpower. It could do anything.

But fucking his fiancée in a tiny dressing room while his stepmother and her dress designer waited outside would certainly get back to Macalister, and the distance Royce put between us cooled our raging bodies enough to see reason.

He raked a hand through his hair and settled the mess I'd created, pulling himself back together. He took a final look at me, all wanton with my kiss-swollen lips and wrapped in his favorite color, and his eyes smoldered. They made a promise he was going to deliver on very soon.

"I should get out of here," a smirk broke on his lips, "while I still can." He strode to the door and pulled it open but hesitated before going through it. "Come find me tonight after your game."

He vanished through the door, and a moment later Donna appeared, gazing into the dressing room to survey the aftermath. She scoured the dress with her sharp eyes, and when she discovered it was unharmed, relief softened her expression.

I hadn't finished recovering, so my voice was shaky. "Do you do wedding dresses?"

The woman's laugh was bright and full. "For you? I'd be honored."

With practice every night, I'd become quite good at chess.

The unfortunate thing was Macalister benefited from the practice as well and was also improving. Playing the same person repeatedly taught him my thought process and my weaknesses, and he used all of it to his advantage.

Tonight, I'd gotten closer than ever to beating him. The

game had taken forever, and I'd put him in check more than once, but then he'd castled his king, and the repositioning move obliterated all my plans.

"You're a worthy opponent, Marist," he said as he took my king.

I mumbled a *thank you* and a *goodbye* before scurrying back to my room, anxious to put on some lipstick and go find Royce. It was a Friday night. Would we go out and make appearances? Or would he carry me off to a place where we could be alone?

There was a black box waiting on my bed, and my heart slammed to a stop before it crashed to the floor. It was roughly the same size as a shoebox, and I approached it with fear until I discovered the handwritten note beside it.

Open me.

I'd seen Royce's scrawling handwriting enough times at the office to recognize it, and I let out a tight breath. My emotions swung wildly from dread to excited anticipation about what could be inside.

The fancy box was closed with a magnetic latch, and I slid my fingers beneath the lid, peeling back the hinged top. The white diamonds glinted and winked brilliantly in the light, set against the black velvet interior, and the beauty of it forced me to clasp a hand over my mouth.

And it grew more amazing the longer I stared at it.

From a distance, the masquerade mask just looked like glittery lace, but up close was where the finer details emerged. Delicate lines of diamonds curved and scrolled, each ending in a tiny head complete with emerald eyes. The half-mask was a beautiful tangle of slithering snakes.

I gingerly lifted it from the box, and another note dangled from the ribbon I'd use to hold the mask in place.

*Leave this here and
meet me where I proposed.*

The girl who loved the movie *Labyrinth* swooned. Emotions surged through me in a frenetic mix of excitement and anticipation. What was going to happen when I found him? Was he going to tell me all his plans? Open up?

Would he show me our future?

The desire to put on lipstick was pushed aside—it'd only slow me down. And it would be wasted, anyway, because all I wanted to do was finish what we'd started in the dressing room this afternoon. I tucked the mask back in the box, placed it on the dresser beside my stack of mythology books, and darted out into the hallway.

Where I faceplanted into Macalister's hard chest.

He gave a grunt of pain, dropped whatever he was holding, and his arms came up around me to stop my fall.

It wasn't the first time he'd had me in his arms. We'd waltzed together the night of the initiation, but as we stared at each other now, I wasn't sure which one of us was more uncomfortable.

"Macalister," I gasped.

I was going to say more and tell him how he'd startled me, but the words died in my throat. Upon hearing me say his name, the glaciers in his eyes melted. His hands clamped down and urged me to stay.

"Are you all right?" He peered down at me like my answer was irrelevant. He'd judge for himself.

No, I wasn't all right because he had his hands on my waist and it was unnecessary. I was steady now. "I'm fine." I jerked out of his hold, and he didn't bother to hide his dissatisfaction. I frowned. "What are you doing here?"

He bent, retrieved the item he'd dropped, and thrust the Greek mythology book toward me. "You seem to be in quite the hurry tonight. You left before I could return this."

He was a voracious reader and had devoured almost all my books. I couldn't tell if he genuinely liked the subject or if he only read them to get under my skin.

"Oh," I said. "Do you want another?"

His expression was ominous. "Not tonight."

"Okay." I took the book from him and added it to my stack in my room, and was dismayed to discover he was still in the hallway when I returned, waiting for me.

He asked it like he somehow already knew the answer. "Where are you off to?"

I was reluctant to tell the truth, but he'd be able to tell if I were lying. "I'm meeting Royce."

"Oh? Where?"

I had to pull the words from my body. "Uh . . . the maze."

Dark clouds gathered in his eyes at my answer. "The hedge maze?"

I nodded and squeezed out a tight smile, trying to inch past him in the hallway. "He's waiting for me, so I—"

"I'll walk with you."

Alarm coasted through me. "Oh, that's okay. You don't have to."

"I insist. It's easy to get turned around, and I believe last time you went in there on your own, my son had to rescue you with an umbrella."

Last time—? I'd been in the maze dozens of times since that stormy night and probably knew it better now than he did. But Macalister often worked late. He wasn't aware I spent most of my afternoons before dinner sitting beneath the fountain and reading.

"Besides," he added, "there's something I'd like to discuss with both of you."

There was no room to argue. He left me and strolled down the hall, wordlessly demanding I go with him, and all the excitement I'd had for my rendezvous with Royce died.

Macalister reviewed the most recent book I'd lent him as we made our way out of the house and toward the maze, but it was hard to focus on what he was saying. Every step brought me closer to a situation I didn't want to be in. What was Royce going to think when I showed up with his father by my side?

And what the hell did Macalister want to talk to us about? I imagined all sorts of new, terrible rules he'd enact. More control he'd try to exert over us. I was so tired of it, and I'd only been living in the house two months.

The sun had set more than an hour ago, and even though the landscape lights were on and the weather was warm, there was a strange menace that lurked in the edges of the shadows. The breeze rustled through the trees and made the branches scrape against each other like fingers trying to claw their way out.

When we entered the maze, I could tell he was frustrated by how slowly I was moving, but he didn't comment. Perhaps he thought my slow speed was because I was carefully trying to learn the correct path, rather than delay the inevitable. When we reached the opening to the center, he made me go first.

Each tier of the fountain was up-lit and glowed, casting amber light onto the cascading water and the ripples in the collection pool below. As he'd done while waiting to propose to me, he sat on the edge of the bench, his elbows on his knees and his head tipped down to the ground.

Only this time he wasn't in a tuxedo or even a suit. He wore a stone blue button-down shirt over pale gray shorts, effortlessly casual. The crunch of my footsteps on the pebbled path drew his gaze up, and when he caught the sight of me, his smile was epic.

He pushed to his feet. "I was beginning to wonder if you weren't—"

Macalister stepped into view, and Royce became a new statue in the garden. It was impossible to tell what he was thinking because his frozen expression was devoid of emotion.

"I'm sorry to interrupt." Although Macalister didn't sound sorry at all. "Marist told me where she was going, and I asked if I could come with her. I believe the three of us need to have a conversation."

Royce must have rebooted himself because he blinked and came back online. Gone was the smile and the warmth he'd had ten seconds ago. He was the prince of Cape Hill now, and he eyed his father with veiled suspicion. "You know what? You're right." He lifted his chin, and his chest expanded with a deep breath. It made him look bigger and more powerful, and his tone was firm. "Marist is mine, and I'm going to buy her back."

I couldn't hear the bubbling fountain or the insects singing in the distant trees. Everything dropped out so the only sound was his statement playing in a loop in my head.

Marist is mine.

Macalister jolted, visibly as surprised as I had been, but he recovered faster. "Oh? And why would I let you do that?"

Royce didn't look at me. He kept his intense gaze fixed on his father. "Because I'm going to give you fifty million dollars."

THIRTEEN

TIME FROZE.

Fifty.

Million.

Dollars.

I couldn't breathe. Couldn't blink. My muscles locked up, and everything stopped working.

Macalister stared at his son with disbelief. "That's . . . a strong offer."

"Well, I wanted to make sure you understood how serious I am." And he was, from his confident posture to his strong voice.

"If you want me to take you seriously," his father said, "then perhaps don't make me an offer with money you don't have."

"What makes you think I don't have it?"

Anger streaked through Macalister's face like a bolt of lightning. "If you're telling me you liquidated stock in the current market, I have serious concerns about your financial acumen."

Royce was offended his father even suggested it. "I haven't touched my portfolio."

"Then you don't have it." Macalister stiffened. "I know your net worth, Royce, because I'm the one who gave it to you."

The smile that spread across his son's face was joyless and cold. "You think you know everything. You've watched every transaction I've ever made, stood over my shoulder, judging each move. But I figured out a long time ago you were never going to give up those purse strings. Not really."

Macalister gave a noise of exasperation. "Ah, I see. Now is where you make a big production out of revealing you have a secret account in Singapore. I'll save you the time. I've known about that account ever since the day my hateful uncle funded it for you. Even if you were smart and invested wisely, you don't have that kind of money there."

He probably expected his son to look heartbroken at this news.

Instead, Royce's dark smile widened. "You're right. I don't—not in that one. But in the accounts you *don't* know about?" He looked so cocky, so sure. "Hell, if we close this, I can transfer funds by the end of business tomorrow." The smile faded. "My offer is fifty million."

"No," Macalister said quickly. "I won't let you bankrupt yourself."

"Oh, spare me. You and I both know I'll be fine." It was as if he'd thrown off his disguise and finally risen to his true form. He was Ares in the flesh, hungry for battle. Starving for war. "Quit stalling and let's fucking negotiate."

The tension between them was a cable stretched to its limit and ready to snap.

Macalister turned his head and looked down his nose at me with shrewd eyes, like he was deciding my worth. Discerning if I'd be a good investment and worth the risk.

Beneath all the shock, I finally found my voice, although it was a broken whisper. "Royce."

I didn't understand what he was doing. If his life's goal was to wrest control away from his father, he'd need every dollar he had, plus considerable help from outside investors. He'd secured that, it'd seemed, given his dramatic attitude shift today.

So, what the fuck?

Was he willing to risk everything he'd ever wanted . . . for me?

There was a tightness in my chest. A pain I couldn't pinpoint as another thought took hold.

Royce Hale was a liar. It was possible everything he'd just said wasn't true. A bluff. Maybe there wasn't enough in his accounts. What if he'd asked for an enormous loan to give him the chance to undo his mistake?

I stared at him as he awaited his father's answer, his hands balled into angry fists and his posture screaming he wanted a fight.

Macalister was the opposite. Calm, indifferent. "No."

The word hit me like a rock to the head, and I stumbled backward. "What do you mean, *no*?"

The older Hale watched me curiously as I wobbled on my feet, barely able to stand. He had so much money, maybe he didn't care to have more, but fifty million? And moreover, it wasn't about that. Royce's huge offer came loaded with power. His father would always be able to lord over his son what a terrible transaction Royce had made, buying me back at five times the price he'd sold me for.

"I'm not interested in Royce's offer." Macalister stood there in his black suit and red tie, looking so fucking comfortable you'd never believe what he'd just turned down. "However, I have an offer for Marist."

My stomach clenched. "What?"

"A new game."

"No." There wasn't any hesitation from me.

He scowled. "You'll listen to me first before making your decision." His gaze flicked to Royce. "Be aware this negotiation is with her and her alone. If you can't control yourself, you can't stay." When he was satisfied Royce understood, his focus returned to me. "If you win, I'll step aside. You can be with Royce in whatever capacity you want. You'll have your car. If you wish, you can return to your parents' home until the wedding. You'll be allowed to make your own decisions, even if they're the wrong ones."

My mouth dropped open.

He was offering freedom. Total freedom from him and his control. It was too tempting to ignore, but such a great prize would come at a terrible risk. "And if you win?"

He was pleased I'd asked, rather than reject him again. But his pause was so long, I could tell a direct answer wasn't forthcoming.

"Do you want to know which of the myths is my favorite?

The story of the Minotaur." He lifted a hand, gesturing to our surroundings. "Fitting, given where we are, don't you think?"

The Minotaur was a monstrous half-man, half-bull creature who'd lived in the center of the complicated Labyrinth.

"There are different versions of the myth," he said. "Some say it's seven men and seven women every seven years, and others say nine, but the rest is the same. They're sent into the Labyrinth and try to escape before the Minotaur catches them." The wind blew through the channels of the maze, swirling around us, but didn't affect him. Like it hadn't been given his permission. His expression was too focused, too intense. "Tonight, I'll be the Minotaur. If you can escape the maze before I catch you, you win."

My breath came and went in short bursts. I was wise enough to know it couldn't be that simple. I had to think two moves ahead. "You didn't answer my question. What happens if you win?"

Wickedness played across his attractive face, accentuating his high, elegant cheekbones. "Then I get the same prize as the Minotaur."

Words choked in my throat, refusing to come out, and my cheeks burned hot like I'd carelessly fallen asleep in the sun.

Royce asked it, although I suspected from his urgent tone he already knew the answer. "What happens when he catches someone?"

Macalister looked at me expectantly. He wanted me to say it out loud.

My voice was hollow. "He eats them."

Royce's eyes widened and his face turned an ugly shade

of red. "*No.*"

"Be quiet."

Macalister's sharp voice might have silenced his son, but it had no effect on the loud voices in my brain. Royce had told me his father didn't play a game unless he thought he was going to win. Macalister was taller than I was, which meant he had a longer stride. On the nights he couldn't sleep, he ran on the treadmill. In a footrace, he'd beat me easily. And he believed I didn't know the path out, at least not that well.

Even with all of that, it still didn't seem like a guaranteed win for him.

"That's it?" I spat the question out. "All I have to do is make it out of the maze before you catch me?"

Once again, a pleased look flashed through his expression. He understood I saw through his offer and needed to know the catch. "Before we start, I'll be allowed to disorient you however I see fit."

I narrowed my eyes. "Disorient me?"

My stomach became an arctic crevasse as his fingers went to the knot of his tie and worked it loose. The silk was the color of blood, and he unthreaded it painstakingly slow from his collar, coiling it over his hand.

"I'll cover your eyes and turn you around. I'll do things to make you lose your bearings." With the tie gone, he undid the top button of his shirt, and an arrogant smile crept onto his face. "The game isn't worth playing if I don't have a fair chance to win."

That definitely made it harder on me, but I'd spent so many afternoons memorizing every twist and turn, each statue decorating the dead ends, that I *knew* this maze. I could conquer it blindfolded.

And Macalister had no idea.

The risk was great, but the promise of freedom was so tantalizing . . . was it crazy to consider playing? I turned and glanced at Royce, who glared at his father with such contempt, it was breathtaking.

I swallowed down my nerves, pushed a wayward lock of hair out of my face, and prepared to negotiate. "I'm not saying yes, but if I were, I'd need a thirty-second head start."

Macalister's lips curled up into something too insidious to be called a smile. "Ten."

The shift in Royce happened faster than a clap of thunder, and his desperate plea tore me in two. "Marist, *don't*."

The anger that radiated from Macalister was so hot, it invaded my senses with smoke. My mouth filled with ash. He glared back at his son. "If she doesn't, I'll strip you of your seat."

Oh, God.

Two months ago, I'd stood in the rain in this hedge maze and told Royce I was going to destroy his life the way he'd done to me, and now I could execute that plan with terrible accuracy. He'd sold me out, and Macalister just presented me with the opportunity to do the same.

If I didn't play his father's ridiculous game, Royce would lose *everything*. The loss of his board seat had the same effect as castling in chess. It'd throw all the plans he'd spent his life building up to into chaos.

Pain twisted in my heart. I'd fought too hard and given

up too much to get Royce that seat, but if I played the game and somehow lost . . . then we'd *both* lose.

The walls of the hedge maze closed in, their prickly branches tearing at my skin. The Minotaur was a much better fit for Macalister than Zeus. He wasn't a god tonight—he was a monster pretending to be human.

Royce cemented back into his statue form, and his stricken face was haunting. He didn't want to lose me, but he didn't want to lose his position on the board either. It was clear all the same thoughts I'd had were running through his mind.

All, except for one.

I'm going to win.

I lifted my shoulders and puffed up my chest, trying to look as confident and intimidating as possible. It was laughable. I was thirty years younger than Macalister, a foot shorter, and wearing a summery gold dress with ballet flats. But I'd negotiated with him before, and I had to try now.

"I need a twenty second head start."

He looked at me with the ruthless eyes of a Goliath CEO crushing a tiny competitor. "My offer is ten, and it's final."

There was no point in bluffing. He knew I wasn't going to walk away. I took in a stilted breath as I repeated the deal. "All right. I escape the maze, and I'm free. You'll stay out of my life and my relationship with Royce."

"Yes, and you understand what happens if I win. I believe I explained it to you the last time we spoke on the phone."

As he forced me to recall his filthy fantasy, trembles shook my knees, but hopefully they were hidden beneath my flouncy skirt.

I stared at him, unable to move, as he extended his hand. "Agreed?"

"Marist." Royce's twisted, tortured word shot straight to my core, and then he uttered the same phrase I'd pleaded the night he'd sold me. "Don't do this."

Couldn't he see there wasn't any other way? We'd both sacrificed too much to have him end up with nothing. I gazed at him, trying to convey it was going to be all right. I was going to save us both, I just needed him—for once—to trust me.

I set my focus back on Macalister and grasped his hand before I lost the nerve. His powerful shake was firm and aggressive, and I pulled my hand free before he wanted to let me go.

His head swung toward his son. "Leave us."

Royce's shoulders shook. He seemed to be vibrating with barely controlled rage and I had to avert my eyes, unable to bear the sight of it. Stones ground together as his feet brought him closer, and each measured footstep mirrored the slowing thump of my heartbeat.

When the sound stopped, I lifted my timid gaze to him.

If looks could kill, Macalister Hale would have been struck dead in the center of his hedge maze, killed by his own son like King Laius in the Oedipus myth. Royce's fury was so powerful, it seared right through his father's icy shell and cracked inside.

"A day is going to come," Royce seethed, "when I'm going to make you regret this, and you should know . . . that day is coming very, *very* soon."

Was that fear edging into Macalister's eyes? He blinked,

and it vanished. "I'm more powerful, experienced, and intelligent than you'll ever be, Royce. Don't be foolish and throw away everything I've given you over someone we both know you won't care about by the time you walk down the aisle." He pointed to the exit. "Leave without another word, or I'll lose my patience and be forced to do something drastic. Something that would include our attorneys."

It wasn't clear if he meant HBHC's attorneys or his personal ones, but the threat was too real to ignore. Royce cast a final glare at his father, then turned his eyes toward me. The fire of violence in them extinguished, leaving behind only the beautiful sapphire blue and all the unspoken words he wanted to say to me.

With his tongue shackled and the order from the king handed down, there was nothing else for him to do but leave. I watched my fiancé go, even after he disappeared behind the wall of evergreen and the sound of his despondent footsteps trailed off to nothing.

Every inch of my body was aware of the man who lurked at my back, waiting on me. When I turned to face him, I was shocked to find the pained expression he wore. Did he feel actual emotion?

Was he regretting his decision?

"Why are you doing this?" I asked.

He closed his eyes and pinched the bridge of his nose in a sign of frustration. "Because this thing between us is unhealthy."

Well, there was an understatement. "Yeah, no shit."

Down came his hand, and his eyes popped open, pinning

me under his turbulent gaze. "It wasn't supposed to be this way. I didn't want to get involved. I only wanted to put distance between the two of you."

I didn't believe him for one second. There were too many times he'd looked at me with carnal thirst or outright desire. There was the day I'd interviewed with the board and stood up to him. The time we'd waltzed together after the initiation. And of course, the evening when he'd bought me.

"I feel infected," he accused. "Thoughts of you take up time I don't have to spare. And you cloud my judgement to the point it has become a serious issue. You've denied me, and more than once, which I believe is the root of the problem. Once we put it right, I can move forward."

My pulse thundered through my body. He was a spoiled brat determined to get his way on an epic scale. I glared at him, dumbfounded. "You seriously believe if you get your 'two minutes' with me, you'll—what? Get me out of your system?"

Had the man never watched episodic television or seen a movie? Because if he had, he'd know that preposterous idea didn't work.

He grew angry, inching toward the edge of his control. "You're a relentless distraction. I spend all day, every day thinking about the moment when I'll see you next. Are you aware I was needed in Helsinki earlier this week for a face-to-face? I pushed the meeting to video conference so I could stay here, with you. Which is entirely unacceptable." His gaze left mine, and he stared at the fountain as he searched for the right way to express himself. When he found it, disgust cascaded down his face. "This thing . . . this fucking *obsession* is beneath me."

I gasped, banding an arm across my stomach. The evening had been one hit after another, and I wasn't sure how many more I could take. I wanted to start the game now, because I was ready to bolt.

He calmed, his posture eased, and his head dipped down so his gaze could find the red tie clasped in his hand. "Win or lose, tonight will give me release."

I shifted nervously on my shoes. I'd abandon them before the race started because I'd have better traction with my bare feet. "Then let's get it over with."

"I agree," he said.

FOURTEEN

It took all of my strength to stand still as he approached. Macalister's steely-eyed gaze weighed a million pounds, pressing down as he stretched the tie out between his hands and lifted it to drape over my eyes.

I sucked in a sharp breath when he leaned in. He smelled like pine and old money as he set about tying the makeshift blindfold, being careful not to catch my hair in its knot. The tie didn't completely block my vision. If I opened my eyes, my eyelashes fluttering against the silk, I could see a sliver of light and make out my shoes on the path.

The heat of his body lingered even after his task was complete, and my blood pressure rose to the stars above in the sky. The blindfold, I'd expected, but I hadn't anticipated how disorienting his presence would be.

"I'm going to catch you." He whispered it beside my ear, and I jerked in response, not realizing he was still so close. His voice was pure sin. "Part of you is hoping I will."

"No, I'm not." I refused to accept any other concept.

I flinched at his touch when cold hands gently gripped my shoulders. They guided me to turn in place. One circle. Another. All of it was an unnecessary excuse to have his hands on me. We hadn't moved from the center of the maze, so when the blindfold came off, it'd only take a single moment to know which way to go.

The hands released me. "Take off your dress."

"What?" Panic dumped over me like a bucket of frigid water.

"You agreed I'm allowed to disorient you however I see fit. So, you will be naked when we do this."

I shook my head furiously. "No."

He was a viper slithering inside my head. "This is not difficult, nor is it something I haven't already seen."

I tucked my chin to my chest and furrowed my eyebrows. He believed this would slow me down and trip me up, but I wouldn't let it. I was going to win, and nothing was going to stop me. I'd spent so long not caring what other people thought of me, I'd lost any shyness, and this included my body. If anything, tonight would be easier than the initiation because it would only be one man instead of nine, and I wouldn't be able to see his reaction.

"Do you want me to do it?" He asked it with an eagerness that sent my pounding heart into overdrive.

"No," I snapped. I reached down and grasped the hem of my skirt, lifting the stretchy fabric. Up I pulled, taking extra care around my face not to bump the blindfold off, until the dress was collected in my hands.

I'd worn the sexy pink lace bra and panties for Royce,

but a tiny inkling deep inside me was flattered when Macalister drew in a sharp, affected sigh. There was power here. Perhaps he'd made an unwise move and my nakedness would be more disorienting to him than it was to me.

The dress was pulled from my grasp, and there was rustling. He must have folded it and then discarded it on the bench beneath the fountain.

"All of it, please." His hushed voice was full of gravel and need.

Unwanted goosebumps prickled my skin.

When I twisted my hands behind my back to undo the bra, I surrendered to the situation. I would pretend it wasn't real. I was in one of the myths I enjoyed, some nymph being chased by a man besotted with infatuation. I'd escape, and he'd be cursed to roam the maze for eternity in search of me.

It was a pleasant night, but the breeze caressed my body and my nipples hardened into points. Taking off the bra hadn't been that much of a challenge, but my underwear was a different story. Which was stupid. The pale pink lace was thin and essentially see-through, and what he'd said was right.

Macalister Hale had already seen me naked. There were no new secrets to be—

His demanding voice cut through the air. "What is that?"

I froze. What was he asking about? A cold finger stabbed between my ribs, and my mouth rounded into a silent 'oh.' And then it curved into an evil smile. "It's a tattoo."

Although I couldn't see his face, I didn't need to. I could hear the contempt loud and clear in his voice. "When did you get this?"

The upside to stripping naked before him was I'd arrived at this perfect moment, and vindictive warmth spread through my limbs. I was proud to show off my statement of defiance. "It's what I needed my car for." My tone was overly bright and fake. "Do you like it? I hope so, because your money paid for it."

I didn't know what kind of reaction I expected from him, but it went deathly silent, and it was far scarier than I would have thought. It was quiet for so long I began to wonder if he'd abandoned me or rage had vaporized him into thin air. I reached out, pawing into the unknown.

"Uh, are you still there?"

"Finish your task." His sharp order was the sting of a crop, and I jumped in response. "We'll deal with your decision to deface your body at a later time."

My expression soured as he sucked all the energy out of the moment, deflating my attempt to get under his skin the way the tattoo was inked in mine.

Hesitantly, I hooked my fingers under the waistband of my panties and slid them down my legs. I tried to be as careless and awkward about it as possible. This wasn't a striptease or a seduction.

I stepped out of my shoes and dropped my underwear on them, leaving me wearing nothing but the engagement ring his son had given me.

There was a reason the Greek gods were usually depicted in the nude when most art from other cultures at the time clothed their subjects. The Greeks didn't see nudity as shameful—it was the body's natural state and the hero's form. Perhaps it was fitting I was naked now.

I was going to be the hero of my story.

Once again, Macalister's cool hands were on my arms, but rather than turn me, this time he guided me to walk. The smooth pebbles weren't too painful as they dug into my bare feet and sensitive arches, but they were cold and foreign, and after several paces I could feel the grime collecting on my skin.

I tried to keep my bearing as we walked, but his hand was on my shoulder, and I knew he was staring at me, and once he began to make me turn in place, it was futile. He led me through switchbacks and reversed directions so many times, I was hopelessly lost.

In the myth, the hero Theseus is saved by Ariande, who gave him a golden ball of yarn for him to use to find his way out after defeating the Minotaur. But I didn't need yarn to escape the Labyrinth. I told myself when the tie was undone, I would know where I was in a single look.

I can do this.

He pulled me to a stop, and his hand was gone. It gave me a moment to try to imagine what we looked like. The high walls of dense green leaves surrounded us. He was the Minotaur cloaked in a designer suit, and I was the shivering maiden, naked except for a strip of red silk covering her eyes.

Macalister's voice dripped with seduction. "Would you like to earn five additional seconds?"

A warning tingled on the back of my neck. This advantage would cost me. I didn't hide the wariness from my tone. "What would I have to do?"

"I'd like to kiss you."

I jolted away from the sound of his voice and fought the need to run, the urge to shake my head and refuse. This was another attempt to disorient, only it was on a much larger scale.

But it was five seconds, and that was huge. It could be the difference between winning and losing, and wasn't I supposed to win at all costs?

"Where?" I demanded.

The pad of one of his fingers brushed over my lips and his voice was hushed. "Here." His rasping voice sounded like sex. "Give me five seconds, and I'll give you yours."

Beneath the blindfold, I closed my eyes.

I'd allow one terrible kiss to avoid another which would be far worse. Five treasonous seconds to prevent two minutes of the unthinkable.

"Fine." I forced air into my lungs. "Do it."

The rocks skittered as he stepped up to me. I stood like a woman about to be beheaded. Strong and tall and brave in the face of utter fear, with only my trembling bottom lip revealing the turmoil raging inside me.

Macalister's touch was more delicate than I'd expected. I was expensive crystal, and he worried he might break me. His cool palm cradled the side of my face and slowly angled me up to receive his kiss.

My insides threatened to shake loose and abandon the rest of my body. I wanted to cower in fear and shame that I was going to let this happen. Every time I gave him an inch, Macalister took so much more, and I was vaguely aware I was on a slow slide to hell. A death by a thousand cuts.

Every shallow breath I took was faster than the previous as I waited for him—to the point my chest was heaving violently and I grew lightheaded. The anticipation was probably worse than the kiss would be. This was only more of his mind games, and I refused to let them have any effect.

But the first casualty of every battle is the plan, and as his lips touched mine, all my ideas of shutting him out died. When his soft, lush mouth moved against me, my eyes flew open and I could see him through the line of vision the blindfold didn't block out.

I didn't kiss him back, but it didn't matter. He invaded. Like his scotch, he was an acquired taste and too expensive for my unrefined palate. His lips teased and taunted, challenging mine to give in to him.

Five seconds was a fucking lifetime. No, longer. Cities rose and fell in the time it took him to kiss me.

He had one hand cupping the back of my neck, but then the other hand slid around my bare hip and onto my back, and before I could retreat, the hard length of his body pushed against mine. My breasts collided with his strong chest and the line of buttons down his dress shirt.

He was cold-blooded and yet shockingly warm.

I gasped, and my hands flew to his shoulders to push him back, but I'd made a critical error. When I parted my lips, he took ownership of my mouth. The hand on the back of my head held me firm so he could deliver a kiss that commanded my lips to move in time with his.

His aggressive, dominating way was a dangerous rip

current. It carried me along unwillingly and without escape. I despised how it forced a shiver up my spine.

It wasn't clear if I'd succeeded in pushing him away or if he'd chosen to end the kiss on his own, but our bodies and mouths separated, and I stumbled back until the sharp edges of trimmed branches gouged into my skin.

"You said a kiss," I accused. "I didn't say you could touch me."

"Most people use more than just their mouths when they kiss," he said dryly. "I thought it was understood."

I shook my head, trying to clear his effect from it. "And it was longer than five seconds."

"Was it?" A wicked smile lurked in his voice. "It felt short to me."

Adrenaline ran hotly through my veins, making me agitated. Couldn't he see how badly I wanted this over with? I itched to tear off the blindfold and take off running. "Can we start, already?"

He inhaled and exhaled, slow and deep, and I had the terrible feeling he was stretching, warming up his muscles. Fuck. Should I do that?

He spoke before I could make my decision. "We'll start whenever you're ready. I'll begin counting when the blindfold comes off."

I wanted it to be a statement, but it came out sounding like a question. "You'll count out loud?"

"Yes."

Oh, my God, this was really happening. I sank my teeth into my bottom lip as I mentally prepared for my task. I was unnaturally tight, and I sucked in what I hoped would be a calming breath. I'd never been a fast runner, but a fifteen-second head start should be more than enough. The hedge maze was big, but it wasn't endless.

You can do this.

My hands shook as I raised them to the back of my head and my fingers found the knot. The silk slipped free faster than I expected, falling to hang around my neck like a loose scarf.

"One," Macalister said.

He stood before me, one side of his rich black suit coat pushed back and his hand resting on his waist. His other was raised in front of him, and as I blinked my newly uncovered eyes, he lifted his gaze from his watch to meet my eyes.

I didn't have time to waste evaluating his authoritative expression. I turned my attention to my surroundings. We were standing in a corridor, and to my right the hedges broke, so I had three options. Go right, go forward, or reverse. I whipped my head around and spied the ornate urn decorating the dead end, a root curling over the edge of the base.

If I'd had time, I would have laughed. Not because this was the same spot where Royce had rescued me in the rain, but because I'd anticipated this move. This place was the farthest distance from the entrance. If I had to chase someone through this maze, I would have picked this as the starting line too.

"Two."

It also meant Macalister was standing in my way, blocking the exit, either hoping to deter or slow me down. *Not a chance.* I grabbed the tie hanging around my front and flung it to the ground as I took off, sprinting past him.

"Three. Four. Five."

Pebbles *whoosh*ed as I skidded around the first turn.

"Six. Seven."

I tore down the path, pumping my arms to propel me faster.

"Eight. Nine. Ten."

I took the next turn so tightly I clipped the corner and rough branches scraped across my arm. It kept stinging as I ran, but I didn't glance down to see if it had drawn blood. It'd slow me down in more than one way, as I couldn't stand the sight of it. It made my knees turn to jelly, and that was the last thing I needed right now.

"Eleven. Twelve." His voice was quieter, muffled by the hedges and the distance between us. "Thirteen . . . Fourteen . . . Fifteen."

When the counting ceased, my heart hammered in my chest. I huffed my breath, ignoring the throbbing scratches on my arm or the painful slap of my bare feet on the errant twigs that had fallen on the path. My freedom was still so far away.

When he'd stopped counting, Macalister became the Minotaur, and I ran from him as if my life depended on it. I didn't hear his footsteps dashing behind me, but each beat of my heart was a cannon booming in my ears, drowning everything else out.

When I made the second to last turn, the muscles in my legs were hot and screaming. There was a painful stitch in my side, right below my Medusa tattoo, as if her snakes were biting at me, spurring me on. I had to keep going. For myself, for Royce, for the promise that we could be more someday.

I raced through the final turn, and hope swelled as the entrance came into view, but I didn't ease up. For all I knew, the monster wanting to devour me was right on my heels.

The myth of Orpheus leapt into my mind. The fabled musician had lost his wife and made the harrowing journey to the underworld to try to bring her back. He impressed Hades and Persephone so much with his music, they released her on the condition she walk behind him and he wasn't allowed to look back until they were safely out of Hades' realm. Too anxious and impatient, the distraught husband reached the threshold for the mortal world and turned to see her.

I would not be Orpheus. I was too close to getting what I wanted to have it all vanish right before my eyes.

The thrill of escape grew exponentially with each step I took. In one more breath, I'd be out. Every cell in my body wanted to sing with elation—

No.

No!

It wasn't possible.

The Minotaur didn't catch me from behind.

He materialized ahead of me, stepping through the entrance, and blocked my escape, all while wearing a smile that announced I was doomed.

FIFTEEN

I STOPPED DEAD IN MY TRACKS, SENDING GRAVEL SKITTERING everywhere. My mind couldn't make sense of what I was seeing, but my body took over. It forced my legs to start churning, only this time, they carried me away from the exit. The only goal now was to blindly *run*.

Panic was a great motivator, but it couldn't do the impossible. It didn't make me as fast as the goddess of speed Nike or give me wings like Icarus to escape the Labyrinth. In fact, I only made it past the first turn before the Minotaur ensnared me in his powerful arms. His hold was a cage, and I ran at the bars, trying to escape.

"Marist, stop. It's over," Macalister said.

"How?" I sobbed. "How did you get ahead of me?"

He turned me to face him, and his pale eyes held me just as captive as his arms. Sweat dampened the hair at his temples, and he was breathing as hard as I was. He'd run in his suit and his dress shoes in the lazy September heat, and it'd taken its toll on him.

His hands were splayed out on my bare back, casing me to him while we both struggled to catch our breath and adjust to the shocking outcome of his game. His eyes hooded and his gaze swept down over my heated face, continuing further south.

I'd thought he was staring at my breasts, but his gaze shifted, and he frowned. "You're hurt."

I followed his eyeline and saw the angry red scratches across my bicep, the thin threads of blood seeping from them, and it pushed me past my limit. My knees gave way, and I sagged into his arms, drawing a startled noise of surprise from him. I clutched at the fabric of his suit as I went down, trying to halt my collapse, but it was pointless.

Macalister fell to a knee with me in his arms, slowing my descent. There was concern in his expression, and I found that more disorienting than anything else he'd tried to do. He wasn't supposed to be capable of feelings.

"Tell me what's happening," he demanded, although there was an edge of nervousness to his voice that made him sound less like the monster I'd pictured him as.

But tell him what was happening? How about the world was upside-down? I'd lost. God, I'd lost *everything*. Instead of admitting defeat, I was a stupid girl and went with the most practical answer. "I don't like blood," I croaked.

He held me firmly as he shrugged out of his jacket, one arm and then the other, until it lay in a heap on the ground. Then he seated me on the path, the smooth stones pressing uncomfortably against my bottom, while he knelt beside me.

He jabbed a finger at the jacket. "Put it on."

I let out a painful breath, a mixture of fear and relief. I didn't look at him as I struggled into his suit coat that was far too big for me and smelled like a man who wasn't my fiancé. But once I had it on and folded across my body, my nakedness and the blood covered, I found myself again. My bones solidified, and fire raced through my marrow.

"How the fuck did you get ahead of me?"

He climbed to his feet and wiped the gray dust marks from his knees before extending a hand to help me up. "I built this maze."

He said it like that should be more than enough explanation. I swatted his hand away and went to stand, but he didn't like that. As soon as I was on my feet, he lunged at me, wrapping his arms around my thighs and lifting. It bent me over his shoulder into a fireman's carry.

"Put me down!" My heart rocketed into my throat, making it hard to talk as he righted himself and began to walk toward the exit.

"I don't believe you're in any position to tell me what to do."

It wasn't just shocking being possessed like this—it was uncomfortable. Every step he took made his broad shoulder dig into my belly, and I felt like a helpless maiden being carried back to the monster's lair.

Except he wasn't going deeper inside the maze; he carried me out the entrance and then around the side of it. What was he doing? I squirmed and wriggled, trying to escape, but his arm was banded tight around the back of my thighs, locking me in place.

He turned the corner, following the outer wall of the

hedges, until he was halfway to the other end. And there he abruptly put me down, setting me dizzyingly on my feet. He kept one arm around my waist, but I wasn't sure if this was to keep me upright or prevent me from escaping. Maybe it was both.

I watched with stunned disbelief as his free hand disappeared into the bush in front of us and a moment later an entire section of the hedge swung open. The fake foliage covering this secret door was the perfect seamless match.

I couldn't breathe, but my voice still worked. "You cheated!"

Macalister had the nerve to look insulted. "Where in the rules did it stipulate I couldn't leave the maze? I only had to catch you before *you* escaped."

My eyes filled with tears of rage. "You *cheated*."

"I did nothing of the sort."

His hold on me changed. It grasped my wrist, covered by the overly long sleeve, and guided me through the passageway. He brought me stumbling into the long corridor that dead-ended with the urn on the other side—the starting line of the race I didn't realize was unwinnable. Then the door swung closed behind, locking us inside.

I couldn't fathom words. All the fury I felt was overwhelmed and drowned out by my trepidation. It kept me silent as I was led down the path and back to the center of the maze. My shoes were there, my bra and underwear discarded right beside them. It was a shocking sight, and I looked away, desperate not to see.

When Macalister pulled me to a stop and turned to face

me, his expression cautiously eager, it broke me.

"I can't do this," I whispered.

Rather than look angry, he looked . . . worried. Like he was confused and unsure and it was fucking terrifying to see him like that. This version of him, I didn't know how to handle. He set his heavy hand on my shoulder, and I was grateful it was covered by the coat to prevent him from making true contact with me.

"I have no interest in forcing myself upon you," he said. "But I can't deny how much I need this." He set his hand on my other shoulder, boxing me in under his hold, and his expression filled with longing. "I cannot deny how badly I want this. Once it's done, I'll be able to let you go. If you honor our agreement, I'll consider the one I made with Royce null and void."

My breath caught. He was saying I'd be free. Not from his house or his control, but at least from his interference with my relationship with Royce.

His hands crept inward, drifting up my neck until my face was trapped between both of his palms, ensuring there was no escape from his hypnotic eyes. He was so close, his warm breath rolled over my skin. It slid down my neck and caressed the bare skin it found between the lapels of the jacket.

"I understand your reluctance. I believe I can make it easier on you."

"How?"

He took one hand off my face, and it glided down my front so it could delve inside the jacket. I flinched at his cold fingers, but he wasn't attempting to touch me. He was only trying to reach into the interior pocket. The red tie spilled out into his hand.

"You want to blindfold me again?" I both did and didn't like the idea. On one hand, I wouldn't be able to see him, which might give me the chance to pretend he was someone else. But on the other, I worried about giving up that much control.

"No," he said. His eyes were cryptic, his thoughts hidden too far behind them. "I'll show you, but I'll have to remove my coat you're wearing."

I bit my bottom lip. It was hot under the coat, and the silk lining clung to my sweat-dampened skin, but it was far easier to stand before him with it on than completely naked. When I didn't say no right away, he must have taken that as a *yes*, because he hooked his fingers under the neck and eased it down. The coat fell in a jerky cascade, catching for a moment on my elbows before falling to the stones at our feet.

His tone was soft but direct. "Give me your wrists."

My blood turned to slush, making it impossible to move.

"If you do this, it's the only thing you have to give tonight. Everything else I will take." I didn't understand what he meant. He slowly blinked his deep and intense eyes. "If you tell me to stop, I'll stop. But I am persistent and patient, and I won't give up until I have what I want. What I'm suggesting is the illusion of giving up control."

It would be just like the hands that had held me during the initiation. All I had to do was say the word, and I'd be released. Even more, with my arms bound in front of me, I'd still have the option to push him away or run. He was offering a false 'out' for my mind. A way to lie to myself so I could let it happen.

"Surrender your hands," he said, "and then tell yourself you had no choice."

I closed my eyes, knowing what he'd said was true. He was a man who wasn't denied anything, so he wouldn't give up until he'd had his two minutes with me. Perhaps I shouldn't have traded them away in the first place.

Macalister was . . . inevitable.

I lifted my hands, my entire body trembling, and heard his quiet, pleased sigh.

The silk draped over my wrists then cinched them together. My eyes fluttered open as the second knot was looped and pulled tight.

And then it was done. My hands were bound, and I'd submitted to him. Dark satisfaction streaked through his expression. Now he'd take what he wanted.

As he'd warned me, it started with his hands. He set his cool palms on my shoulders and glided them down my arms, his fingers flowing like water. His touch was meant to be sensual, and my body tried to like it, but my mind refused.

He commanded it in a hushed but powerful voice. "Look at me."

I'd been staring off into nothingness, not seeing the fountain or the hedges, and avoiding him. My reluctant gaze shifted his direction, working slowly up along his fitted white dress shirt until I reached his face.

His expression was the same one he'd shown me only a handful of times. It was full of shameless desire. He looked at me like a king surveying his new bride.

"Some part of you wanted to lose," he said, just loud enough to be heard over the dripping fountain. "You secretly hoped this would happen."

"No," I blurted. It came from me in such a rush, to him it probably sounded forced. Like I was overcompensating, but what he'd said wasn't true at all.

Right?

His half-smile said he didn't believe me.

His hands were firm but not rough as I was turned to face the fountain. Its steadily flowing water was hypnotic, and I fell into a kind of trance as I stood on the path and endured Macalister's reverent caresses. He gathered my hair in his hands and pushed it gently over my shoulder, exposing every inch of my back to him. It was his favorite part on a woman's body, he'd said.

A fingertip traced a line across my shoulder blades and down my spine, moving like a slow drop of water finding its path down into the hollow of my back. It drew a shiver from me, and he gave a soft noise of satisfaction, enjoying my body's response.

When his hands slid around to cradle my hips, he moved in. The length of his body pressed to mine, emphasizing the opposition between us. I was shorter, he was tall. I was nude, he was clothed. And I was female, while he was male.

Distinctly *male.*

He wasn't physically aroused, but the shape of him pressed to me made all the air vanish from my lungs. The line of buttons down his shirt and the buckle of his belt kissed my skin, and as his hands continued to rise, I pressed my lips together.

It'd been two months since anyone had really touched me besides myself, and since I wasn't facing him, I tried to think these hands didn't belong to Macalister. But every time I attempted it, it was like he knew. There was the flash of his Cartier watch, or the smell of his cologne, or his heavy sigh of contentment in my ear that couldn't be anyone but him.

His hands stroked up over my breasts, and I swallowed an enormous breath. I didn't want to like the way it felt, but my neglected skin enjoyed the sensation. My nipples firmed into tight points as he massaged and explored. I issued a sound of surprise when he pinched one between his thumb and forefinger, hard enough to verge on pain.

It was shameful how I felt the sensation between my legs in a dull ache.

He didn't follow his script exactly as he'd laid it out, because his mouth came down on the curve of my neck while his hands encased my breasts. He'd told me he wasn't going to start with his mouth until he was done with his hands, and there was a very crucial place he hadn't touched yet.

Was he not going to? The thought caused the faintest of whines to float through my mind. What the fuck was wrong with me?

It was undeniable how his kisses on my neck felt, coupled with his sensuous hands, and I gave up fighting. My hands were tied, after all, so I allowed myself to acknowledge I liked what he was doing—only a little.

Try to enjoy it.

It was what Alice had whispered to me before the initiation, when she knew what was going to happen. What her own husband was planning on doing to me. What a fucked up blessing she'd given that day. Would she feel the same way if she found out his two minutes had been deferred?

"Alice." I said her name like a safe word, and it had a similar effect. He paused.

His lips moved against my skin as he spoke. "What about her?"

I had a million questions about why their relationship was the way it was, but it was doubtful he'd tell me. None of the Hales seemed to think much about each other's feelings, but that wasn't how I operated. She'd been aloof and direct, but nice to me in her own way. "I don't want to hurt her."

His hands started again, abandoning my breasts and inching downward. "The only person who can hurt Alice . . . is Alice." His tone was ironic. "Believe me, I've tried. She's unbreakable."

Was this why they'd fallen out of love? Had Macalister tried to conquer her and failed? I didn't get any more time to think about it because his hands spilled over my stomach and then the knots at my wrists, gliding lower.

The muscles in my belly clenched at his touch. My breath went ragged when he sucked on a tender spot just below my ear. I didn't want his fingers to move any lower, but goosebumps marched up my legs.

He teased me. His palms slid over and between my thighs while avoiding the most intimate spot. My chest was tight with anxiety and anticipation, and he dragged the moment out for a lifetime. Long enough for my traitorous body to settle back against his and subtly encourage.

His voice was seductively evil. "It's all right to want it," he whispered. "I won't tell anyone."

Oh, fuck. I hated him. I couldn't stand how he twisted me up to the point of ripping me apart or how—

"Oh," I gasped, a mixture of horror and pleasure.

His fingers brushed through where I was hot and damp and throbbing in a way that made me uncomfortable. The tie seemed to grow tighter around my wrists, but maybe that was because every muscle in me had tensed.

His fingers were tentative at first but grew bolder when a panicked whimper eked from my throat. It was clear he enjoyed what he was doing. He made a thick groan of satisfaction, and his erection began to swell behind the fly of his pants. I felt it harden against my hip, and once again, I had two opposing emotions at the same time.

First was fear. He was a powerful man, and my hands were bound. I wondered if there would always be a hint of danger tied to this event, or if it would go away as I grew more experienced. Instinctively, I couldn't trust any man with a hard-on.

The second emotion was pride, and it was fucking pathetic. Touching me had turned Macalister on, but so what? I hadn't done something special or unique that any other woman wasn't capable of. So, why did I feel flattered that he found me arousing?

The pads of his fingers rolled a slow circle over my clit, and another panicked moan welled up from deep in my stomach. I used my bound hands to grab his wrist to try to stop him, but there was no power in my attempt.

It was all for show.

My sex-starved body was greedy. It would humiliatingly accept pleasure from any hand right now.

The stubble dotting his jaw was rough against the side of my neck as he kissed and nipped at me. And his hands. Those *fucking* hands rubbed against me, making it so damn hard to stay quiet. I didn't want him to know it felt good, which was pointless. He seemed to know everything.

He ground his palm against my center, and tremors worked up my legs, making it hard to stand. I sagged back against him, concentrating on not letting a moan pour from my mouth, but then abruptly the hands were gone.

I swayed as he bent and retrieved the suit coat from the ground and brushed the dirt and leaves from it. It was cool without him against me, and the breeze blew, which helped to cut through the haze of unwanted desire he'd worked up in me.

Was that it?

No. He walked around to face me, taking in my undoubtably flushed cheeks and heaving chest, and gave me a look that said we'd only just begun. He used his free hand to grab one of the tails of the tie and, like a leash, he pulled me along toward the base of the fountain. As if he were my master and I were his pleasure slave.

It was erotic and obscene.

He laid his coat down open on the bench, and my heart thudded as I recalled what was supposed to happen next.

Since my hands were tied, I couldn't resist when he scooped me up in his arms and lowered me onto my back, down on the suit coat.

The cement was rough and gritty against my bare legs, and as we closed in on the part I most dreaded, I lowered my bound hands to cover my nakedness. As if it would give me protection. I pretended that when he got to my hands shielding my most intimate part, he'd stop, even though I knew he wouldn't. Not unless I said to.

This was my feeble attempt to not just give myself over so willingly.

Macalister put one hand and one knee on the bench and hovered over me. His gaze raked down my body, tracing the swell of my breasts and the flare of my hips and the junction of my thighs that was hidden beneath my hands.

"I couldn't see beyond that ridiculous green hair you used to have." He leaned down and brushed his lips over mine. "But you're stunning."

I turned my head away from him, not wanting his kiss or the reminder of how much control I'd given him.

But he grasped my chin and turned me back to meet his gaze, and irritation flashed in his icy eyes. "I gave you a compliment."

My voice was empty. "Thank you."

He stared at me like a puzzle he couldn't solve. He could only see things from his perspective. He probably thought he'd transformed me like an ugly duckling, and I should be grateful. But was the opposite true?

I lay perfectly still as his mouth roamed over my skin.

He tasted my lips again before carving a path down my body. Anticipation needled at me as his tongue swirled over my nipple and drew wet tracks from breast to breast.

Since we were beneath the fountain, whenever the wind blew, water would faintly mist over us. It sheened my skin and gave me a chill, and I told myself it was the cause of the shiver that shook my shoulders. It couldn't be his hot mouth biting and sucking and devouring.

When he'd had his fill, Macalister snaked down to kneel beside the bench and between my legs. He pushed my outside knee off the stone and onto the ground to give him more room, and I began to quake. This hadn't been so hard with the initiation. I'd been caught off guard, and Royce had started, and—

None of the other men had said they were obsessed with me.

His hands stroked up and down my thighs, followed by his lips. He kissed the length of my calf, the inside of my knee. Each one was an electric jolt, both pleasant and unpleasant. I stared up at the sky, full of sparkling stars and a bright moon, and chased my ragged breath.

When his hands scooped under my legs and he pulled me closer to him, positioning me right at the edge of the bench, I wasn't sure where to put my foot that had been resting on the stone. He straightened for a moment, dropped a kiss against my ankle, and set it over his shoulder.

His breath was warm against my skin in juxtaposition to the cool, misty breeze, and then suddenly there was fire. It scored along the insides of my thighs as he dug his sharp fingers in and raked them down. I hissed at the discomfort and lifted my head to glare at him—

Big mistake. He watched me with longing as he pressed his lips to the red lines blooming on my skin. The track marks he'd created and said were necessary to intensify my orgasm. It was as if he wanted to soothe the pain away. I couldn't watch. My head thumped back against the unforgiving stone, and I swallowed huge gulps of air.

He moved closer to my hands, and my heart beat furiously. Blood roared through me, fueled with anticipation and unwanted need. Could he feel every tremble in me? Did he think he was the cause?

I held my body uncomfortably tight when his mouth arrived at my hands blocking him from his destination. He didn't push them away. Instead he continued to kiss, outlining each finger. It simulated what he wanted to do. His head between my thighs, his mouth at my center, his palms smoothing seductively over my legs.

By making Royce his father's proxy the night of the initiation, at least I'd spared him from having to watch what was about to happen. My left hand was on top of my right, and Macalister ignored the ring there the same way he ignored the one he wore on his own hand.

He peeled my left hand back and laced his fingers with mine. It was disorienting and intimate, but I couldn't focus on it. There was still my right hand covering myself from him, but he was only a breath away.

Everything froze like an ice storm, a moment trapped under glass.

An alarm sounded in my mind, reminding me to keep fighting, and it came from me between panted breaths. "It's been . . . more than . . . two minutes."

His eyes were so hooded, so drunk off desire, he didn't understand what I was talking about at first. But a smug smile burned across his lips, like a banker excited to tell a rude customer their account was overdrawn.

"It has." His voice was rich and dark. "You owe me interest, though. One minute for each day you denied me."

SIXTEEN

I FLINCHED AND TRIED TO SCOOT AWAY, BUT MACALISTER'S grasp on my hips stopped me.

"No," I said.

"Or I give you an orgasm," he added. "Whichever comes first."

I'd hoped to outlast him. Two minutes I could endure, but it had been two months since the initiation, and there was no way I'd survive an hour of his torment. "I didn't agree to—"

A trill erupted from the phone he had tucked in his pocket, shattering the ice that had trapped me. He unlaced our fingers and sat back on his heels as the phone was answered and brought to his ear.

"What?" he barked.

He'd been furious to be disturbed, but as he listened to the other side of the conversation, his expression changed.

His eyes widened, then narrowed.

His posture stiffened. The muscle running along his jaw flexed.

Whatever he was hearing, it was serious and urgent. Hope sparked inside me. Was I about to get a reprieve?

"How interesting." Macalister's tone was sharp as a dagger. "I appreciate you letting me know." His gaze swept down over my naked body, my bound hands clasped between my legs, and he seemed to be weighing his options as if deciding which he wanted to deal with first—the new information or the trembling girl in front of him.

"No," he said. "We need to consider how to respond. Find Richard and bring him to my office."

The phone call ended as abruptly as it had started.

He stared down at me with a hard look, full of disappointment, and it was clear he hated the words coming out of his mouth. "We'll have to continue this another time."

"There's nothing to continue." My heartrate flew as I scrambled toward escape. "I gave you your two minutes." Counting the phone call, I'd given him even more.

His face turned so ugly, I shivered. He grabbed the knot where he'd bound my hands and jerked to get my attention. "You made me wait, and therefore you owe me interest."

I shook my head. "I never agreed to that. Untie me. We're finished."

"We're finished when I say we are."

Strong, rough hands lifted, and I was pulled down into Macalister's lap so I was straddling him as he sat back on his heels. He ducked his head into the circle created by my bound arms, and my eyes went painfully wide.

This position was terribly dangerous.

First, because my naked body was positioned over

his significant erection and I could feel every inch of him through his pants. Second, escape was virtually impossible, from both his grasp and his bottomless eyes. And third, because while he'd kissed his way down my body, he'd undone the buttons of his shirt. It hung open at his sides, exposing his toned chest and taut stomach.

His hands were splayed on my back, and he urged me forward before I could stop him. His kiss landed on my lips at the same moment my bare skin pressed to his, and between my legs, there was the subtle jerk of his cock. He liked the way I felt against him, my breasts flattened to the faint dusting of hair on his warm chest.

"No. *Stop.*" I jerked away and struggled to get out of his lap, but his arms tightened around me. It didn't seem to be to restrain me so much as it was to try to get me to calm down.

"You promised me," I reminded. "I'm saying 'stop.' Let me go."

There was a long, scary second where I believed he considered ignoring me, but then his mouth brushed over the shell of my ear. "All right. I'll release you as soon as you kiss me."

What? No. I shook my head.

"Then we'll stay as we are until I have what I want." He shifted me in his arms, reminding me of all the indecent places we were connected. "It's a simple kiss."

"Nothing with you is simple," I hissed.

He drew back so I could see him. He liked hearing what I'd said, judging by his expression. It was pure arrogance. I wanted out, to be free from under his command and away from the Minotaur's ravenous eyes. I had to be practical. This wasn't nearly as bad as the alternative and the fastest way. I shut off my brain, leaned forward, and flattened my mouth to his before he could react.

I hated him.

He pushed, and pushed, and as his kiss seared across my lips, I wondered how much longer it would be before he wore me down. Before he broke me. He'd already turned my body against me. His tongue swept into my mouth and coaxed me to join him, and although I refused, the sensation of it wasn't . . . unpleasant.

He clearly enjoyed it, and like a true Olympian, Macalister didn't give a fuck about how wrong it was.

Finally, he released me from his thorough kiss, lifted my arms over his head, and set about undoing the tie.

"We can take as much time as you'd like," he said softly, "but be aware you're putting off the inevitable." His eyes darkened as they filled with power. "I've negotiated billion-dollar mergers and destroyed every company that tried to take what's mine, Marist. People far more powerful than you have surrendered to me." He lifted an eyebrow in a soft taunt. "Do you believe you can refuse me forever?"

No, I didn't.

But I sure as hell was going to try.

Macalister tried to help me get dressed, but I scooped up his suit coat, shoved it at him, and ordered him to go. He didn't like being told what to do, but he must have sensed I was on the edge of a total breakdown, and emotions made him uncomfortable. It was better for both of us if he disappeared.

I clutched my dress over my body and stood stock-still as he went, waiting until I couldn't hear his footfalls anymore before returning to life. Perhaps 'life' wasn't the right word. I didn't feel alive. I was numb, an empty vessel as I pulled on my clothes and trudged through the maze, avoiding using the dishonest door I now knew existed.

When I neared the house, I looked up at Royce's window and saw the light on. Was he in there? Oh, my God. He had a view of the maze from above. Had he seen what his father had done? My dinner roiled in my stomach and threatened to come up. The shame was overwhelming. It made my joints hurt, my bones ache.

The house was quiet as I came inside. Only a step on the back staircase creaked as I made my way up them. It was the longer route to get to my room, but I wanted to avoid running into Macalister.

And I didn't run into him. It was the youngest of the Hale men who I encountered in the dark hallway as he slipped out of Alice's room. Vance's startled expression was guilty for a moment, before it filtered out and he returned to normal. We gave each other a hard, evaluating stare.

"Hey, Marist." He forced casualness into his voice. "I was helping Alice with something. You okay?"

I couldn't get the chill of his father off me. Maybe I'd never be warm again. But I fed Vance the lie automatically. "I'm fine."

We both began moving toward our rooms at the other end of the long hallway.

"Must have been some fight."

"What?" I asked.

He looked at me skeptically. "I assumed that what's happened since Royce lost his shit."

Nervousness quicken my breath. "What do you mean?"

"Oh. Uh . . . I guess I'll show you."

Down we went, past my room and his, to the closed door of Royce's. Vance didn't knock. He gripped the handle, turned, and pushed the door open. I made a horrible, choked sound of surprise, and my hand came up to cover my mouth.

The room was a disaster.

Furniture lay on its side, lamps were broken. The black coffee table looked like it had been flipped over and gouged a chunk out of the wall when it had fallen. The mirror that had once hung above the dresser was shattered, and a hundred tiny reflections of my stunned face stared back at me, more pieces scattered across the carpet.

"He was upset." Vance's statement was simplistic, but his voice had gravity that carried the seriousness. "He didn't exactly know how to deal with it."

My heart slowed, petrifying painfully. "Where is he?"

"He called for a car a little while ago. I asked Tate to check on him, and he texted back that he was already with Royce."

My eyes stung as they filled with tears, but I blinked them back. "Is he okay?"

Vance couldn't have looked more surprised if he'd tried. "Yeah, he'll be fine. He'll probably need a day or two to get over himself, but then I'm sure he'll apologize."

I didn't understand. "Apologize?"

"For whatever he did that made you guys fight." He crossed his thick arms and leaned against the wall beside the door, setting his full attention on me. "Look, I'm sure he wasn't your first choice, and at times my brother can be a real asshole, but I'm pretty sure he cares about you. Like, a lot." His boyishly handsome face was uncharacteristically serious and genuine. "I don't know if that's ever happened before."

I'd thought it was impossible to feel any worse, but I'd been wrong. I couldn't bear to look at him as he pleaded his big brother's case. I traced the scrolling pattern in the hallway carpet and tried to hold myself together.

"I don't know the details," he said, "but I'm hoping you don't give up on him just because he screwed up."

"He didn't screw up." Shame made my voice small. "I did."

When my gaze returned to him, he gave me a look that said he didn't believe me. "Well, this conversation never happened, and I definitely didn't show you what his little temper tantrum did to his room, okay? Because if the roles were reversed, I'd be pissed."

I understood what he meant, and I appreciated him showing me. I faked confusion. "What conversation?"

He gave a tight smile, straightened from the wall, and closed Royce's door before moving across the hall toward his own. "I'll see you later."

"Hey, Vance?" He was halfway into his room and turned to look at me. "Your shirt's on inside out."

He paused and his focus dropped down to the navy

t-shirt he wore, the serged seams facing outward. "Son of a bitch," he muttered.

When he disappeared into his room, I did the same. I shut the door, rested my forehead against it, and closed my eyes. I'd become a cold furnace, the pilot light blown out and no way to restart on my own.

I could blame Macalister all I wanted to, but in my heart, I knew the truth. I'd caused the destruction in the room next door. Royce was trapped by his father just as much as I was, if not more, because at least I could walk away if I wanted to give up. I could scurry back to my family. We'd be broke and desperate, but we'd still have each other.

There was no running from Macalister when your last name was Hale.

And now I'd betrayed and hurt Royce worse than he'd done to me.

It wasn't the angry red scrapes across my bicep that made me fall to my knees in the center of my room. The sight of blood didn't faze me right now. No, it was the open black box I'd placed on my dresser earlier and the custom piece of jewelry he'd likely had commissioned just for me.

I didn't need to wear the mask to become Medusa. I already felt like a monster.

It wasn't clear if Royce had come home last night. Maybe he'd stayed with Tate, or else he'd slept in one of the guest bedrooms, but at seven the next morning, I heard staff inside his room, working to clean up the mess.

I'd left my door unlocked and stayed awake most of the night, foolishly hoping he'd come to me. I didn't care if it was to yell at me or ask for his engagement ring back. It didn't matter. I just wanted to see him again.

He didn't answer the single text I'd sent him. I'd typed a hundred different things and deleted them all before sending, unable to find something remotely adequate to express how I felt.

> Me: I'm sorry.

I was a zombie in the back seat of the black Mercedes that took me to and from my classes at Etonsons. I sat shell-shocked in my lectures, taking notes like a transcriptionist and not absorbing any of it. My phone was on silent, so every vibration of a text from my sister or an email from someone about the wedding plans had me racing to check my screen.

When I returned to the house after my last class, it was empty except for the staff. I went up the grand staircase, shivering in the cold despite the fact it still felt like summer outside. Macalister kept the house colder than a doctor's office, convinced the low temperature kept the mind sharp.

I caught my reflection in the mirror over the dresser as I packed my mythology books into the suitcase I'd used to bring them here. Even though I was a college kid, I was no longer allowed to look or dress like one. I had on a gauzy black button-down blouse and camel brown cigarette pants, and my hair and makeup were done, and I looked more likely to go to a corporate event than a lecture on campus.

When everything was done, I perched myself on the

edge of the bed and waited.

It wasn't that much longer before I heard the security system chirp, the front door swing open, and slow footsteps on the stairs. Whoever it was, they were alone, and I swallowed thickly. Alice and Macalister usually rode to the office together, but Royce went on his own.

When he materialized in the shadow of the hallway, I rose to stand, and we stared at each other through my open doorway. Would he come in? Or would he turn and go into his own room, forcing me to follow him?

His expression was unreadable as he took a few hesitant steps my direction, stopping when he stood at the threshold. He was wearing my favorite of his suits, the cobalt blue one he'd worn during the awful luncheon where I'd made the deal with Macalister that I'd marry his son.

I opened my mouth to speak, but no words came out. They hung in my throat, fighting over which line was the best to open with. When my eyes grew damp with tears, he moved into the room and pushed the door closed.

He asked it so softly, it broke my heart. "Are you all right?"

"No," I said. "Are you?"

"No," he admitted. His intense stare was like the sun. Too hard to look at for more than a moment at a time. His tone was hesitant. "I'm sorry I left last night. I thought you wouldn't want to see me."

"What?"

"After what you had to do for us. For me, really." He looked tortured and ashamed. "I tried, Marist. I tried so fucking hard, and it still wasn't enough."

I inhaled so sharply, it hurt. Everything *hurt*. He thought he'd failed me? "Oh, my God, Royce. No, I'm sorry. I didn't see another way, and I thought I could beat him, and—"

He came at me like an unstoppable hurricane, his hands diving into my hair and forcing me to look at him. His voice teemed with determination. "Don't. You think I blame you? I *can't*." He took in a deep breath. "Watching you make that deal was almost as hard as the one I had to make. The only person I blame is *him*." His focus dropped down to my lips like he was thinking about kissing me, and his voice rasped. "You? You did what you had to."

When I closed my eyes, it unleashed the tear that had collected, and it rolled hotly down my cheek. Then his thumb was there, brushing it away a split-second before his lips settled on mine in a chaste kiss. This wasn't him manipulating me, or even about desire.

It was two people enduring the same pain and finding relief in each other.

When our kiss ended, I pressed my forehead to his and kept my eyes closed because I was too scared to look at him when I asked it. "What happened after you left the maze?" My tone was terrified, and a shiver glanced down my spine. "Did you watch?"

"No."

I let out a tight, stuttering breath, not caring if this was true or he'd only said it to spare me. For once, I was happy he was a spectacular liar. He ran his hands over my shoulders, down my arms, all the way until he had my hands grasped in his.

His fingers toyed with mine, and then he went wooden. Hurt and betrayal twisted on his face, and he stepped back, staring at me with new eyes. Like I had deceived him.

"You not wearing the ring."

I swallowed a breath. "I'm leaving."

Fire blazed in him and spilled out onto his face. "No."

"I don't belong here, and I don't know how I can stay with what's happened."

Royce was stone with an angry cast to it. "No. Don't let him win."

"This isn't a game!" I snapped. A glacier crept over me, making my toes and fingers numb. "I'm not a pawn for you and your father to play with."

"I didn't mean it like that. Just wait—"

"I already told you, I'm done waiting."

He tilted his head as if noticing something alarming. "You're trembling."

I wasn't. I was *shivering*. "I can't seem to get warm since . . . last night."

"Fuck, Marist," he said softly. He tried to put his arms around me, but my hands came up and stopped him.

"Give me a reason to stay."

He looked grim. "He'll destroy your family if you leave."

It was true. Besides the fact my father had worked for HBHC his whole career, Macalister was connected. He'd not only blacklist my father, he'd go out of his way to make sure it was impossible for my parents to find work.

"Give me another reason to stay."

He didn't understand what I was really asking. "Because

he'll destroy *me* if you leave."

Also true, but I shook my head. "Try again. Tell me why I should stay."

Royce's exasperation made him put his hands on his waist, showing off his broad shoulders and lean form. "Because you're mine. Because I want you to."

Air caught in my lungs. "Why?"

His eyes narrowed at my challenge, and he volleyed his own back at me. "Give me the ring, and I'll tell you."

I gestured to the dresser. "It's in the box with the mask you gave me."

He went to it, opened the black box, and stared down at the delicate masquerade mask before fishing out the ring. "Do you like it?"

"The mask?" I could barely find the words. "Yes. It's beautiful."

He stalked toward me with the ring clasped between his fingers. Last time he'd come at me like this, he'd been nervous. But not today. He was filled with determination. He glanced down at the ring and back to me. "I need to know why you took this off."

I shifted awkwardly on my feet, not wanting to say, but my silence only made it worse. "I don't deserve to wear it after what I did."

My answer made his eyes go wide. "That's the reason?" He lunged forward and seized my left hand. "Put it back on."

Instead, I drew back my hand. I was so cold, I left him standing there and strode into my bathroom, determined to find heat.

"Where are you going?" he asked, chasing after me.

His expensive brown dress shoes made loud clops on the tile floor as he followed me toward the glass walk-in shower. I cranked the handle, and seconds later water fell from the rain showerhead, sending steam wafting in the tiled space.

His voice was heavy with disbelief. "You're taking a shower? Now?"

"No." I gave him a stern look. "I will when you leave." He stared at me like I was crazy, and, yes. I was acting like a girl on the edge of her sanity because I was. If I got any colder, I might die.

Or maybe I'd become Macalister. Cold-blooded and unfeeling.

I didn't know which one was worse.

Royce's voice was gentle. "Tell me what you need to make you stay."

I stilled. "Was Sophia lying when she said you weren't with anyone last year?"

He blinked his blue eyes that perfectly matched his suit, considering his answer carefully. "No."

I rolled my eyes. "I don't mean dating, I mean sex too."

He didn't want to reveal it, like this was somehow embarrassing. "There wasn't anyone else."

My pulse quickened with unexpected excitement. "Seriously? Why?"

"I don't know." He combed a hand through his hair. "I told you to wait for me, and after that, I felt . . . weird. I didn't want to get into something with anyone else. You were my end goal."

His statement put me off-kilter, but I tried to stay strong and not fall for his manipulation. "I'm supposed to believe that Royce Hale has a conscience? Because I don't."

"We said we wouldn't lie when it was just us."

"All right." He'd walked right into my trap. "Are you planning to buy Ascension Bank?"

I watched the shields go up in his eyes, covering how nervous he really was. "What gave you that impression?"

"The fact that you own a four-point-nine percent stake in them was a big clue. It was buried in your email to Frank."

The shower was steaming up the room, making him hot, although it didn't touch me. I was still frosty cold. He shrugged out of his suit coat and hung it on one of the towel hooks.

"Did you mention this to my father?"

I pulled my chin back. "No."

His expression was cryptic. "How do I know that's true? You're not wearing the ring anymore. For all I know, he's turned you against me, and now you're his spy."

"He didn't turn me against you, and I didn't tell him."

"Why not?"

I gave him the same answer he'd given me about why he hadn't slept with anyone last year. "I don't know."

"I think I do," he said. His face was as gorgeous and perfect as one of the statues in the hedge maze. "Maybe you're in love with me."

SEVENTEEN

ROYCE'S LUDICROUS STATEMENT PUNCHED AN EMPTY LAUGH from my chest. "I'm not."

His eyes went loud with a challenge. "Then why didn't you tell him?"

I ignored him. My gaze swung longingly to the shower as I crossed my arms over my stomach and held in what little warmth I had.

But Royce wasn't going to let it go. He stepped between me and the water that rained from the ceiling and gurgled quietly down the drain, blocking my view so he was all I could see. Nothing but high cheekbones and full lips and eyes that stared relentlessly.

"Why'd you go through with the initiation?" His voice was steady and calm, but there was power buried in his words. "Why'd you play his game and save my board seat after I'd sold you to him? I mean, if you wanted to fuck my life over, that was your opportunity—but you didn't. Tell me why."

Everything was unraveling. "I don't know!"

"Sure you do." His cocky expression was seriously hot but also infuriating. Heat sparked inside me, and I latched on to it. He tilted his head and gave an impish smile. "You're not the first girl to fall in love with me."

"I'm not in love with you," I hissed.

"We said no lies," he reminded.

Oh, my God. I was going to murder him. Flames licked at my body, melting the ice.

His hand slipped inside his pocket and produced the ring. "You're not the first girl to fall in love with me, Marist. But you're going to be the last."

My heart skipped and tumbled, wanting to believe, but my brain knew better. It flew into protection mode, refusing to accept what he'd said. "Now who's lying?"

"Not me." His conviction was absolute. "Put this ring on, back where it belongs."

"This isn't real," I cried. "You're just saying what you think I want to hear. Anything to keep me in check so your dad's satisfied and everything goes according to your plan. This isn't what you want."

Heat flared in his eyes, two torches burning as he closed the ring up in a tight fist and began to toe off his shoes. "You want to know what I fucking want? I'll show you."

The ring was jammed back in his pocket, freeing up his hands so he could use them. One banded around my back and the other grabbed my ass, and a startled noise squeaked from me as I was lifted into his embrace. His face was furious. Resolute. He carried me into the shower, his feet splashing into the water pooled around the drain.

Hot water sluiced over our bodies. It drenched us and the clothes we wore in a matter of seconds, but not before I'd gasped in shock. Royce didn't waver. Like he'd done in the rainstorm, as the water poured over him, he didn't appear to notice. He'd ambushed me, and once I'd been captured, there was no escape.

Not that I wanted to.

He dropped me on my feet beneath the showerhead, and I only got a flash of his hungry look as I brushed a sopping lock of hair back out of my face. It was because his hands curled around the undone neckline of my shirt, and then he pulled the sides apart so hard, it sent buttons *ting*ing and skittering across the tiled walls. Water slung everywhere.

It was . . . violent.

Primal and fucking *erotic.*

A muscle deep between my legs tightened and pulsed at his breathtaking action.

With the shirt out of his way, he hooked his fingers into the cup of my bra and jerked it down, setting my breast free. I bit my lip and threaded my hands in his soaked hair as his greedy mouth latched on to my nipple.

"Fuck," I groaned. The throaty word bounced and echoed in the shower.

He was rough and wild, like a man pushed beyond his breaking point. Careless hands pawed at me, yanking the ruined shirt off my shoulders and down my arms until it fell into a sodden heap.

The other cup of my bra was jerked down so my breasts were pushed out over the tops, and he gave a sexy grunt as he bit the newly exposed flesh.

I wasn't cold anymore. It was scorching in the shower. I arched my back, jutting my breasts into his face so he could better tease me. His tongue slid over my slick, glistening skin, flicking angrily back and forth over my distended nipple, punishing me with each lash.

I loved it.

But it wasn't enough for him. He stood, slung back the water off his intense face, and seized my shoulder. It was so he could turn me around and get at the clasp of my bra. He undid the two hooks, releasing the tension on the band, and as soon as the bra began to slide down my arms, he was there, cupping my breasts with his hands, squeezing hard and cruel.

Royce brought our lower bodies together, pushing his hips into my ass. The thrust had enough force I had to slap my hands against the glass wall that looked out into the bathroom to stop myself from going headfirst into it. When he ground his erection against me, simulating what he wanted to do without clothes in our way, my body went white-hot.

One of his hands grasped my hip, and his fingers dug in, holding me as he rubbed the protruding zipper of his pants over my ass. His tone was merciless. "You want it?"

Oh, God, how I did. I matched his aggression, becoming a snarling, desperate thing. "Give it to me."

He grabbed a fistful of my hair and yanked me toward him, curving me uncomfortably back so he could growl it in my ear. "After you put on my fucking ring."

He released me with a shove, and my elbows banged into the glass, but he didn't care. This was a man with purpose and drive, who'd spent too much time under his father's rule. He was an alpha off the leash, determined to reestablish his dominance.

Royce grabbed my left hand, and then the ring was there, being jammed back down on its home on my finger. He let out a heavy sigh when it was done like he'd just defused a bomb.

His fingers scored down my back and skimmed around my body, flowing over the waistband of my pants until he found the snap at the top of my fly. It popped open with a soft crack, followed by the *vrip* of my zipper, and his deft hand shoved down the front of my panties.

"Oh," I whispered.

My fingers squealed against the glass as I tightened my hands into fists. His touch lit me up, made pleasure burst inside my core. The rough, mean stroke of his fingers over such a delicate part of me felt good. Dirty. Deserved.

Our hurried breaths competed with the sound of the water beating down on us.

I tipped my head forward, resting it against the glass, and although the shower was steamy, I could make us out in the mirror across the room. Me, topless and slumped over, him behind me, one white-sleeved arm cutting across my body as his hand disappeared into my pants. They were so drenched they almost looked black.

His stirring hand made me mindless. I moaned and sighed in bliss, rocking back against his hips to try to signal what I wanted.

He straightened and withdrew from me. "Get those pants off," he ordered. "Show me your ass."

It was strange how I welcomed his control when any other time I would've hated it. His commands set my blood on fire and made my fingers clumsy with lust, but I was able to work the tight, wet pants down over my hips, one side and then the other until they were bunched at my knees.

Threads ripped as he hurried to undo his cuffs and then the buttons of his shirt before flinging it to the floor. It made a wet slap against the tile. I closed my eyes in a slow blink, caught under his spell as his large palm wandered apprecia- tively over my backside. He squeezed the round globe of one ass cheek and muttered something unintelligible under his breath. Whatever it was, it sounded complimentary.

His belt buckle rang out. Then his zipper. In the shapes in the mirror, I saw the blue color of his pants fall halfway down his thighs.

The ache for him was awful. It made my knees wobble and my chest tight. The only relief was him and the connec- tion of our bodies. He raked his fingers down my back, grip- ping my underwear and tugging it down my ass until it was just out of his way.

Heat engulfed me as the thick head of him stroked through my slit, preparing, and in one quick move he rammed into me, all the way to the base.

"*Fuck.*" Everything tensed from the ache.

He froze. "Too fast?"

It was only the third time I'd had sex, and never in this position before, which made him feel huge and like he went on forever. It was uncomfortably tight and full, and I swal- lowed hard. Yes, it was too fast, but I also liked it. His urgent need to have me mirrored my own. It felt dire the moment before he'd shoved himself inside me. So, I bit the inside of my cheek and shook my head, hoping he'd keep going. I needed him to show me the truth with his body, since it was the only way I believed him.

His first thrust was brutal and splashed water onto the glass. It cascaded down, showing us our image in distorted ripples. I cried out with both agony and ecstasy. Fuck, it felt good. Like scratching an itch until it was raw.

Royce's hands were firm on my shoulder and my hip, holding me steady as he pushed himself ruthlessly inside my body, so hard the slap of skin meeting wet skin clapped in the air. He grunted with satisfaction as he found the tempo he wanted to fuck me at. It was savage. Unforgiving. Hardwired and driven by thousands of years of instinct to claim and own.

We moved as one, grinding and sliding and pushing our bodies together. Moans poured from my lips and dripped down my neck. Tremors shook my legs, but I supported myself with my hands flattened to the glass.

"I'm so fucking deep inside you," he growled.

I exhaled loudly, my body clenching and gripping the cock sawing between my legs.

He was the only man I'd been with, but I couldn't imagine how it could get any better than this. He leaned forward, putting his splayed fingers on the glass beside mine, and canted his hips, rocking himself against me like we were both at war and yet partners moving toward the same goal. The warm skin of his soaked chest flattened to my back, and his mouth crashed down on the side of my neck.

"Oh, my God," I said. My eyes wanted to roll back in my head, but if I let them, I wouldn't be able to see the sexy picture playing out in the mirror. I swiped my palm over the steamy condensation, clearing a spot to look through.

"I'll fuck you like this every night if I have to, Marist, so you don't forget who you belong to." Like that was a threat instead of a reward.

And, please. Like I could ever forget.

His labored breathing ratcheted up, as did his moans, and one of his hands snaked between my thighs, finding the place where we were utterly connected. He rolled two fingers over my clit, spinning circles of pleasure and bliss.

"Oh, *fuck*," I whined. It was the only word I could find. A blunt hammer to use to try to express so much.

He sucked on my earlobe and released it with a soft *pop*. His voice was domineering. "Tell me you love me."

What? Even if it was true, I wasn't going to say it now, like this. "No."

"Tell me, and I'll make you come," he offered.

His fingers and his thrusts slowed to a crawl, and in an instant, the heat I'd had for him flipped upside down. He thought he could coax those three little words from me by withholding pleasure.

By manipulating me.

I pushed his hand out of my way and took over. "I don't need you for that."

He stopped moving, still lodged deep inside me, and must have realized his mistake. "Wait, I'm—"

But it was too late. I'd been on the cusp, and with my

new agenda, I entered the endgame. I rubbed furiously back and forth, the swell of my orgasm building to a roar. Pinpricks and tingles washed down my legs, both hot and cold as my vision narrowed.

I panted, drinking in the humid air while my climax bore down.

And I fell over the edge, flying and coming and moaning my release, my ecstasy-filled cry echoing over the rain. The pulse of my body set him in motion, milking him until he had no choice. My orgasm vaulted him unwillingly past the point of no return.

"Jesus, fuck," he spat.

Rough hands locked onto my hips, pushing and pulling. He went from not moving at all, to a breakneck, frantic speed, and the motion prolonged my orgasm. It went on and on, with crests and valleys like a yacht rolling through the sea.

He seized, his body cording with satisfaction, and his thrusts became jerky and shallow, slowing to a stop. He groaned into the side of my neck, his chest shuddering against my back. I wasn't happy with what he'd tried to do, but this? Feeling him lose control was sexy as hell.

And it made me feel powerful.

I was bent awkwardly with my forearms against the glass and his body over mine, but I wasn't in a hurry to pull away.

"Okay," he said between deep, recovering breaths, "I fucked that up at the end, there."

I didn't give him a response, letting my silence speak for me.

Finally, I went to move, and he straightened, giving

me room to stand. We'd been in such a rush, my pants and underwear were down around my knees, and I worked to strip them off.

Royce did the same with his suit pants and underwear, and then we were both naked, standing in the shower and looking at each other with unsure eyes. He made a face like he wanted to say something, but it took him forever to get it out.

"I'm sorry." He moved in until his shadow fell over me, blocking the light overhead. "I didn't mean to be an asshole and push." He hesitated, like he wasn't sure if he should confess it. "I, uh, haven't heard anyone say that to me since my mom . . . It's been a long time."

Only fifteen years.

My heart ached for him, both the loss of his mother and for the family who never said they loved each other. So, I understood why he was eager to hear it again.

"I get it." I reached up and used my fingertips to trace his strong jawline. "But you can't make me. When I say it, it'll be on my terms."

He nodded in understanding. He slipped a hand behind my back and fitted me against him. His other hand palmed mine, his thumb flicking over the engagement ring.

We hadn't kissed. Not since the dressing room yesterday, and so when his lips covered mine, electricity flowed through me. It sizzled across my skin, drawing goosebumps and delicious shivers.

The kiss deepened, thickened. A different kind of longing made my body heavy and weightless at the same time. I didn't just want him like this, a rough fuck in the shower. I wanted all of him.

He turned us under the steady stream of water, so my back was against the tile, and I could see around him while his mouth traveled down my neck. We looked amazing like this. My hand draped over the muscles of his back, my eyes lidded. Two lovers unable to control the passion between them.

Tonight, I wasn't Medusa. If he was Ares, then I was Aphrodite.

I closed my eyes and hoped our love story wouldn't suffer the same fate theirs had.

EIGHTEEN

THE LIBRARY WAS FOREBODING TONIGHT. THE GOLD lettering on the spines of the books glinted razor sharp, and the unused fireplace was a wide, dark mouth threatening to devour me.

I'd arrived early for our appointment, even though it had taken every ounce of strength I possessed to get me through the doorway. I hadn't seen Macalister since last night. The mere thought of him made ice crawl down my spine.

And this evening he was late.

It was exhausting sitting here, waiting while tension held me in its stiff grasp. Was this his intent? To remind me who was in control since he'd supposedly relinquished ownership over me?

I wasn't about to text him and give him hard evidence I was waiting for him. He'd likely take it the wrong way.

So, I was just about to leave when he finally arrived and stalked into the room, bringing a cold draft with him. He undid the button on his suitcoat before he lowered himself into the seat across from me. "Excuse my lateness. There was an issue I had to handle personally."

His focus went to the board, and then to me expectantly. I always played white, which in theory had the advantage of the first move, but I hadn't been able to capitalize on it yet. He waited impatiently for me to pick up a pawn and make my opening, acting like this was all normal and everything in the hedge maze had never happened.

Like the Minotaur didn't exist.

I toppled over my king, letting it clatter to the desk. "I resign."

He was prepared for this. Perhaps the only thing that surprised him was I'd waited this long to try it. His demeanor was calm and controlled. "No. You're not allowed."

"I'm done. I'm not playing anymore."

Cold drifted through his expression. "We made an arrangement, and you'll honor your word, as I did mine."

"I won't." I felt small but tried not to show it. "I can't after last night." If he was truly obsessed as he'd said, then there was a small chance he cared for me. I pleaded to that side of him. "Let me go."

His eyes were murky water moving beneath a thin layer of ice. "No."

My heart sank to my toes, but what did I expect? He'd turned down fifty million dollars for me. "Then . . . I'm going to resign every night."

His frustration could have been masking his desperation, but if so, he hid it well. He leaned back in his chair, crossed his arms, and peered at me with tight eyes. "I'm disappointed in you, but I may be willing to compromise."

"You mean, renegotiate."

"Yes," he said.

I shook my head. "No, I'm not interested."

I'd finally learned to stop digging myself into a deeper hole. Any gains I'd made were short-term and followed by terrible consequences. I wasn't too proud to admit he'd bested me, but I wasn't going to feel shame over it. He had thirty more years of experience than I did.

When I rose to my feet, genuine alarm coasted through his face. "Where do you think you're going?"

"I made my move and the game is over, so we're done here."

He stood so quickly the chair banged back against the bookshelf. "One game a week."

My hesitation made him elaborate.

"We'll revise our agreement. Instead of every night, we'll only play once a week."

I was so tired. "In exchange for?"

"Nothing." He let out a begrudging sigh. "I can't make you enjoy the game, and certainly not if we stop playing altogether."

This was a better outcome than I'd hoped for, but I gave him a discerning, wary look. What was the catch?

"This is more than fair," he added with irritation. "I've allowed you multiple times to change the rules. Last night, for example."

I sucked in a sharp breath. He'd given me partial freedom, even when I'd lost. "Fine," I snapped. "But tonight counts."

Meaning I had a whole week where I didn't have to see
him. I walked toward the door, no longer feeling like Atlas
holding up the sky on my shoulders. I wanted to hurry out
before he changed his mind.

"Marist." Macalister said my name like he was summon-
ing a servant. "You may want to say your goodbyes to Royce.
There's a financial reporting symposium in Sydney next week
that I've decided to send him to. I think he could use the
experience."

I turned in place, staring at him with wide eyes. "What?"

"He'll be back in time for the anniversary gala next week-
end, but he'll need to leave tonight." Macalister picked up the
white king and put it back in its spot.

I ground my teeth and swallowed my anger. It was absolutely clear what he'd done, and I wasn't going to let him get
away with it. "You said you weren't going to interfere."

His dark expression pinned me in place. "And I haven't.
I don't see how I can do anything if he won't even be here."
He smoothed a hand down his tie as if he could brush away
my feelings that easily. Desire seeped in and pooled in his
eyes. "I look forward to our next game."

I fled the library without another word.

Ironically, I saw Royce more the following week than I
did Macalister, even though my fiancé was on the other side
of the world. He'd FaceTimed me twice during the week. Because of the time change, I'd come home from class in the

evenings, and he was just waking up and preparing for his days at the conference.

Now, it was Saturday. He'd landed late last night, come to the house, and gone straight to his bed. He'd likely sleep until it was time to go to the gala. I wouldn't see him until he was wrapped in a tuxedo and wearing his mask.

Alice's hair and makeup team had dismissed me from her room ten minutes ago. I'd fought hard to wear my hair down, and she'd finally agreed when the hairdresser backed me up. Medusa's snakes shouldn't be pinned away.

But it meant I had to don my mask hours before the party tonight, so the woman could style my hair around it and hide the band that held it in place. I was still adjusting to its heavy weight on the bridge of my nose as I stared at my reflection in the full-length mirror in my room.

I didn't think any jewelry could compete with my great-grandmother's necklace, but I'd been wrong. I was wearing the necklace now, the diamonds draped around my throat like a wreath, but my gaze kept working its way back to my face. I loved the way the delicate snakes weaved and chased each other in a lacy pattern.

The only color on me right now, besides the tiny emerald eyes of the snakes, was my vividly stained red lips. I had on a short, white silk robe over my black strapless bra and panties. I'd been instructed not to put on my dress until it was almost time to leave. Alice didn't trust me to keep it free of wrinkles and accidents, and it was of the utmost importance we all looked flawless when we arrived at the venue, according to her.

But I longed to put on the dress. I eyed it hanging on the door to my closet, itching to finish my transformation. How was I going to survive another thirty minutes?

There was a short knock on my door, but it pushed open before I could acknowledge it, which meant it couldn't be anyone else. Macalister didn't wait. He owned this house and this room, and he felt he should be able to come and go as he pleased.

I spun to face him, my hands immediately going to the sash of my robe to make sure it was cinched tight. It didn't matter that I was covered—I felt naked.

I wasn't; I was just horribly underdressed.

Was it the same tuxedo he'd worn during the initiation? It was a rich black, and the lapels had a faint sheen to them. Black buttons dotted a line up his white shirt, ending in a perfectly tied black bow at his throat. He wasn't wearing his mask yet. Perhaps he thought it was beneath him and would only put it on when we were in the limo, heading to the Harbor Plaza.

His gaze roamed the room in search of something, and when he discovered me, he studied me carefully. He catalogued my bare legs, the silk robe, my red lips, and the glittering mask around my eyes.

I forced myself to sound calm rather than terrified. "What do you want?"

His expression gave nothing away. "I have something for you in the library."

"What is it?"

He didn't answer me. He disappeared from my doorway,

demanding I follow him. Anxiety clung to my skin. I was chilled in the persistent air conditioning Macalister required, and yet I began to sweat. What terrible thing awaited me in the library?

He stood facing the window, his hands clasped behind this back, and he didn't turn when I entered the room, but he must have sensed it. "It's on the desk."

The only thing resting there was a large and flat wooden box with a metal clasp. It looked similar to the one my mother stored her best silver flatware in. The grain of the wood was inlaid to create a beautiful pattern.

Fear gripped me. It was another Pandora's Box, and I wasn't interested. "No, thank you."

He turned to look at me over his shoulder, his eyebrow lifted in displeasure. "There's nothing *inappropriate* inside, and you're being rude."

I held in a tight breath and plodded to the desk, my suspicion-meter all the way in the red as I cautiously undid the clasp and lifted the lid.

Black and white alternating squares were bordered with scenes from the ancient myths I adored. The chessboard was seated in deep blue velvet, a darker shade than the eyes staring at me as I curled my fingers around the edges of the heavy board and lifted it to get a closer look.

"Oh," I sighed.

Beneath the board, the thirty-two chess pieces were displayed. Zeus and Hera as the black king and queen, Athena and Poseidon as the white pair. For both colors, Ares was the bishops, Pegasus the knights, and two Greek columns served as the rooks. Below, eight satyrs were pawns, half-goat and half-man with tiny horns on their heads. I put down the board and picked one of the pawns up, marveling at the weight and detail.

"This is beautiful," I said. "They're so intricate."

When I looked up from the piece, I found Macalister viewing me with fascination. Like a starving man watching someone else eat. It made my heart beat faster and my nerves rise. He'd given me a gift. What was he going to want in return?

"I thought we could play a quick round."

There it is. "Thank you, but I don't think we have time. We don't want to be late for—"

"They won't start the party without me."

I'd left the door open. He strode to it and pushed it closed, and the action made alarm spike through me. As much as I wanted to see this gorgeous chess set arranged on the board, it felt dangerous. I wasn't mentally prepared to spar with him right now, when I was barely dressed.

But he didn't care. He sat in his seat and began to pull the black pieces from the case, arranging them on their squares. My options were limited. I could play the game and get it over with or argue and waste time and have to play the game anyway. He'd get his way, regardless.

I plunked down into my seat, gingerly extracted my white pieces to set them up, and when we were both ready, I made my first move.

"Your mask is stunning," he said as he moved his pawn. "Medusa?"

"Thank you. Yeah, it was a gift from Royce." I moved another piece. "What's yours? Zeus?"

He took his turn and gave a faint, enigmatic smile. "No, not Zeus."

A stone turned over in my stomach. I had the terrible realization of who he was going as and couldn't bring myself to say it. I tried to steer the conversation away from the subject.

While we played, he talked about how proud he was of his company and that HBHC had reached such a milestone. They'd survived the Great Depression and the global financial crisis in 2008, and under his leadership, stock had soared.

Well, up until last month.

"Shareholders love to panic at every minor detail," he mused. "We'll be fine." He confidently slid Ares three spaces diagonally and took my satyr pawn, placing it on the desk with the other pieces he'd captured.

Hairs on the back of my neck tingled. Something was wrong. I stared at the board in confusion, trying to figure out where I'd made a wrong move—

Holy. Fucking. Shit. I hadn't.

But Macalister *had*.

He realized it at the same moment because he launched forward in his seat and tried to put my pawn back in play.

My breath was hurried. "No, you took your hand off. Your turn is over."

He looked furious, but also like he was about to be ill.

His chest lifted in an enormous breath when I moved my knight. "Check."

I'd never seen him take so long to make a move. He

stared at the board with hostility, as if it had somehow caused his situation. No doubt he was running different scenarios in his head, trying to compute a way out that didn't end with his defeat.

He slid his rook forward like every square it crossed was painful. It probably was to him. I'd spent the last few months suffering in his endgame, and he didn't like the roles being reversed.

I took his rook with Hera. "Check."

My heart beat like a war drum, and it was fitting, because my Ares was going to deliver the fatal blow. Macalister only had one move left, and yet he didn't make it. Had my Medusa mask turned him to stone? Or was he simply sitting there, contemplating his defeat?

I'd done it.

Finally beaten him and released myself from our arrangement. All he needed to do was move, and then I could utter the word I'd wanted to for so fucking long.

But I didn't get to tell Macalister *checkmate.*

He gave me a look of pure malice before he violently swung a hand across the desk and sent the pieces flying off the board. Some slammed into the bookcases and others crashed loudly to the floor, and I was up out of my chair before I could take a breath, stumbling back away from him.

"We'll play again," he exploded. His expression was cold fury as he slapped his hands on the desk and used them to help push to his feet.

"But I won."

"No, it doesn't count."

When he lost the game, he seemed to lose everything, including his control. He charged at me, and by the time I realized what was happening it was too late to run. His arms closed around my arms and waist, and we stumbled backward, all the way until my back slammed into a bookcase.

His mouth crushed down on mine, stopping my panicked noise from escaping. As he pressed his lips against me, he used his body to drive me back into the shelves, the wood digging in. It was uncomfortable in every sense of the word. He smothered me. I felt each button of his shirt, my breasts flattened by his wide chest, and the swell at the center of his legs that pushed greedily at my belly.

I tore my mouth away from his, smearing my red lipstick across his lips, and tried futilely to catch my breath. "Macalister, stop."

He left our lower bodies connected but drew back and looked at me like prey he'd trapped and wanted to toy with before finishing off. He was wild as he stared down at me with his messy lips and savage eyes. "I don't want to."

What the fuck was I supposed to say to that? When I tried to squirm away, his grip tightened and locked me down. Blood roared and banged frantically in my head. Should I scream? My hands were trapped at my sides, and I reached behind me, my fingers catching on the edge of a book. Maybe if he let me go, I could pull it from the shelf and swing it at his head.

Abruptly, his face twisted with torture, then it melted and he sobered. He didn't release me, but tension faded from his arms. "I'm sorry. I was upset and . . . handled it poorly."

The image of Royce's destroyed bedroom flitted through my mind, but I had more urgent things to think about. Like how Macalister was still holding me captive. "Let me go."

"I will in a moment." He regained his composure, his cold veneer snapping back into place. "I tried to rid you from my system, Marist. I told myself I couldn't want you because you don't exist. That once I was clear of the fog of you, this *desire*"—he said it like it was distasteful—"would cease."

He let go of me, only to put his hands on the bookshelf beside my waist, squeezing until the wood groaned in protest. His eyes were devastating, and I wanted to stop looking, but couldn't. He was a violent crash on the side of a highway, a siren's song for attention.

"But in your absence," he continued, "the desire worsened, and I'm willing to acknowledge I cannot master it. So tonight, after the anniversary gala is over, you will come to my room, wearing only this mask." His voice was full of dominance and power. "And then you will give me *anything* I ask for."

My knees buckled, but he caught me by my hips, pinning me to the bookcase so hard the shelf rattled. "No," I spat at him. "I won't."

He sounded genuinely offended. "Why not? I'm attractive and powerful. I can please you sexually, and there's so much more I can—"

"I'm in love with Royce." It came from me with no hesitation, the raw truth.

He flinched as if I'd slapped him, and then a nasty expression painted his face. "I don't believe you. You're too smart to do something as stupid as fall in love. If you did, then you wouldn't have done what we did in the maze."

His words cut deep, flaying me alive. "You left me no choice. I had to save him."

Macalister lifted his chin but peered down at me, judging me critically. "Then do it again. Come to my room tonight and submit to me. He can keep his seat, and I'll show you how I'm a better version of him in every way."

I glared at him with the darkest look in my arsenal. "Fucking *no*."

He sighed loudly and with reluctance, about to play a card he didn't want to. "I had Nigel schedule an appointment with a dermatologist for you. I'm told the process of removing a tattoo is far more painful than receiving one, and it will take several treatments."

I froze in place, barely able to breathe. "No."

"Don't look at me like that." His voice was so stern, I struggled not to cower. "I do not approve of the choice you made. If you want to keep it, you'll have to earn it."

My eyes filled with hot, angry tears as I looked around the room frantically for escape. "I'll leave," I blurted.

"Where would you go?" He wasn't cruel when he asked it, but it stung, nonetheless. "Do you think he would give up everything he has for you? As you've done for him?"

One lone tear spilled out from under my mask.

No, Royce wouldn't. He'd told me so the night of our first date.

Macalister softened into something slightly more human. "You know better. He's not worth tears." He took a hand off the shelf and cupped the side of my face. "It doesn't have to be complicated. Say yes, and I will satisfy you in all the ways he can't."

The word *no* bowed on my lips. Not just to his offer, but to the way he was closing the space between us, his kiss threatening like low storm clouds coming in from the ocean.

But before I could issue the word, the library door creaked open.

In my struggle, the sides of my robe had come open under the sash, and I stood beneath Macalister with my bra and panties exposed. His hand was on my jaw and my lipstick smeared over his lips. I could claim it wasn't what it looked like, but what person in their right mind would believe?

He took his time straightening away from me, not even a little bit embarrassed to have been caught.

Not even when it was by his own wife.

NINETEEN

ALICE STOOD IN HER BEAUTIFUL PEACOCK BLUE DRESS, FROZEN with one hand still on the doorknob. For an agonizing moment she didn't move, as if a mechanism inside her had broken and all her systems ceased functioning.

But Macalister had said she couldn't be broken, and she proved it when she snapped back to life. Her gaze turned to her husband, and her face went sour. "We don't have time for this. Look what you did to her makeup."

He swiped a palm over his mouth in an attempt to remove the red stain from his face. At the same time, I grabbed the sides of my robe with trembling hands and pulled it closed, overlapping the fabric as much as possible like it made any fucking difference now.

When Alice charged at me, I wanted to run, but she grabbed my wrist and pulled me toward the exit. "Come on. I can fix it, but we need to get you dressed if we're going to stay on schedule."

Her grip was unbearable as she led me toward my room.

Not just emotionally, but physically too—her thumb dug deep into the pressure point just above my wrist. I didn't complain. I was too busy trying to figure out what the fuck I was going to say to her.

Thankfully, we didn't see Royce in the hallway. She got me into my room and sat me on the bed, acting like I was the victim and not her. I couldn't stand it. The guilt, the wrong assumption, the hurt it must have caused her.

She was unbreakable, but I wasn't, and my voice cracked on her name. "Alice."

She emerged from my bathroom with a makeup removing wipe and dabbed at the edges of my lips. "This stuff was supposed to be color stay."

I grabbed her wrists, getting her to stop. "*Alice.*"

She finally looked and really saw me, not just the problem of my makeup. Her tone was sad but plain. "It's all right, and not that surprising, if I'm being honest. You talk to him the same way I do, and he's always liked it when he's challenged." Her focus went back to the makeup, and she traced the edge of my lip with the wipe, creating a sharp, defined line. "And I've seen the way he watches you."

"I don't feel the same," I said. "It's one-sided and—"

"He wouldn't be interested if it wasn't." A bitter smile widened on her face. "He lives for the chase, and he grows bored once he has you."

She was speaking from experience.

Alice finished her task and straightened. "Did Luc give you the lip color?" She didn't wait for my answer, just assumed it was a *yes.* "Don't bother putting more on right now, unless you think Royce can control himself."

Overload made my mind blank when I removed my robe, stood before her in only my undergarments, and allowed her to help me into the green dress. She zipped up the back, her cold fingers hooked the clasp at the top, and then she grabbed my heels and set them on the floor for me to step into.

"Thank you," I mumbled. Although it was obvious she wasn't doing this to be nice. She was more concerned about the schedule.

When it was done and I stared at my reflection in the mirror, I tried to become the fierce monster I was portraying, the one who turned men to stone with a single glance. I wouldn't crack under the enormous pressure, nor would I flinch when I saw the rest of the board members again this evening. They'd undoubtably be in tuxedos like they had been during the initiation, but at least they'd be wearing masks.

When there was a knock at my bedroom door, Alice pulled it open. Royce gave her a once-over and then a friendly smile. "You look beautiful."

She was so impatient it was like she didn't even have time for his compliment. "Thank you."

His gaze swept past her, landed on me, and Atlas set down the sky and heavens.

I'd forgotten the effect he held over me when he was like this. A tuxedo was just a style of suit, and I'd seen him in plenty of those over the last few months, but this was decidedly different. More refined and elegant. The clean lines and stark contrast of black on white emphasized the breathtaking man beneath.

Alice had been concerned about Royce controlling himself, but she'd been worried about the wrong person. I stormed toward him, the train of my green dress dragging behind me, and flew into his arms. I wasn't sure if he'd put his hands on my waist to embrace me or to slow my attack, but I hooked a hand behind his neck and pulled him down into my needy kiss.

He issued a soft sound of pleasant surprise.

I'd started the kiss, but he took command. His mouth roved against mine, matching my intensity and then exceeding it, like he craved it even more than I did. It couldn't be possible. I needed to reaffirm my connection to him after what had happened in the library.

Alice's voice interrupted with a joking tone, although it sounded forced. "Okay, save some of that for the gala, please. We need to get going."

We separated reluctantly. I grabbed my clutch while he retrieved his mask, and then we strolled to the staircase, my hand clutched in his.

Macalister stood at the bottom of the steps with his back turned so he was merely a figure in black. We couldn't see his mask, only the black curved horns of the Minotaur protruding upward. Royce felt my steps falter, but he squeezed my hand, wordlessly trying to convey it was all right. He was at my side.

It was harder to descend the staircase in this dress than it had been in the red one, made worse because of the man waiting for us. He turned when we'd reached the entryway and cast his judgmental gaze down upon us.

His mask only covered the top half of his face, so it was clear he'd scrubbed the rest of my lipstick from his lips. The horns were a glossy black while the mask itself was feathers layered upon feathers—black on the outer edge, bronze around his eyes.

It was frighteningly beautiful.

And it made it that much more difficult to read what he was thinking. His gaze scoured over me and Royce, and our hands intertwined, and something like a sneer lurked on his lips. It vanished as footstep rang out.

Alice strolled down the stairs with her mask in place, and we stared up at her like we were receiving a queen. Which made sense, for she was Hera, queen of the gods. Her mask was a dark gold, and each point along the top was decorated with a glittering star, creating her decadent crown.

I was struck by how she looked. Not just gorgeous, but powerful. Beyond desirable. Men would kill other men for a chance with her. Why on Earth was her husband not brought to his knees by her? Why was he fixated on me when I didn't compare to what he already had?

He didn't compliment her. He offered nothing, not even a smile as she joined us. Instead, he glanced down at his watch impatiently. "We need to leave. I told Vance's driver to meet us at five-forty."

Royce let go of my hand only so he could pull on his mask.

When it had been decided we'd use the mythology theme, he'd asked me who he should go as. My original answer had been Hades, the king of the underworld, but I'd been wrong. I saw him as Ares now.

The black leather mask was molded to his face and then flared out like sharp pointed wings. Red notched upward at the corner of his eyebrows and down from the center of his eyes, exaggerating a menacing scowl. The mask was full of aggression and dominance. He looked ruthless. It was undeniably sexy as he pulled it into place.

So much tension filled the back of the limo, it was difficult to breathe. Royce and I sat on the side bench while Alice sat next to her husband on the back seat, and for a long time no one said anything. Macalister's dark gaze kept returning to me every few minutes, as if checking to see I hadn't vanished from the car.

We'd made it into Boston before the silence was broken.

"How was the conference?" Macalister's focus shifted to his son. "They seemed quite pleased you could attend. You'd think you were a celebrity from the way they fawned over you." He was smiling, but there was zero warmth. "I'm sure you enjoyed that immensely."

Royce let the comment roll right off him. "It was fine, but I would have rather stayed here and dealt with stock price crisis."

"It's a situation, not a crisis," Macalister said dryly.

"We're down three percent over the month. Pretty sure *crisis* is the word the shareholders are using."

Macalister was a god, but even he had to answer to someone, and he did not like Royce reminding him of that.

When the limo parked and the door opened, fresh air poured in, dispelling some of the thick tension that clogged the back seat. The limo had pulled up in a parking garage alongside another, although this car wasn't as big. We all got out, doing our final checks to make sure we were camera-ready, and I stood still as Alice applied more lipstick to my already red lips. I tried not to think about how cruel the situation was for both of us.

Vance had taken a car to pick up Jillian, but neither got out of the limo we'd parked beside. Was it possible this was someone else's car? I didn't recognize the driver standing beside it, but there were quite a few on the Hales' staff. Macalister marched with frustration toward the back door and reached out to open it—

"Sir." The driver stepped in front of him. "They're not ready yet." His expression was heavy, filled with what he was trying to say while staying professional at the same time. "I think they might need another minute."

The single word from Macalister fell like a hammer. "Move."

The driver scrambled out of the way as his boss lunged for the handle and jerked it open.

Light from the parking garage splashed inside, revealing two bodies connected. Vance knelt on the floorboard, his black pants undone and down around his knees. He had one hand across his belly, holding his shirt up out of his way, and the other behind him on the seat, supporting himself as he leaned back. Jillian was in front of him on her hands and knees, her silver dress hiked up around her waist.

"What the *fuck*?" Vance cried, jerking out of her and turning away at the same moment he grabbed the back of her dress and yanked it down, covering her naked lower half.

"We're all waiting on you," his father growled before shutting the door with force.

The slam of it echoed in the parking garage, and then plunged the space into horrible silence. The image was seared in my brain, but what about Alice? I snuck a glance at her, but unless she was hiding all her emotions under her mask, she didn't have any. She looked exactly as she had earlier when she'd caught her husband looming over me.

Vacant.

The limo rocked. Not from sex, but from the occupants' panicked hands as they hurried to dress. Raised voices came from inside the car, but it was too muffled to make out the words and understand what exactly they were arguing about.

The door shoved open and Vance stepped out, his tuxedo in place and a mask pushed back on the top of his head. It allowed us to see his expression, which was a mixture of guilt and exasperation. His blue eyes focused on his father as he shut the door. "She's not coming."

"Apparently not," Royce said.

Macalister ignored the comment and leaned over his youngest son. "Excuse me?"

For a brief moment, Vance flashed daggers at his older brother, but his attention swung back to his father. "She's too embarrassed."

"Fix it," he ordered.

"I tried. She won't come out of the limo."

When Macalister turned his demanding gaze toward his wife, everything went cold inside me. He needed to smooth things over with Lambert's daughter and have her walk in on

Vance's arm, and he expected Alice to handle it for him.

"I'll do it." I stepped forward, grabbed the door, and ducked inside before anyone could stop me. Maybe if I got her to come out, Macalister would owe me. I could use it to buy myself some time until I figured out what to hell I was going to do about his demand in the library.

At the least, it should spare Alice from having to talk to the girl who'd just been caught fucking her lover.

Jillian sat at the front of the back seat, as far away from the door as possible, with her face in her hands, and she didn't look up when I pulled the door closed and locked us in together.

"Hey." I gave her the most soothing tone I had. "Hey, it's okay."

She lifted her head, and her face was a mess. Black smudges collected under her eyes from her tears, and rather than worry about her . . . I wondered if her mask would be able to disguise it. God. What was wrong with me? This would have been the last thought on my mind four months ago, back before I'd agreed to become a Hale.

Her voice wavered. "Please tell me you came in here to kill me."

I opened my clutch and pulled out a tissue, extending it out to her. "Nope. I came to tell you that Macalister wants you and Vance together so badly, he'd probably be thrilled right now, except he's too busy worrying we're going to be late."

Her movements slowed as she took the offered tissue. "What?"

"I get that you're embarrassed, but what just happened is

seriously no big deal. But if you don't walk in with Vance . . . that's a very big deal." I scooted closer to her on the side bench. "So, I'm here to help. You're going to sit beside me when we all go together in the limo. You'll put your mask on and hide behind it if you want to, and I promise everyone will act like nothing happened. Big, fake smiles for five minutes while we walk in, and that's it. Easy."

Knuckles rapped on a window, announcing I was running out of time.

"Everyone saw me naked," she whispered.

"Not really. It was a lot more Vance than you." I quirked a smile. "Even if they did, who cares? You got this. Show them you don't give a fuck."

When I climbed out of the limo, Macalister was right there, and I sucked in a breath. "We can go. She's putting on her mask."

He straightened with surprise, and relief edged across his expression. I gave him a look that told him I hadn't done it out of the kindness of my heart. He was now in my debt.

While I'd been coaxing Jillian from the back seat, Vance had lowered his mask. It was a dark green with brass highlights, like the algae had been worn away from those spots. Curling tentacles spread out and hung down, four octopus arms on each side.

He spent so much time on a yacht these days, maybe he didn't need the mask to feel like Poseidon. He helped Jillian out of one limo and straight into the other, larger one. I darted in right after them, taking a seat beside her as I'd promised to do.

The ride to the red carpet at the front of the gala was quiet and blissfully short.

There wasn't really supposed to be media at the event. Photographers had been hired to take promotional images for the brand, but there was a velvet rope on either side of the red carpet, and several media outlets had shown up. So, when we emerged one by one from the back of the limo, there were cameras and flashes and cries for our attention.

I was the fake, Instagram Marist. I pasted on a smile and clung to Royce with an iron grip, then forced myself to walk with a normal gait and not sprint to the safety of the building at the other end. Inside, I was Medusa and he was Ares, and everyone should fear us, rather than us fearing them.

Not that Royce looked at all uneasy. He grinned and kissed my hand, playing it up for the cameras. Selling the story of our fairytale romance.

The expansive ballroom of the Harbor Plaza Hotel was bathed in purple and magenta lights, giving the room a surreal quality. Tall candelabras, draped in crystal beads, sat in the center of each table, flickering whispers down on the tablecloth.

I successfully survived dinner seated at the same table as Macalister, as had Jillian. Perhaps the three glasses of wine she'd consumed had helped. But I hadn't been able to talk to Royce alone and tell him what had happened. Part of me was too scared to. Not because I worried he wouldn't believe me, but because if I threatened to leave . . . he might let me.

He'd choose his goal over me.

There was music from a live band following the dinner,

and as we danced, I couldn't help but notice Mr. Lambert and Macalister tucked in a corner, deep in conversation. At one point, Macalister smiled and laughed. To anyone else, he might look charming, but it left me horribly cold. Royce and I had our fake personas, and it was clear his father did too.

I grabbed Royce's hand. "Let's go out on the balcony."

I'd put in my time during the cocktail hour and schmoozed with Royce's employees. I'd sat with the rest of the Hales for a family picture. I'd even been able to chat with my parents for a few minutes before dinner, and once again, my mother had been more focused on the necklace I wore than her own daughter.

Now I wanted five minutes alone with my fiancé, who I hadn't been able to touch for a solid week and was desperate to be away from the board members milling about the party.

We each snagged a glass of champagne and strolled out onto the balcony that overlooked the harbor. Despite the nice October weather, it wasn't crowded out here. The music thumping from inside was muffled behind the windows, and there was the occasional horn from a boat, but it was relatively quiet.

He looked out over the water and said it right before he took a sip of his champagne. "I almost didn't go."

"What?"

"To Sydney. It was hard to leave."

I rested my hand on the cold railing lining the balcony, not sure if he meant because he'd miss me, or because he wanted to protect me from his father.

"Hey, I need to tell you something."

He turned and put the full force of his intense gaze on me. "Yeah, me too. But you go first."

"I played your father in chess this afternoon, and I won."

Beneath his black mask, surprise washed through his eyes, and a cautious smile lifted his lips. "That's great. That means it's over, right?"

I took in a preparing breath. "He didn't take the loss well."

His smile died. "What'd he do?"

I figured he only needed the broad details. "He kissed me. He told me I had to come to his room tonight and if I don't, he'll make me get rid of my tattoo." His mouth opened, maybe to tell me it wasn't the end of the world, but I kept going. "And he'll take away your seat."

Royce's chest rose and fell with an enormous breath. Then he tilted back his champagne flute and drained it in three big swallows. When his gaze settled back on me, it was impossible to read. "He's bluffing."

"What if he's not?"

He shook his head. "I know him. He's invested too much effort in his legacy to do that."

I wasn't stupid enough to ask Royce to give everything up and run away with me, but I wanted to. Macalister had invested in his legacy, and Royce had in his plan, and neither was going to walk away. They were on a collision course.

I could only hope we would survive it.

There was a boom overhead that made me flinch, and as I gazed up, gold rained down. Fireworks. There was a boat in the harbor setting them off, and it took me a moment to realize these were for the HBHC gala. The chandelier fireworks lit up the night sky and reflected in the bay water below. Their slow descent made them golden weeping willows until they faded away.

It was a beautiful, lavish display.

As he watched them, his elbows resting on the railing, I studied him. He looked so handsome and sure, and the words bubbled up, unstoppable.

"I love you."

His head snapped to me, the fireworks forgotten. "What?"

"I said I love you."

At that exact moment, Sophia Alby materialized from fucking nowhere. She must have come up behind me like a ninja. Was this how she got the bulk of her information? By eavesdropping and perfect timing?

She wore a black dress, a mask like Catwoman, and an epic grin. She'd heard what I'd said and was eagerly awaiting Royce's response.

He rose to his full height, his eyes pure and determined, and placed a hand on my waist. "I love you too."

It was effortless. Easy for him. His lips brushed over mine in a sweet kiss that asked for more, and I obliged. His second kiss was hungry. It tasted like champagne and passion, but emotions swirled uneasy inside me.

I had no idea if he meant what he'd said . . .

Or if it was a lie.

He could be in his prince persona, only saying it because if he didn't, the repercussions would be disastrous. Sophia would start a whisper campaign within the hour that our fairytale wasn't exactly as it seemed.

"You two are adorable," she said. "I just came by to say 'hi' and tell you I love your mask, Marist. Can we grab a picture together?"

"Uh . . ."

Like last time, she didn't wait. She pushed in between Royce and me, held her phone up, and prepared to take the selfie. "Smile!"

The version of myself on her screen looked normal, but beneath my dress, my knees knocked together. She captured all three of us smiling, the fireworks lighting up behind us. Satisfied, she lowered the phone, and the hairs on the back of my neck stood on end. A blast of cold hit me like someone had opened a freezer door, and although I didn't want to, my attention was pulled that direction.

Macalister was on the balcony, coming toward us like he was on the hunt. Or perhaps he was the Minotaur, even though his mask was pushed back on his head, revealing his full face. All the conversations going on around us ceased. Every pair of eyes was on him instead of the bursts of gold in the sky. They lit him in warm flashes.

"See what I mean?" Sophia whispered seductively before floating away. She was gone by the time Macalister reached us.

"Why are you hiding out here?" he asked.

Royce's lips pressed into an irritated line. "We're not hiding, we're watching the fireworks."

That was the moment Macalister Hale realized there were fireworks going off over the harbor. Maybe he didn't know about them beforehand, as Alice had been responsible for the gala planning. He gazed up at them and watched the grand finale with a critical eye, but when it was over and the crowd who'd gathered to watch gave their applause, he looked pleased.

It was as if the show had given him more power. "Marist, may I have a dance?"

"No," Royce said.

His voice was cold and deadly. "I don't recall asking you."

Before Royce could say anything else, I put a calming hand on his arm, and my tone to his father was firm. "No, thank you."

Macalister's expression was hard to read. Was he angry? Or just disappointed? "Very well. In that case, you two should make your final rounds. Royce, you'll be needed after. Since most of the board is here, it's the perfect opportunity to discuss an acquisition I think is in HBHC's best interest."

Royce made a face. "You think we should try to acquire someone *now*? With the stock already down?" He was skeptical. "That's going to be a tough sell. Who's the target company?"

There was no mistaking Macalister's insidious smile. "Ascension."

Oh, shit.

He knew.

TWENTY

My hand rested on the railing, and instinctively it clenched. Macalister had figured out Royce was planning to buy Ascension, and he was cutting his son off at the knees. Without that company, Royce had no shot at taking over HBHC. All those years he'd toiled to bring this into fruition, and now it was . . .

Gone.

A sickening feeling overwhelmed me. I was sinking into the bay. I didn't know how Macalister had figured the plan out. That information certainly hadn't come from me, but . . . would Royce believe that?

I hadn't been wearing his ring when I'd asked him about Ascension.

There was no reaction from him. The revelation had turned him into a statue. He didn't blink and didn't seem to be breathing either. My heart was beating fast enough for both of us.

Finally, he sighed, but it felt forced. Like he was trying to act natural. "The rest of the board won't go for it."

"You're underestimating how convincing I can be."

Royce narrowed his gaze. "You want to tank our shares even more, go right ahead. You'll have a revolt on your hands, and as the second largest shareholder, keep in mind I'll be leading the charge."

Macalister waved the comment off. "We'll discuss it, but I'm thinking about the long-term. This is a smart move."

There was so much subtext there, he might as well have come out and said he wanted to buy Ascension simply to prevent his son from doing it. I despised how smug he looked about the whole thing. Pleased with himself.

He glanced at his watch. "We have fifteen minutes before we're due in the business office. I had the team set up in there." He tugged at his shirt sleeves, straightening the shirt beneath his jacket. "Marist, I've called a car for you. When I return home later, we can replay our game of chess since we didn't get a chance to finish our last one."

My mouth dropped open, and in that moment, anything could have come out. Fire. Expletives. A scream. But it all tangled together and clogged my windpipe, preventing a single sound.

It wasn't until Macalister was gone that my words began working again. I clutched Royce's arm, squeezing the tuxedo fabric in my fingers. "I don't know how he figured it out, but I didn't tell him."

His voice was cool and indifferent, and it hurt like a fist to the chest. "You sure about that?"

"Yes, Royce. I swear." I'd told him everything, even the

stuff that was hard and made me look awful. "You believe me, right?"

The hesitation in his distant eyes was painful. "Yeah, of course."

He'd told me he wouldn't lie when we were alone.

And yet he just had.

Royce and Macalister weren't back by midnight, and even though I was still in my dress, I went downstairs seeking a late-night snack. Or maybe a drink.

But the kitchen wasn't empty.

Alice sat alone at the table and in the near-dark, an untouched mug steaming in front of her.

"Marist." She put her hand over her heart. "You startled me."

"Sorry, I was hungry." I bit my lip and inched toward the table. "Are you okay?"

"No." She didn't look at me. Her eyes were out the window, staring at the gardens she loved to maintain. "I'm leaving."

I nearly asked where she was going before her meaning sank in. "You're leaving Macalister?"

She nodded. "If I'd known it was going to be like this, there's so much I would have done differently."

I lowered myself into a chair across from her, feeling like she wanted to talk, even if it was with the girl her husband was fixated on. The lights weren't on inside the kitchen, but my eyes had adjusted, and there was plenty of light coming in from outside. She looked tired. Weary and maybe broken.

I hurt so badly for her.

"I tried to give him everything he wanted," she added. "But I couldn't. I was never going to be *her*."

She had to be talking about Macalister's first wife, Royce and Vance's mother. She lifted a hand and delicately wiped it under an eye. Was she crying?

"I'm sorry, I don't know why I'm telling you this. I don't mean to put it on you."

I wanted to help, to make her feel better. "No, it's okay."

"Do you want some tea?" She gestured to the cup in front of her and then the teapot still on the counter. "I think I made enough for two."

"Sure."

Her blue dress swished as she went to the cupboard and pulled down a mug. "I tried to leave him once before, a little over a year ago." She filled the cup and handed it to me. "We were separated for three months. I think the rumor was I'd been sent to rehab."

She'd been gone when Royce graduated with his MBA from Harvard. That felt so long ago. "But you came back."

"I was unhappy no matter where I was, and decided I'd rather be unhappy with him around."

I took a sip of my tea and made a face at the bitter taste. Normally, I loaded it with sugar and milk, but it seemed rude to get up in the middle of her conversation.

Her eyes were sad as her gaze settled on me. "I'm not proud of it, but for a time I found someone else who made me . . . less unhappy."

"Vance," I said.

It didn't surprise her that I knew. "Yes." Her fingers traced the handle of her mug. "We both wanted to hurt him in our own way. You've seen how hard Macalister can be on his sons."

"Yeah." I took another sip of my tea.

"Part of him died when Julia did." I froze mid-sip, but Alice was very matter of fact about it. "A lot of the good parts, from what I've heard."

"Hmm," was all I could find to say from under my mug. I didn't remember him much from before the accident.

"I knew the thing with Vance wasn't going anywhere. It couldn't. But Macalister lost interest in me years ago, and Vance was all I had."

Until Jillian Lambert.

The image flashed through me of Vance's hips pressed to Jillian's ass. I drank my tea to try to wash it away.

"I can't be here anymore, not when no one wants me."

"That's not true."

She looked dubious. "Oh? Don't tell me you want me around. We're not friends, Marist."

"We could be," I offered. It wasn't the most convincing I'd ever sounded.

She shook her head then reached behind it and began to pull out the pins in her hair, dropping them onto the table in a neat stack. "No, I really don't think we could."

"Why not?"

Her blue eyes were full of turmoil and irritation. "You know why."

My pulse quickened, but I tried to remain calm and stared at the woodgrain in the table. Was she talking about the initiation? Macalister's obsession with me? Or had she seen us in the hedge maze the night I'd lost to the Minotaur?

"My options are simple. I can watch the two men I've had as they cast me aside to pursue other women, or I can leave."

My stomach hurt. A dull sympathetic ache because I knew what it was like to have no good options.

"I'm strong," she said, "but I'm not strong enough to stay. Not if you're here."

I frowned, not liking how her tone seemed to have a threat laced to it. I took a final sip of the tea, set it down, and stared at her. "Will he let you go?"

She shrugged. "Royce and I are his two great failures. We never surrendered complete control."

The statement hung for a long while, leaving us sitting in silence.

"Can I be honest?" I whispered. "This tea isn't my favorite."

She laughed with her whole body, so long I wondered what the joke was that I wasn't in on. "The funny thing is I've always liked you." She smiled, and her eyes gleamed. "You're not afraid to say something direct."

"Thank you." My heart fluttered, causing a strange sensation. It was like I was running down a hill and my pulse couldn't keep up.

"I don't mind being direct either. There's a third option I can consider. It's one where you're not in the picture." Her face went so cold, it was nauseating. "Care to guess which one I chose?"

Visually, she was peeling apart, creating two Alices instead of one, and I blinked rapidly to try to put them back together. It didn't work, and it didn't make sense.

"I don't feel right." My heart was out of sync with my body.

"No, I wouldn't think so."

It was hard to make myself stand, and when I did, everything became much worse.

She rose to her feet as well, moving effortlessly. Like it was easy and the floor beneath her feet was stable. "I've been sitting down here for almost an hour, not sure if I was going to drink this tea or not. And then you showed up."

Blood screamed in my ears, so loud it drowned out whatever else Alice was saying to me.

Wait—no. Hera, not Alice.

She was taking her role a bit too seriously. The jealous queen of the gods punished all the mortals Zeus slept with, even the ones who were unwilling. Except Macalister wasn't Zeus.

"He's the Minotaur," I mumbled.

"What?" She stared at me like I was crazy, and maybe I was. Things moved around me in unexpected ways.

I stumbled away from the table. I'd only come downstairs for a snack, so I'd left my phone in my bedroom. Now it was so far away.

"What did you . . . do to me?" I tried to cross the kitchen, but the floor pitched and rolled like a ship in violent seas. It took all my effort, and when I reached the counter by the door, I clung to it and struggled to catch my breath.

She didn't say anything.

Or maybe she did. The room was darker now and growing smaller every second. I hurled myself out the door and into the dining room, but all-new terrors waited for me in here. I saw the board members as the gods on Mount Olympus, eight feet tall and horrifying, and when I knocked one of the chairs over, pain shot up my leg.

I was going to throw up. Or pass out.

Or maybe die.

Time slowed and then lurched forward like an arrow pulled back in a bow and set loose. Hera didn't seem to be here anymore. I'd made it out of the hellish dining room, and now I was in the entryway, facing the grand staircase, where all the lights had halos. At the top of the landing, the Hale family portrait watched me with their intense eyes, taunting me to come join them.

I climbed a million steps until my legs quit working.

And then I crawled.

The stairs grew steeper, and I clung to the carpet, worried I was going to fall.

Keep moving!

I slithered as Medusa up the next step, fighting for every inch and against my heavy eyelids that wanted to close. I had to get to my phone. I had to tell Royce again that I loved him and make sure no one was around this time so I could hear if he'd say it back.

I wasn't to the landing yet, and there was still another flight of steps to go after that. I'd never make it. Tears welled in my eyes, and the pounding in my head was too powerful and crushing to go on.

I didn't want to give up, but this was checkmate.

Marist Northcott was going to die halfway up the staircase on her quest to becoming a Hale, her beautiful green dress splayed out around her. I dug my fingers into the thick carpet, anchoring myself as best I could, and let the darkness have me.

"Marist!" a male voice shouted.

Hands scooped up my shoulders, forcing my eyes to crack open. Everything was blurry and indistinguishable, like I'd put on a pair of my sister's glasses. I tried to speak, but it was a garbled mess in my head.

Then Royce came into view. I reached up, wanting to touch and make sure it was really him. "I love you," I croaked.

My hand landed on the face, but it wasn't his.

It was the Minotaur.

TO BE CONCLUDED IN

The DECEPTION

FILTHY RICH AMERICANS | BOOK THREE

OTHER BOOKS BY NIKKI SLOANE

ACKNOWLEDGMENTS

Thank you so much to my gorgeous husband Nick for everything. And I mean, everything. He helped brainstorm, supported me at every stage, and encouraged me when I was stressed out about making my deadlines. As is with every book I write, this one would not have been possible without him.

Thank you to my friend Andrea Lefkowitz. She is a voice of reason who has twice now saved this series from crossing a line a lot of readers would have found intolerable. She was also there for me during a difficult time and kept me together, and I owe her so much.

Thank you to my editor Lori Whitwam. I turned this in five days late and she still got it back to me on time, and then even let me sneak in a second round of edits. Sixteen projects together and she still wants to work with me, LOL.

Thank you to my publicist Nina Grinstead for all her hard work and support, and making this series the best it could possibly be.

Thank you to my beta readers Aubrey Bondurant, Casie Lanham, Rachael Leissner, Theresa Martin, and Tara Slone for their help and great notes.

I owe a huge thank you to so many bloggers and author friends and there are too many to name. If you're reading this, picture your name here! I am so incredibly grateful to anyone who shared their love for this series, their uncomfortable feelings for Macalister, or who supported my writing at any stage of my career. I'm weird and awkward and not good at saying the right thing at the right time, but everything you've done means so much to me.

ABOUT THE AUTHOR

Nikki Sloane fell into graphic design after her careers as a waitress, a screenwriter, and a ballroom dance instructor fell through. For eight years she worked for a design firm in that extremely tall, black, and tiered building in Chicago that went through an unfortunate name change during her time there.

Now she lives in Kentucky, is married and has two sons. She is a three-time Romance Writers of America RITA© Finalist, also writes romantic suspense under the name Karyn Lawrence, and couldn't be any happier that people enjoy reading her sexy words.

Website: www.NikkiSloane.com

Printed in Great Britain
by Amazon

64954879R00173